Sharnel

Showing Your Cards

By: A Lady on Her Way

Copyright © 2025 Bank On Yourself LLC

Sharnel
Showing Your Cards
By: A Lady on Her Way

ISBN: 979-8-9990106-0-5 (Electronic)
ISBN: 979-8-9990106-1-2 (Paperback)

The characters and event portrayed in this book are fictitious. Any similarity to real persons, living or dead, is entirely coincidental and not intended by the author.

Printed in the United States of America

Sharnel
Showing Your Cards

This book is dedicated to the artist within; this is your time…Welcome! #BankOnYourself

TABLE OF CONTENTS

Third Floor
Sharnel
Regina
Second Floor
Tonya (Mrs. Nash & The Family)
Miss Kena
Mr. James
First Floor (Top)
Rayna
Miss Chyna (Mr. Tony)
Donte
Keith (Keithy Face)
Not in Our Building
Preston (P)
Mr. Charles
Paul
Trina
Trav
Fat Mane
Tammy (Cousin of Rayna)
Royal (Roy)

BACK STORY

There are some things you can explain and others that just feel right. Now, what's right? You be the judge or not. Let me formally introduce myself: I'm **Sharnel.** This is my story, my truth. I've lived a life that worked for me. I've been grown all my life—there's no sob story, but shit happened. Life was not 100% easy despite living in the suburbs. It was safe, but it had its rough spots. Think of it as the place they send the Black people when gentrification takes over their city. You get the picture—enough said.

Anyway, I'm a beautiful medium brown girl, about to graduate high school with my girls—you'll meet them later. Although I'm only 5'3" don't let height fool you. I ain't never scared and never backed down from a fight—no matter the opponent. Which is why I always keep my naturally curly hair tucked away in braids or a weave because let's face it, if I slay ready…I can stay ready. I've been physically mature since age 11, so attention (good or bad) is nothing new for me. I learned early on to wear my ass, hips, and breasts with pride—despite what others "attempted" to make me think or feel.

If I had to describe my best asset it would be my smile and sparkling brown eyes. My granny used to tell me my smile and eyes alone shine bright enough for the world to see. I don't know how true it that is, but she was my person; So, I'd take it from her rather than some rando on the street.

I've lived in the same apartment building, on the third floor (the basement) all my life. It was fairly small, with only 11 apartments across 3 floors. My floor is considered the musical chairs of apartments—people move in and out every couple of years, so it's not worth noting any of them.

I lived with **Regina** (my mother) and her rotation of **"Uncles of the Week"**—you know those "uncles" that you see one day and the next you don't. I personally could've cared less; they didn't appease me. Hell most of the time, I barely saw her, which made me the ideal child for Regina: not seen or heard, just staying out of the way. Regina lived her life, and I lived mine. As long as the lights, heat, water, and rent got paid and she left money for food, I was cool. The rest I figured out on my own.

Moving on the second floor was the Bebe's kids section, where the laundry room was located. The three families on that floor had four to six kids each, which usually consisted of a rainbow coalition of mothers and fathers—except for the Nash family. My homegirl **Tonya Nash** lived there. We'd been tight since I was 10 and Tonya was 12. She was 5'5" with cocoa-colored skin and a slender frame, Tonya didn't have much in the ass or breast department, but she was still fire and she knew it. Problem was, she flaunted her body more than her mind. Despite failing two grades, she wasn't dumb; she just didn't apply herself. Tonya belonged to the sheltered-kid-gone-wild club, sometimes pushing her freedom too far. You will see what I mean later.

Tonya lived with her mom, her dad, five siblings, and her big mama in a three-bedroom apartment. Can you imagine? Tonya was 19½, still sharing a bedroom with her two sisters until she went to college in the fall, while her brothers slept in the living room. Even with a lot of bodies, the house was always clean and orderly, and everyone treated each other with respect for the most part. Mr. and Mrs. Nash were nice but strict. Tonya still had a bedtime and could only hang out occasionally—probably, for the best. We clowned her about their rules; however, I respected her parents for the structure they provided.

Also on the second floor was **Miss Kena**, a Jamaican lady, the neighborhood braider with four young kids. She always had her hair wrapped, with a deviant smile that seemed to read your soul. Sounds weird, but she was dope. When doing my hair, she always talked about protecting my femininity and gave tips on natural products to cleanse my mind and body. However, she always scolded me (with love) especially when talking about boys. She'd say, "Watch out for dem boys; they prey on the flesh of the un-tinkered." Sidebar: Yes, I am a virgin, shut up! I have had a few close encounters but never completed the action. Anyway, Miss Kena kept me in stitches with her fables; there was always some hidden truth in them, which I appreciated.

Finally, **Mr. James** also lived on the second floor. He was the neighborhood watch—he knew and saw all. Most days, he was on his porch observing the daily dealings. He had six kids with five different women, but wasn't what some would call a holiday father. He was an active father. His kids (including their mothers) rotated staying at his house. He was declared mentally disabled from his time overseas, but he also owned several local businesses. Like anyone with PTSD, he had good days and rough ones. Life had aged him beyond his years, but sweetness remained—a big, tall man sporting a long salt-and-pepper ponytail. He used to crack us up bragging that his "good hair" was how he fathered all those children. Word on the street was that he and Miss Kena had a thing going on, but that's grown folks' business.

The first floor was the party floor—someone was always playing music, cards, smoking, or sounded like they were having a good time. Since I only frequented one apartment there, that's all I'll cover. My day one, **Rayna Wright**, lived on that floor. We've been friends since embryo. Her mother (**Miss Chyna**) told me that when Regina and I moved into the building, our moms met while pushing us in our strollers. When our little hands touched…they knew we would be trouble. We've been friends ever since. Our upbringings were similar, except her mom was a single mom of three (Donte, Rayna, and Keith). **Mr. Tony**, her dad, lived in Miami but visited several times a year. He was always a blast and treated me like one of his own.

Rayna was 18, 5'5", dark brown, with sparkling brown eyes. She was thick in all the right places with a small waist—another one who knew she was gorgeous. She was sassy, loud, and never short with her words. If you hung around Rayna, it was never a dull moment. She had a boyfriend named P, whom she had loved since the 7th grade. When we were in the 9th grade, he declared she was his woman, and she bought into it. He made sure everyone knew it too.

Miss Chyna was like Regina in that she wasn't always at home. Unlike Regina, Miss Chyna worked all the time but partied even harder on the weekend. As a single mom, she was proud to provide for her children. Since she knew Regina was never home, I stayed at her house a lot, and she treated me like one of her own. Miss Chyna made sure I had dinner with them as much as possible. She even taught me to cook. She wasn't very tall, but she was a redbone with short hair, although she mostly rocked wigs. If you saw her, you'd think she was a sibling to her children and not their mother.

On some Saturday nights, Rayna and I would sit on the edge of her bed listening to her rant while she got ready. She even went into depth about life experiences, including some "grown-up advice." Her rationale was, "I'd rather you hear it from me than some chlamydia-having hoochie on the street." I'd always crack up or blush; she was a trip. Her motto was, "Hold on to nothing because unreliable people get weak! So, stand on your two feet; don't let your knees get weak."

Donte Wright, Rayna's brother and the oldest child of Miss Chyna, was 20, 6'3", skinny but ripped with muscles, chocolate brown, with the haziest dark brown eyes I've ever seen. Not much to him other than his hair, which was always cornrolled straight back, and his voice was deep. Despite having nice white teeth, he rarely smiled—maybe a smirk here and there. He took man of the house to a new level; since he contributed to the bills, that was all he felt responsible for. If Rayna asked him to do anything, he'd remind her of that and walk away.

Donte didn't talk much but was always ready with a quick comeback. If he did laugh, it was likely at something fucked up or after saying something fucked up—pick one! He always looked like he was deep in thought. Even when we were kids, he didn't talk much; he just had this man of the house stature. Although he dropped out in the 11th grade, he wasn't stupid—just bored with school. He got his GED and started working on cars at the local shop, and he had done well so far. Needless to say, I hate him! One thing I didn't understand about Donte was his local hood booger girlfriend (if you want to call her that), **Trina**. They were polar opposites, *BITCH!* I'll address that later.

Keith Wright (*Keithy Face*), my favorite little guy and the youngest of the bunch, was 5 going on grown! What can you say about this handsome caramel baby with curly brown hair? He kept us all grounded by always asking questions and pointing things out, especially if you said a "bad word." He was a surprise to us all when Miss Chyna told us she was pregnant. However, we immediately embraced him and spoiled him rotten, which annoyed the hell out of Donte. Beyond questions and sarcasm (thanks to Donte), he believed Thomas the Tank could do no wrong—just a typical baby with lots of love and innocence.

Although he lived in the next building, **Preston (P)** might as well have lived in ours. He was always there to see either Rayna or Donte, who was his right-hand man. P was 20, 5'11", medium brown skin, and always rocked a low-cut haircut with deep waves. He had the greatest smile but always talked major shit! P should have stood for petty instead of Preston since he was an instigator. But what I loved the most was he's a protector and my "big brother". He never graduated from high school and didn't have a GED, but he still made money working in the warehouse and occasionally hustling weed. He had plans to open a dispensary one day. Despite not completing school, he was truly a businessman. He understood the dynamics of running a business at a high level and sometimes helped Mr. James with his dealings in terms of negotiating contracts and purchases.

He lived in a two-bedroom apartment alone. It was smaller than the ones in our building but still very nice. He and Donte were extremely close. He was as crazy about Rayna as she was about him. He brought her gifts, and drove us to school sometimes, but what I admired was that he always respected her. Miss Chyna said they couldn't date officially until Rayna was 16, and even then, she had rules. P honored that; he respected Miss Chyna, but he also respected Donte. He asked for permission before "officially" dating her. Although Rayna would never say it, I know it meant a lot to her. I don't know if it's true, but it's rumored that Donte threatened to hurt him if he ever disrespected Rayna. P promised to break up with her before bringing harm to her.

CHAPTER 1

Hanging out on the front step was a norm for those of us who lived in the building and for others we hung out with. We'd sit outside and just talk mess, listen to music, or gather before heading out. If you were ever looking for anyone, it was the spot to check first. For me, it was also a getaway, especially late at night. I'd sit outside for hours and let my mind drift away. But we will talk more about that later.

Before Miss Chyna headed to work, she always stopped to give "marching orders" for things to be done before she returned home. This not only included her children but also me. I didn't mind; I was always there and eating her food, so I felt like a part of the family. Hell, I even had keys to her house, so it was nothing for me to come and go. Rayna and I were sitting out front with Tonya, talking as usual, when Miss Chyna came out of the building. She came down the five steps before stopping in front of Rayna and me as we watched Keith and Logan (Miss Kena's son) play kickball in the courtyard.

"Here's today's chores. Rayna, you need to clean that kitchen! I'm over it…get it done ASAP; I wanna see my face in everything." Rayna rolled her eyes, but Miss Chyna didn't care; she knew it was going to be done or else. "Sharnel, give my baby Keith a bath and don't let him stay in there too long. Make sure you brush his hair. Lord knows he only lets you do it. Put him to bed at 7:30 PM, and y'all feed my baby; he's small enough."

I nodded; I didn't mind. Keith was my baby, like literally. I remember when he came home for the first time five years ago. He was so small and cute; he literally tore my heart open. I didn't have any siblings and barely any cousins, so I'd never felt close to anyone other than my girls, my granny, and Papa, God rest their souls. So, I was glad to take him under my wing. I'd babysat for Miss Chyna plenty of times at my house and hers.

After the chore speech, Rayna always had to add something extra. "What about Donte? What is he gonna do?"

Miss Chyna flipped the switch real quick and got into Rayna's personal space. "Don't worry about Donte; he has his marching orders." Miss Chyna immediately smiled and then kissed us both on the cheek. "I love y'all; be good, look out for one another," then walked off to her car.

"Dang, that nigga Donte ain't never gotta do nothing!" Rayna complained, as always.

"You know he's your mama's favorite," I laughed, "besides, he's probably with that hood booger!" I rolled my eyes at the thought of Trina. However, no sooner than I could finish my sentence, he came out of the building.

"You worried about the wrong thing, ain't you?" he replied as he held the building door open for Logan. Donte stood watch as Miss Kena opened the door for Logan, then walked down the building steps to stand on the sidewalk next to Keith, who had just walked up.

In response to his comment, I looked at him and rolled my eyes in disgust. As I sat on the second-to-bottom step, I found myself staring at Donte. I couldn't figure him out. I could never say it to him, but his presence alone did something to me. He didn't have to say much; being around him made my whole-body tense up. It was weird, but I could feel him before I saw him sometimes. Donte didn't say anything. When he realized I was looking at him, he walked away and left Keith with us. "Wonder where he's going?" Apparently, I said it out loud since Rayna responded, "Urgh, who cares? He comes and goes as he pleases."

Donte wasn't very emotional and definitely wasn't messy at all. If anything, he avoided drama, which I appreciated about him. However, it was another reason why I couldn't understand why he liked Trina. Trina was cute, about the same height as Tonya. She was medium brown, skinny, and could dress her ass off. But she was loud, always at the center of something, and did too much, in my opinion. She quoted stupid stuff she heard other people say as if it were the gospel truth. She couldn't stand me, partially because I checked her little sister for trying to clown Tonya at school one day. However, the feeling was mutual, so anytime we saw each other, it was always a problem… for her, and I made sure of it!

Keith jumped on my back and knocked me out of my trance as he squeezed my neck. Then he proceeded with his usual routine questions and demands for me. "Shar Shar, what time is dinner? When is bath time? Don't brush my hair too hard!"

"Ahh, young sir, where are our manners?" I laughed.

He acted like he was pondering my request by turning his head to the side before starting again. "Can you make me dinner, PLLEEAASSEE? Can you give me a bath with bubbles, PLLEEAASSEE? Can you brush my hair not too hard, PLLEEAASSEE?" I matched his stance and acted as if I was considering his request by humming and raising my eyebrow.

"Okay, I can make these things happen for you, sir; can you give me 30 minutes?" He mocked me and acted as if he was considering my request.

"Did you say PLLEEAASSEE?"

"I'm sorry, PLLEEAASSEE," I laughed and replied. He nodded in agreement.

"Y'all some cornballs, team too much," Rayna replied as she rolled her eyes.

As I watched Keith play with his toys and the bubbles in the tub, I started to think about motherhood. Can I do this? Do I even want kids? Every day? At that moment, he looked up and smiled at me, and my heart melted. If I did become a mom, I would be a better mother than Regina. Marriage was a requirement though because I don't want to be a single mom! My child would have a true family. "Y'all almost done?" Donte was standing in the doorway. I looked at Keith as he held up his hands to show me if they were wrinkled. "Yep, just a few more minutes, then he's all yours!" Donte nodded and went into his bedroom across from the bathroom.

I washed Keith up, combed his hair, and dressed him for bed, then sent him to Donte. Keith only allowed Donte to brush his teeth, so I wasn't even going to attempt that battle. I washed my hands, picked up the towel and clothes, and headed to Miss Chyna's room in the back of the apartment. As I headed back toward the living room, I heard Donte and Keith doing their brotherly chant. I stopped and listened outside the door.

Donte asked, "Who are you?"

Keith replied excitedly, "A Wright man!"

Donte responded, "That's right! What do we do? Say it with me!" Donte started, and Keith followed.

He got a little lost but jumped back in when he remembered. "Respect God and ourselves, hold our heads high, take care of our family, and never disrespect but protect our women!" I heard them do their brotherly handshake once they finished.

When they walked out of the bathroom, I was leaning against the wall. I smiled and acted like I was wiping a tear.

"Looks like we got nosy ears, Keith!" Donte looked in my direction.

"Shar Shar, not nosy ears!" Keith laughed as I kissed his face and picked him up.

"That's right, Keithy Face! But that was dope!" Donte nodded and went to his room.

It was already 7:00 PM, but I told Keith if he sat quietly, I would let him watch TV until I finished cleaning. Since Rayna wanted to hang out with P and suckered me into cleaning the kitchen, I washed the dishes, wiped the counter, and began sweeping. However, I stopped when I felt a presence behind me.

"Rayna's ass ain't never gonna do nothing if you keep doing it for her." I turned to look at Donte and rolled my eyes, then continued sweeping the dust into the dustpan.

"Well, maybe if you helped her, I wouldn't have to."

When I finally stood up and faced him, he said, "Shit, you're the one who wants to be a part of this family, so you gotta contribute too." Typical Donte, always with the bullshit.

"Whatever, Donte, you're supposed to be the man of the house, right?"

"Right, so that means I pay bills, and you women fix my plate!" I just shook my head as Donte walked off to put Keith to bed, as he had fallen asleep watching TV.

When I finished in the kitchen, I walked into the living room to gather my things. As I was about to make my way down the hall to tell him I was leaving, he was headed into the bathroom.

"I'm out; tell Rayna she owes me!" He nodded.

"Hold up, I'll walk you down." I was over Donte for the night and didn't need any additional commentary.

So, I politely and sarcastically replied, "I'm grown; I don't need an escort, Sir!"

Not to be outdone, he shook his head and snapped back, "You heard what I said, Sharnel!"

"Urgh, get on my nerves," I said as I folded my arms and stomped toward the front door.

He followed me. "Man, hurry your ass up before I change my mind."

He couldn't be serious! "I didn't ask you to walk me in the first place, sir; you volunteered!"

Putting my hand on the doorknob, he popped my hand, which pissed me off. I knew better; he was a man… I should have waited for him to open the door. Donte reached for the knob again, and I sucked my teeth and went out the door. Once we were outside, Donte locked it, and we headed downstairs in silence. When we reached the front door of the building, I stopped.

"I'm good; thank you."

Donte grunted and just stared at me. "Why you always gotta do the most, Sharnel? Keep walking, fuck!" He motioned for me to walk down the last four steps.

When we reached my door, I stopped, placing my hand on my hip. "I'm at the door… you can go now!" Obviously frustrated, Donte waited for me to open the door. I purposely took my time as I opened the door while mumbling, "Urgh, always gotta get your way!"

"Whatever, man, just hurry up before Keith wakes up!"

I opened the door to the dark, cold, empty apartment and stood in the doorway. "You happy now?"

After peeking inside, he adjusted his tone and spoke somewhat calmer. "You sure you're good?"

Now he wanted to act all concerned; please, who was he fooling? So, I called his bluff. "Aww, since when do you care?"

After snorting, Donte dryly replied, "I don't!" then headed toward the stairs.

What was new? He didn't care about anything… least of all me. But part of me wished someone did. Lately, the apartment reflected what I felt: empty and alone. I wasn't necessarily cold, but some places inside couldn't… wouldn't be touched. What I needed I hadn't found yet, nor was I ready for it to find me. But I knew one day (prayerfully) God would send it to me.

Hearing Miss Chyna's apartment door close, I made a beeline to the front steps. In addition to the laundry room, it was another safe refuge. If anything, ever happened, I knew someone would hear me. I sat outside and just vibed out to music. It was after 9:00 PM, so it was early enough for me to sit and just enjoy the weather. My problem was as the nights got longer; I couldn't pull myself away from the outdoors since the nights were warmer. After I put in my earbuds and selected a playlist, I closed my eyes to let whatever artist came on just take me away.

After a while, I was annoyed that I didn't bring something to drink. Alcohol wasn't my thing, but anything with ginger would do. As I let my mind wander, I felt a presence get closer. There was no need to be scared; I already knew who it was and what was about to happen. The same thing happened every time I was outside at night alone. Donte reached for my earbud. I opened one eye, and he stood in front of me.

"Not smart," he said, holding my earbud as he frowned. "Didn't I take your ass home an hour or so ago?" Not dignifying his response with a reply, I didn't say anything but just turned down my music and waited for him to return my earbud. "What, you scared or something?" he asked with a slight bit of concern.

"Nigga please, what the fuck I gotta be scared of?" I snatched the earbud out of his hand.

Uncaringly, he shook his head. "You act like a little girl, so I assume you are one," then he sat on the steps.

I was over him and wanted to storm off, but I honestly welcomed the company. "Why you in my business?"

"What you doing out here?"

I said more calmly, "Rayna's on her way home, so I came outside to meet her… now who's being nosey, smartass?"

We sat silently, looking at the parking lot a few yards ahead of us. I loved that he cared enough to protect Rayna like that. I just nodded and wished I had a brother to look out for me. "That's nice of you!" I mumbled. Donte just looked at me and then back at the parking lot.

When we heard a car pull up, he stood up and watched P's car approach. P helped Rayna out of the car, and they headed in our direction. "Hey y'all," Rayna said as they approached the steps, "what y'all doing?"

I shook my head, indicating nothing. P and Donte dapped each other up, and Rayna came to stand next to me. She leaned her head on my shoulder and then whispered too loudly, "Shar, why are you out here… one of those nights?"

Looking at me, Donte gave me *the really face* and shook his head. He knew I lied to him. I just shook it off, "Nah, girl, just enjoying the night air," I smiled, slightly embarrassed.

Rayna yawned, "Okay, well I'm about to head inside," then hugged me goodbye as P escorted her upstairs.

Donte didn't move but then turned toward me, "One of those nights?" he grunted.

"You don't care, remember!" I reapplied my earbuds.

He was still waiting for me to explain. There was nothing to say. I didn't want to talk about it, nor was I ready to. So, I returned to my music. He finally took the hint and made his way toward the front door. Just before walking into the building, he replied loud enough for me to hear, "Don't let it be one of those nights too long." There was still no reply from me; my only thought was that he was getting on my nerves. But what was I expecting him to say or, better yet, do?

After staying outside for another hour, I decided to go home. Sitting outside always gave me the relief I needed. It rejuvenated my mind and soul; it provided the clarity I needed. As I entered the building, I dropped my keys and bent down to pick them up. However, when I looked up to the first floor, Donte stood leaning over the railing. I was waiting for him to say something smart, but he didn't. I appreciated his silence and mouthed the words *thank you*. He nodded, then went to his apartment, and I went home.

CHAPTER 2

I never gave much thought to what was next after graduating high school; I just wanted to get out. I wasn't stupid; I got decent grades, not that they mattered or were really expected in my house. Regina expected the minimum and told people as such! As long as the average was achieved and I went to school, she was cool. The one time I missed class, there was a phone call from the school. Then Regina turned into mother of the year and began ranting and yelling. To avoid that shit, I did what I could to keep her at bay.

Academics were never my thing; all that structured shit like formulas, rules, and that other nonsense never made sense to me. I just enjoyed writing and being creative, so I could get into hypotheticals and theories, which allowed my mind to wander. One thing I was sure of was my pen game was fire! My dream was to be a New York Times bestseller, but that was a dream deferred since "academic or scholarly" writing wasn't my thing. So, I kept my writings to myself.

I never went to any school events or participated in any clubs. They were pointless and an extra expense I didn't have the money or time for. So, I skipped all the senior events, including prom. However, on prom night, I agreed to help Rayna get dressed since she and Tonya were going. Rayna went with P, of course, and he convinced Paul, a guy from the neighborhood, to go with Tonya. Paul was another tall cutie—5'10", light-skinned, with wavy long hair he usually kept in cornrows or braids. He was the type of guy who knew he was cute because girls (like Tonya) fell at his feet. He was 19 and graduated two years before us. Paul was a decent basketball player, but after he injured his knee senior year of high school, he quit playing. He got a job working with P at the warehouse. He still lived at home, but you could find him crashing with P from time to time. Anyway, it was a hard sell, but he also knew Tonya was easy, so he could get some if he played his cards right.

On the day of prom, I ran around with the girls to get their last-minute items. Although I didn't go, I did get my hair and nails done with them. However, I soon regretted going as I hated the mall and shopping. But I would do anything for my ladies. To make matters worse, we had to take an Uber since P was getting his hair cut—the freaking worst! When the Uber driver tried to flirt with us, Tonya entertained him, which caused him to take the scenic route to the mall. I couldn't get out of the car fast enough. I was already over the trip. When we got to the mall, we went from store to store because Tonya couldn't afford much. After walking in and out of three stores, I told the ladies I'd wait for them outside. The mall was crowded, and we needed to hurry back so they could get ready.

I decided to put in my earbuds and zone out. I closed my eyes and let the sun beam on my face. I used to do that as a child; it was a mini-escape when things got too tough. I loved to feel the warmth and just let my mind wander. I was really in my zone and lost in my thoughts when I felt someone in my personal space. I knew it wasn't the girls; they would have been loud enough for me to hear. When I felt someone reach for my earbud, I was about to get mad, but I knew who it was. I immediately opened my eyes.

"Not smart," Donte held the earbud in front of me. I rolled my eyes and snatched it out of his hand.

"What are you doing here anyway?" I said in a smart tone. He just lifted up his bag with the latest sneakers inside. I shook my head; if I knew anything, he was going to have the latest shoes.

"Why are you out here?" he asked slightly annoyed.

"When did you suddenly become so concerned?" I shot back. It was clear Donte was reaching his breaking point, so I took a breath and adjusted my tone. "I was over walking from store to store…I hate shopping!" Donte just nodded, looking at me. He didn't say anything, but his stare was a bit much for me.

"See something you like?" I frowned. Donte just shook his head; he was over my antics, but what was new? He was about to walk away when I remembered we had to take an Uber.

"Wait!" I yelled. He stopped and didn't turn around. "Can you give us a ride home?" I snapped. He started to walk again, now he was pissing me off, so I had to swallow my pride and yelled, "Please!"

He stopped again and hurled, "Hurry up or I'm leaving," then kept walking. I ran back inside to get the girls. When we came back, he was parked in front of the mall door. Rayna got in the front, and I sat behind her while Tonya sat behind Donte. Donte pulled off, and we headed home.

"Urgh, can you roll up the window?" Rayna whined over the music that was blaring. Annoyed, Donte hit the button to roll up the windows. Tonya was trying to show me all the costume jewelry she bought. I tried to act interested, but I wasn't.

Rayna turned around and smiled at me. "Shar, I wish you were going with us. You know it's not too late."

I immediately motioned for her to stop. "Not my speed, boo, but y'all have fun."

She turned around, defeated. Donte lowered the music and looked at me in the rearview mirror. "Aww, couldn't find a date? That sucks," he chuckled.

While looking at him, I roared, "Urgh, always think you're so damn funny! I turned down several dates, and even if I hadn't, I ain't willing to whore myself out to the highest bidder for some dusty-ass dude!" I knew that last part stung Tonya. I didn't mean it about her, but Donte pissed me off. He turned the music back up, and we rode the rest of the way in silence. He always had something to say.

After Donte parked in a space in the parking lot, Rayna and Tonya got out immediately and headed toward the building. But I dropped my phone, so I was looking for it. My not moving resulted in Donte not moving. However, he watched me continue to reach for my phone in the rearview mirror. "You getting out or nah?"

Now I was truly over him and wished I hadn't dropped my phone. So, I immediately snapped back at him, "I dropped my phone, and I'm trying to grab it without getting hepatitis from touching anything in your slut mobile."

"Yo, hurry up and get the fuck out, you got too much fuckin' mouth!" he yelled back, cutting off the car and getting out.

After finding my phone and opening the door, I stared at Donte, whose face pissed me off. I was about to slam his door. However, he peeped game, "Don't slam my damn door either!" I was about to do it anyway, but I decided against it. Walking to the building, he continued ranting as he walked behind me. "Young ass always got something to say," he mumbled.

"If that's how you feel, kiss my young ass, Donte," I just put in my earbuds, turned up my music, and stuck my middle finger up as I walked to the building. If he said anything else, I didn't hear it, but I could feel him watching me.

When we reached the building, I stopped at the door, waiting for him to open it since he was right behind me. "Fuck, I look like the doorman?" he asked, looking at the door.

"Nah, I guess I mistook you for a gentleman, douchebag." Reaching for the door, in midair, he popped my hand and grabbed the handle before I could. Donte's action insinuated a shouting match between him and me. "I know you ain't just hit me," I yelled.

"Yo, Sharnel, I ain't in the mood, get through this damn door," he snarled. I walked through, and he continued, "Why the fuck you always gotta say something, acting like a little ass girl all the time!"

"I ain't no little ass girl; you're always bothering me. Try being nice once in your life!" I yelled.

Stepping into my personal space, he was calmer but stern. "Why the fuck would I do that?"

He had never been this close to me. I just looked at him. My thoughts were stuck along with my words. So, all I could muster up was, "Fuck you, Donte!"

Still looking at me intently, he backed up and headed toward the stairs, leaving me. "Yeah, I bet you ain't got nothing to say."

Gaining my composure, I began walking downstairs to my apartment. "Whatever, tell Rayna I'll be there later!"

"Ain't you helping her get ready, Einstein?" he continued walking up the stairs.

He was right, "Urgh!" Making my way upstairs, I murmured and stomped, "Get on my damn nerves."

"See, proving my point," he said.

I knew he meant stomping and ranting, so I stopped. When Donte got to the top of the stairs, he opened the door. I was still a few steps behind him, but he could see me. He entered the apartment door and stood inside as if to wait for me to enter.

He smiled before growling, "I don't indulge little girls," and slammed the door in my face.

"URGH, I hate you," I yelled before opening the door and going in. When I entered the apartment and locked the door, he was already headed toward his room and closed his door. I made a beeline to Rayna's room; she wasn't there, so I checked Miss Chyna's room and found them prepping.

"Damn, what happened to you, girl?" she said as she unzipped her dress.

"Your damn brother happened… my bad, Miss Chyna, I meant no disrespect."

She laughed, as did Rayna, and waved me off. We helped Rayna get ready, and she looked amazing, like a princess in her teal blue ball gown, which consisted of silver embroidery and some clear crystals. We heard someone at the front door and knew Donte would open the door for P.

"Shar, you sure you don't…" I held up my hand, and Rayna left it there.

We exited Miss Chyna's room so Rayna could make her grand entrance. She and P took several pictures; they matched perfectly as his vest, tie, and shoes matched her dress.

"Okay, all my babies get in the picture with Rayna," Miss Chyna said. Donte grunted and went over to Rayna while Keith took his spot front and center with Rayna. However, I stood next to Miss Chyna and waited for her to take the next picture, but she didn't move.

"Umm, do you have a key to this house?" Miss Chyna said, looking at me.

"Yes, ma'am."

"Then get in the damn picture," and she pushed me forward. I made sure to stand on the opposite side of P, away from Donte. "Aww, perfect, now everyone smile," Miss Chyna said. We all smiled, and Donte smirked as usual.

"Shar Shar, you not going?" Keith asked.

"No, Keithy Face, I'm not going," I said and smiled.

"Her ass couldn't get a date," Donte chuckled.

"Shut the fuc…" I stopped when Miss Chyna swatted at me and him for our remarks.

"You said a bad word, Donte," Keith chuckled.

We all headed outside so Tonya, Paul, Rayna, and P could take pictures. I was officially over all the prom-ness. Everyone was outside to see them off. I got a lot of stares, and I knew everyone wondered why I didn't go.

"Can't wait to go home," I mumbled.

"Well, go. No one's stopping you," Donte mumbled back and kept walking.

I was so over him! We walked the group to the limo and waved them off. I walked back with Miss Chyna, Keith, and Donte. Keith was practicing his karate moves, so we stayed away from him.

"Well, y'all, dinner is at 8, so you know the routine," Miss Chyna said.

"Umm, Miss Chyna, I'm…"

She looked at me. "You've eaten with us without Rayna, so don't even finish your statement…plus I know your momma ain't home. So come on; I don't want you by yourself," she finished.

I thought Donte would laugh or make a comment; he just looked over at me and then kept walking.

"Yeah, Shar Shar, we can watch movies," Keith yelled cheerfully.

Donte laughed until Miss Chyna chimed in, "Yeah, and Donte can join y'all too, 'cause I'm going out!"

His smile disappeared, and I shook my head in annoyance. "Oh great, an evening with Thomas the Tank and Oscar the fucking Grouch."

When we made it inside, I sat on the sofa while Keith played with his toys and Donte went to his room. "Okay, dinner is ready, y'all," Miss Chyna yelled.

Keith took off to get Donte, and I headed to the bathroom to wash my hands. Donte and I ended up at the bathroom door at the same time. Keith was already in there, so I just stood and stared at him. "Man, go ahead," he said, then headed to Miss Chyna's room.

"So rude; I was willing to wait," I said as he kept walking.

When we were all finished, we headed to the table and sat in our respective spots: Keith in his highchair and Donte across from me. Miss Chyna instructed us to hold hands while she prayed. I didn't want to hold Donte's hand, so I gave him two fingers.

"Really? Ain't no one trying to hold your hand either," Miss Chyna looked at us both, and he grunted. Then he snagged my hand so he could hold the whole thing. Once the prayer was over, he dropped my hand. "Sweaty-ass palms!" Miss Chyna swatted at him, and I laughed, acting like I was going to touch his face, then sat down.

We ate in silence since Miss Chyna went to get ready. When Donte was finished eating, he left his plate on the table. "You gonna get that?" I asked.

"Ain't you on clean-up duty? You get that shit," he said and walked off.

"Urgh, you get on my nerves!" He was about to walk back towards his room. "Can you at least get Keith ready for bed then? Do something useful," I said.

He stopped in his tracks and came back to get Keith. "C'mon, man, since someone's being lazy," he said while looking at me. I cleared the table and cleaned up the kitchen.

When Miss Chyna came out, everything was done. "You look pretty, Mom Mom," chimed Keith. She modeled her all-black form-fitting jumpsuit, which hugged in all the right places, and matched it with a red jacket and open-toed booties. As she twirled and smiled, Donte entered the living room, shaking his head.

"Okay, babies, I'm out! Donte, help Shar with Keith…you know he will tell me." Donte just shook his head and didn't respond, and Miss Chyna headed out.

As soon as the door was closed, Donte said, "Aight, y'all have fun," then he headed toward his room.

"Really, Donte? You heard what your mother said," I snapped. He mocked me and laughed as he kept walking, then closed his room door. So, it was me, Keith, and Thomas the Tank.

We sat on the sofa; I turned on the video and pulled out my phone. After an hour, I was over the video, but Keith was excited and kept looking to make sure I was still smiling. Then my phone chimed from an unknown number: *Shar, it's Rayna. I left my phone at home, and P doesn't have his…can you please bring mine to the prom…pleassee!!! Just text when you're outside. Love you.* I was instantly annoyed because she knew I didn't have a car and would have to Uber or ask. "Fuck," I said. Keith immediately looked worried and confused, thinking I was referencing him or Thomas.

"You said a bad word, Shar Shar!"

I kissed his head. "I know, and I'm sorry!" When he smiled, I knew he was good.

How the hell am I going to finesse this? I took a breath and headed toward Donte's room with Keith in tow. When I knocked on the door and he didn't answer, I took another breath and was about to knock again, but he opened the door and just stood there. "Look, Rayna left…" Before I could finish, he said, "Nope," and closed the door in my face.

"This is the second time today!" I mumbled. I went to Rayna's room, grabbed her phone, as Keith stood outside Donte's door. As I passed by his door, I yelled, "Keith is all yours since I gotta…"

Just then, he opened the door with his shoes on, ready to go. He motioned for me to keep walking. Keith was still in his pajamas, so I just picked him up with his dinosaur slippers, and Donte grabbed his car seat, and we were off.

He put the car seat in, and I strapped Keith in and closed the door. As I was about to walk to other side of the backseat, he barked, "Get up front, man. Your ass ain't Miss Daisy!" he said before opening his door.

I hadn't noticed he had already opened the passenger side door. I rolled my eyes and headed toward the front seat. I had never sat in the front seat of his car, so I just observed it and immediately started touching buttons to adjust everything to my comfort. Donte just stopped and watched me as I adjusted the seat, turned on the seat cooler, and adjusted the vents.

"You comfortable now?" he asked with a frown.

I adjusted my seat a little more and said, "Now I am." I put on my seatbelt and pulled out my phone.

"Nah, you navigating," he said instantly. I just rolled my eyes and immediately touched his home screen on his dashboard, putting the address in his GPS. "Yo, why you keep touching shit? At least you could ask first, rude ass!" he said, annoyed.

"What, your bitches don't like their settings adjusted?" I snapped.

"There you go, always loud and wrong…first," he said before he stopped. "Da fuck, I'm not explaining shit to you. Just stop touching shit!" he said as he pulled out of the parking space. I just laughed and looked out the window.

We rode with the music low, hoping Keith would fall asleep, but he was wide awake, asking us millions of questions and pointing out everything he knew. As Keith kept talking, a song played that I hated, so I turned it. "Really, ma G? You ain't hear nothing I said," Donte snapped while he looked at me like I was crazy.

"My bad, I hate that song," I said while laughing. He just shook his head and accelerated ahead.

When we arrived at prom, I texted the number, and Rayna responded. However, in true Rayna fashion, she was taking forever. Donte turned off the car and rolled the windows down, then got out. He leaned against the back of the car on the passenger side. Keith was getting antsy, so I got out and took him out of the car seat, hoping he would burn some energy.

We could hear the music from the venue, so I danced with Keith. He tried to get Donte to join, but he was not having it. "C'mon, Donte," I said and tried to pull his hand. He never looked up from his phone; he just said, "Man get your ass on, man. You know that ain't me." He just leaned against the car.

"It's okay, Keithy Face will dance with me," and I stuck my tongue out and danced with Keith.

"You better keep that shit in your mouth till you learn what to do with it," he said, looking at me before closing his phone.

I just laughed. "Oh, you gonna show me!" I snapped back.

He just chuckled and said, "Shar, please, you ain't grown enough to even consider that thought," shaking his head with a straight face.

Before I could reply, Rayna came out. We had been outside for 20 minutes, and Donte was pissed. I knew if he got close enough, he would let her have it, so I rushed toward her with Keith and handed her the phone.

"Aww, don't y'all look like a happy couple," Rayna joked.

"Girl, take this phone and get gone before he cusses you out," I said. She gave me and Keith a hug, and then we heard Donte start the car, so we rushed off. I snapped Keith in and got back in the passenger seat, and he pulled off.

"Did she say what took her so long?"

"No, and I didn't ask," I said plainly.

He just shook his head. "Where we going now?" Keith chimed.

Donte said sternly, "Home!"

"I don't wanna go home!" Keith whined and began to cry.

"Omg, not now," I said, hoping he would stop before Donte got upset.

"Yo, stop all that!" Donte fussed.

Normally, Keith would have straightened up, but he leaned into his reaction. "NOOOOO!" Keith yelled and cried harder and louder.

I could tell Donte was reaching his wits' end. So, I leaned closer to him, then tapped his arm. "Hey, let's just drive around for a bit…he's just tired. You know he's gonna be out in like 15 mins. Look, he starting to fall asleep now."

Donte looked in the rearview, and Keith was fighting sleep in between his sobs and sniffles. He glanced over at me and mumbled, "Spoiled ass," and kept driving.

Donte let the windows down and turned the music up just enough for us to vibe out. It was perfect; I just leaned back and turned my head toward the window without a care in the world. After a while, Donte chimed in, "You good?"

"Yeah, just enjoying the escape." I reflected on how good it felt to just ride, vibing out to nothing but music and the wind.

"Don't do that often, huh?" I was surprised by his question; Donte wasn't much for small talk, yet here he was talking.

"Nah, which is weird. I'm always by myself, but yet I still need an escape," I said, pondering my thoughts.

"What you running from?" Donte asked while looking out of the side of his eye. Da fuck! What type of question was that? Who did he think he was, Dr. Phil? If I needed a therapist, I damn sure wasn't gonna talk to him!

"Running? Who said I was running? I just…" I was annoyed but stopped and really processed his question. Was I running? Is that what I've been doing? I sat quietly as I processed my thoughts.

"Continue," he said as he drove and awaited my response.

Although I felt uncomfortable, I just said what I felt: "I guess myself, my thoughts, home life, the unknown…I just wish things were different, you know! Seems like everyone got something or someone but me sometimes. Don't get me wrong, I'm thankful for Rayna, Tonya, Ya mom…but they got their lives. Just wish I had someone just for me, ya know?"

Donte just nodded and didn't say anything.

"I know that sounds stup…"

"Nah, I get it…sometimes I wish the same," he said, looking over at me, then back at the road.

What did he mean? He had Trina, although I wouldn't classify her as a true mate. After considering who she was, I guess I saw his point.

We were quiet again, then he asked, "So, what does that person look like?"

I just looked out the window, thinking about the question. I wasn't 100% sure, so I said what came to mind: "Man, someone I can talk to without judgment, someone who will support my ambitions and isn't threatened by my independence, someone who's patient, I can trust, loyal to me, believes in love, believes in me, a protector, believes in a higher power… the exact opposite of what I've had before" As the words came out, I started to smile. I'd only had one real boyfriend and he wasn't anywhere close to what I just described. Eric was more like the Mr. Hyde of the neighborhood, evil and wasn't shit and didn't plan on being shit. But we will talk about him later, unfortunately.

In that moment, I knew if I could manifest even half of what I said, I'd be more than happy. "So, you looking for a boyfriend or just a person?" Donte said, slightly confused as he glanced over at me, then back at the road.

Another great question. The truth was, I needed someone—a permanent fixture. I was over temporary people with short-lived intentions in my life. "Honestly, I hadn't thought about that…but maybe I'm looking for true love, I guess." The tone of my response expressed my uncertainty. Why couldn't I just say what I thought? I knew the answer; it was a level of trust.

Donte's motives were typically riddled judgment and sarcasm, but he allowed me to freely express myself. "You believe you deserve that?"

I just shrugged. "I hope so, trying to be at least! I know I can be a lot sometimes…I don't mean to, but that shouldn't stop it, right?" I said unsurely. He didn't say anything initially, but I really wanted to know his opinion. Part of me didn't expect him to answer; at any moment, I almost expected him to laugh or tell me to grow up, but he didn't.

"You deserve it, and you're worth it." Then he looked over at me, then continued, "You'll find it…sometimes that shit's closer than you think." Donte sized me up and then looked back at the road.

I nodded my head and wondered if that was true. Seeing me ponder his words, he added, "Don't search for that shit; it will find you."

I nodded slightly, as I had heard that before. "Easier said than done when you've already found your one!" I smiled a little, but Donte didn't; he just reflected on my statement and remained quiet. I didn't know where those words came from. Trina might deserve someone, but I didn't believe it was Donte. So, I cleared my throat and spoke again. "Thanks…I appreciate it."

Donte nodded, and by the end of our conversation, he and I had reached a new level of comfort with each other. Maybe I underestimated him. Maybe I could trust him; only time would tell.

Donte kept nodding, then turned the music back up slightly and continued driving.

After an hour, we were back home. Donte parked the car and rolled up the windows. "Thank you for this," I said, and he just nodded as I opened the door.

"No problem," he yawned, and I went to pick up Keith, who was knocked out, while Donte grabbed the car seat. As we headed toward the building, Donte's phone went off. I was about to keep walking, but he held up his hand to stop me. He sat down the car seat, then mouthed, *hold up real quick!* Then walked in the opposite direction as I stood waiting with a sleeping Keith.

Moments later, a car pulled up with dark tints, and someone got out. "What's up, babe!" Trina said as she looked at Donte. He didn't even acknowledge her. As she went to hug him, but then stopped as she glanced in my direction and frowned. "What's she doing out here? Why is she holding your brother?"

Donte shook his head, "Look, don't worry about that…we had to make a run!" He pulled what appeared to be $20 from his pocket and handed it to Trina. She snatched the money.

"A run where, Donte? What was so important that you needed her and your brother to go?" Trina put her hands on her hips, waiting for him to respond. Donte stood emotionless and grunted. I knew he was over Trina, but what I couldn't understand was why he bothered with her at all.

"Man, take your ass on; you got the bread, now go!" he said, motioning for her to walk back toward the car. She glanced at me again, then rolled her eyes. As she attempted to hug him again, he caught her hands midair and gently placed them down.

"Oh, so we doing that now?" she yelled.

Donte shook his head and walked back toward me and Keith. Typically, I would have egged her on or rubbed it in, but I was confused, despite trying not to show it. Trina just stood there watching him as he approached us. Donte picked up the car seat. "Let's go, man!" He touched my shoulder, and we made our way toward the building. As we walked, he never turned around, but I pondered why he reacted like that. Better yet, why did she indulge in his behavior? Come to think of it, in all the years they dated, I never saw Donte show any affection toward Trina, despite them having been together for a while. It didn't make sense…but what did with Donte?

When we reached the building, he said, "I got him," but when I tried to move Keith, he started to whine.

"I got him," I said and we headed up the stairs as Donte followed behind me. I thought back to all we had talked about as we walked. When we made it to the top, Donte opened the door. I took Keith and put him in Miss Chyna's bed, then gently closed the door.

Donte was in his room, so I stopped and leaned my head in the door. "Hey, I'm gonna head out," then made my way toward the front door. However, I heard him behind me. Donte grabbed his keys, and I turned around.

"I'll walk you home." I was going to protest, but I stopped; there was no point. He locked the door, and we headed down the four flights of stairs to my apartment.

He didn't say a word, and neither did I. When we reached my door, I opened it, and the apartment was dark. "Thank you again," I said as I faced him.

He peeked in. "You sure you're good?"

I nodded with a half-smile. "Yeah, this is the norm." We were both quiet and looked away, so to break the awkwardness, I asked a burning question. It wasn't my business, but the curiosity was too much. "Can I ask you something?" He nodded yes and waited for me to speak. "Why haven't I ever seen you be affectionate with Trina?"

The question caught him off guard, and he frowned but relaxed his face as he thought about it. I wanted to say more, so I did. "I mean, outside, you didn't even hug her. Come to think of it, I've never seen you kiss her or anything." He looked away, slightly chuckling, then looked at me again as if to ponder where the question came from. I knew it was unusual for me to have anything nice to say about Trina of all people. But part of me felt bad for her. "She deserves love, right?" Donte straightened up and just nodded. She did deserve love, even if she was a raging bitch.

Donte spoke frankly. "I don't have an answer for you, Shar…things are the way they are with Trina." He never confirmed or denied showing affection for Trina. However, I could respect it; different strokes for different folks.

"Well, I hope my person doesn't treat me like that." Donte cocked his head to the side and stared. "I want someone who would be affectionate toward me no matter where we are. That's some deeper-level shit that exists only between two people."

He nodded again and partially smiled. "Didn't know you cared so much," he smirked, and I shook my head.

So, I replied, "you wish" then walked inside the apartment.

He made his way to the stairs, then blurted out, "Maybe I do."

The comment caught me off guard, and I turned around, looking back at him. I smiled, knowing he was being funny. I put on my Mr. Rogers voice and replied, "You know, Donte, you are worth it too! You too can find your someone. At least someone you can be affectionate with in public!" I said, laughing.

He acted like he was wiping a tear and smiled. "Maybe one day I will, Shar," then kept going. I wondered if he meant to say *maybe I do* out loud. I tried to shake the comment off, but I couldn't help thinking what if he did?

CHAPTER 3

Unlike most of the girls in the neighborhood, I didn't have too many boyfriends. Technically, I only had one if he counted. Most guys who were interested in me saw me as arm candy or wanted to be my "first." So, I didn't entertain them. However, when Eric approached me, he came off differently. He was a year older than me. One thing that stuck out was he didn't have the same upbringing as most guys in the neighborhood. He came from a respectable two-parent household, lived in a townhome, and traveled to places that only I could dream of. In the beginning, I hung onto every word he said. However, when the math stopped mathing, I saw the real Eric.

Not only was he not cultured, but he was a complete clusterfuck who robbed me of three months of my life. Eric told so many lies in the beginning that it was hard for him to keep up with them later. For instance, he told me he went to private school, but the truth was he dropped out and never bothered to at least get his GED. The car he sported turned out to belong to some chick who lived in the next county. He tried his hand at being the local weed man but failed at rule number one: never get high on your own supply. So, that was short-lived. When we started dating, he said he wasn't interested in sex and that it made him *feel* special that his girl hadn't been "touched." However, when I caught wind of him telling people we had sex for bragging rights, I broke up with him immediately, but he refused to believe that and kept living in the façade of us dating. When it was over, I didn't even know why I agreed to date him. Maybe I felt lonely or left out; either way, I should have let him go sooner than I did.

One evening, walking with Rayna and Tonya, we had just come from a local party and were headed home. We were talking smack like usual about our day. As we headed toward the building, I heard Eric yell my name. I didn't bother to turn around; there was no point because he was headed in our direction anyway. He walked up with P and Paul. P didn't like him, and Paul barely knew him. So, I knew he just happened to be with them. I wasn't in the mood to argue; he was still pissed I broke up with him. Plus, I'd been ignoring him all day because he wanted some money, and I wasn't about to make that mistake again. When we were together, I loaned him $20 after he assured me he'd give it back; however, he didn't, so I vowed I'd never do that shit again. If you've ever dated a weed fiend, you know they have a chemical reaction when they don't get their smoke. Eric would become frustrated, angry, and sometimes enraged. Based on his behavior, I knew he was itching, and my hope for him to go away quietly was very unlikely.

"Yoo, you don't hear me talking to you?" Eric said as he grabbed my shoulder to face him.

"Nah, I don't…you ain't my man anymore, so don't touch me!" I yelled as I snatched away from him.

"Why don't you leave her the fuck alone, Eric?" Rayna yelled as she stepped closer to him.

P put his hand on Rayna's chest to back her up while everyone else looked on.

"Look, Rayna, I don't have a problem with you," Eric said, looking at P. "I just need to talk to Sharnel, please!"

Rayna and P looked at me, and against my better judgment, I said, "Give us a minute, y'all…I'll be upstairs in a minute."

Rayna gave me one more look to make sure I was certain. When I nodded back, everyone went inside, leaving me and Eric alone.

Eric grabbed my arm and led me to the middle of my and P's buildings. We stood under the light as I snatched my arm away and waited for him to speak. When he hesitated before speaking, I knew he was embarrassed by my words in front of the group, and this argument would be no different than before. Eric finally whispered while pointing his finger in my face, "We ain't done until I say we're done, Sharnel, so get that shit correct!"

I was over him and this conversation. He was doing too much; I had already said my piece, so I laughed and smacked his finger from my face before I addressed him again. "Eric, get the fuck on! I'm done! We're not together! I don't fuck with you, and we have nothing else to say to each other!"

I turned to walk away, but Eric grabbed my arm again. However, this time I could feel his nails beginning to dig into my arm, and it hurt.

"Eric, if you don't get the fuck off me," I snapped and tried to pull away, but his grip got stronger. My arm started to feel numb, like it was in a blood pressure sleeve the more I tried to get away from him.

"Where you going, Shar? Huh! What you gonna do?" he said, laughing.

I kept fighting to get away, but he was not having it. "Fuck you, Eric!" I yelled and spit in his face, hoping he would loosen his grip enough to let me go.

Eric wiped his face, and with a sinister laugh, he then raised his hand and punched me.

The feeling of the heat from his fist, followed by the impact of the punch, sent me to the ground. Feeling completely stunned, I couldn't process what just happened, but I acted in rage. Eric hovered over me and kept taunting me.

"Oh, what you gonna do? Huh? Call your mama…daddy? Ain't no one worried about you! You ain't shit…"

Him mocking me pissed me off, and I was now infuriated. Before he could say anything else, I kicked Eric in his nuts, causing him to back up. I got up immediately and started swinging. However, he regained his composure, blocked one of my swings, and was about to rush me to the ground. But this time, he was shoved to the ground by Mr. James.

"Da fuck wrong with you, huh? You a real man hitting a woman! Come on, I'm time enough for your ass!" he said.

Eric just groaned on the ground. I seized the opportunity to jump on him and start pounding.

"You son of a bitch! I should fucking kill you for hitting me!" I yelled.

I kept hitting, punching, and scratching Eric until Mr. James pulled me off mid-swing. Mr. James locked my arms around me and picked me up. However, the rage in my body sent an adrenaline rush through me, and I couldn't stop fighting even while

Mr. James held me. My tears were mixed with sweat, dirt, and whatever else I kicked up.

"You bitch-ass nigga, I'm gonna make your life a living hell!" I yelled, tears streaming down my face and my fists on fire.

"Calm the fuck down, Sharnel!" Mr. James said with bass in his voice.

"That son of a bitch hit me!" I yelled.

As I said the words, I felt ashamed and broken; I couldn't believe Eric hit me. I couldn't believe I let it get that far. The one thing I believed I had going for me was that I never allowed any man to hit me. However, that was now shot to hell. If Mr. James had not arrived, he might have done worse...or I would have.

Still holding onto me, Mr. James walked in the opposite direction of Eric, who still lay on the ground.

"Let me go, Mr. James!" I sobbed.

"Nah baby, you don't fight no man! Especially that piece of shit!"

He just kept walking until we reached the steps of our building. I didn't even know Mr. James was outside, but he was the neighborhood watch; he didn't miss much, so I was grateful for him. By the time he guided me to sit on the steps, I had calmed down. Mr. James let me go and leaned against the brick wall in front of me. I couldn't look at him—one, I was too mad; two, I didn't want him to see my tears; and three, I was embarrassed.

"How did it ever get this far?" I asked.

He didn't say anything, but I heard him texting on his phone right before he lifted my head to look at my face. "You might have a little redness and some swelling tomorrow, but you'll be okay," he said with a slight smile.

My face and my knuckles hurt; I knew I had hit the cement or rock a few times while punching Eric. I put my head in my lap and just cried. Mr. James placed his hand on my back and rubbed it gently. I couldn't believe what had just happened.

"I can't believe he fucking hit me," I mumbled. "Fuck, Shar, fuck!" I said to myself.

"Now baby girl, don't do that! You were defending yourself… you didn't do anything to deserve that!"

I tried to dry my tears quickly so I could get up and leave. However, when I went to stand, Mr. James put his hand on my shoulder and motioned for me to stay seated.

"Hang out here for a few more minutes."

I wanted to protest, but I didn't; I just put my head in my lap and covered my face.

A few minutes later, I heard Rayna, P, and Paul come out the front door.

"Hey y'all, what happened?" Rayna asked, concerned.

Mr. James didn't say anything, but when Rayna looked down at my hands, which were now swollen, she flipped out.

"Shar! What the fuck happened?" she yelled before removing my arms from my lap so she could see my face. "That mothafucka hit you!"

Rayna immediately went down the steps to look for Eric. P matched her steps and held onto her hand in case Eric was still around.

"Babe, relax, she's good… ain't nothing to worry about!" P said, looking at me with fury in his eyes.

However, that did nothing for Rayna; she was on fire and kept looking around for Eric.

"I can't believe he raised his hand to you! When I see him…" Rayna yelled.

"Settle down, Rayna; she's alright!" Mr. James said calmly.

Rayna took a seat on the opposite side of me. I leaned my head against the brick wall and closed my eyes. I was finally settling down emotionally and wanted to go home. However, that was not possible with everyone surrounding me.

A few moments later, when I heard the building door open, I took a breath. Urgh, one more person to see my pain. I opened my eyes, when I felt someone gently grab my hands and lay them flat on my knees. Donte put an ice pack on my knuckles. I looked at him, and then he took Mr. James' place in front of me. He examined my face and nodded, then looked away. I didn't want him, of all people, to see me like this. He didn't make a joke or even say a word—not that I thought he would. He just looked ahead, occasionally glancing down at me. After Rayna calmed down, she sat closer to me and leaned her head on my shoulder as I continued to rest mine against the wall.

"Shar, I'm so sorry; we should never have left!" she said remorsefully.

I soothed her as best as I could. "Ray, neither of us would have ever thought he was going to do that!" I knew that didn't make either of us feel better, but it was the only thing I could think of.

We sat in silence for a few minutes.

"Fuck, what does this nigga want now?" P mumbled.

He motioned toward Donte, who looked behind him. Mr. James, who had been sitting, stood up and stared in silence. Sitting on the step, my view was blocked by the wall. So, I stood up and saw Eric coming back toward us. Rayna stood up and immediately jumped three steps to meet Eric. However, P, who was already at the bottom of the steps, caught and held her.

"Relax, Rayna! Chill the hell out!" P mumbled.

He whispered something in her ear, and she calmed down, even relaxing her posture. Donte didn't say anything or move; he just looked in the direction of the steps while still standing in front of me. Eric walked boldly to the building and stood about ten paces from the steps. I could see that I had landed a few punches on Eric's face and scratched him. He had not calmed down; if anything, he was still furious.

"Shar, let's go!" Eric demanded, unfazed by anyone.

"Fuck you, Eric! You ain't shit for hitting a woman!" Rayna yelled as P continued to hold her.

When she tried to lunge at Eric, Donte made eye contact with P and motioned for him to take her inside.

"We're gonna fuck you up! Bitch! Just wait!" Rayna promised as P guided her inside.

Once Rayna was gone, Eric went back to his rant and took one step closer.

"Sharnel!!! I said let's go!"

I was about to yell back, but Donte put his hand in front of me, and Mr. James took a step closer to Eric.

"Son, take that shit elsewhere… you done said enough for the evening! Go on home now," Mr. James said calmly.

Eric turned to Mr. James and just laughed, using his hands to make his point.

"Man, mind your business; you intruded enough! I'm talking to my girl."

Mr. James just nodded and smiled as Eric turned back toward me.

"…now, Sharnel, bring your…"

Before Eric could finish, Mr. James went down the two steps from the bottom. He gripped Eric's shoulder, causing him to yell each time he tightened his grip. Mr. James looked like he had blacked out; his face was red, and his eyes looked glazed over.

"Now she done told you y'all are done! So, it's nothing left to say! I seen you come and go like you own shit!" Mr. James squeezed a little tighter, causing Eric to fall to his knees. "Ain't you Etta's boy?" he said, looking at Eric, who was nodding and now sweating. "You see, I know your peoples… all of them!" Mr. James put his face close to Eric and smiled. "Ask about me, and if you dare, come on back around here, and I'll show you what everyone knows about me!"

He let Eric go, and he winced in pain while trying to adjust his shoulder and catch his breath. Mr. James extended his hand and helped Eric off the ground.

"You see that girl," he said, pointing at me, "I ain't her daddy, but that there is mine! This building and everyone in it, they mine too!" He stepped in front of Eric, getting close enough to whisper, "Don't EVER fuck with what's mine, okay?" Then he patted Eric on the shoulder he had just gripped and motioned for him to leave.

Eric stumbled then kept walking and never looked back. A few days later, I heard Eric got jumped while on his way home. Maybe it was a weed deal that had gone wrong; it didn't matter; I could care less. After that, he went to live with his father in Texas, and I never heard from him again.

I stood stunned. I'd heard about Mr. James but never saw him like that. Mr. James returned to the steps, happy and calm. He looked at Donte, and they both just nodded. When he walked past me, I kept looking for any sign of him being the angry man I had just seen. However, he just smiled.

"Go get you some rest, baby girl! You alright now."

He patted my shoulder and entered the building, going to his apartment. I couldn't believe it and tried to process what I had just witnessed. Donte, on the other hand, didn't seem surprised and looked down at his phone. Moments later, Donte walked toward the building door and opened it.

"Come on, let's go."

I entered the building and was about to walk down the stairs, but he gently grabbed my arm.

"Nah, you're staying with us tonight," he said and waited for me to head up the stairs.

I was fine; Eric was gone… was this necessary? I was too tired to argue, and, truth be told, I was grateful not to be alone tonight. So, I headed up the stairs without a word of protest, for once. He didn't say a word, and neither did I. Once we reached Miss Chyna's apartment, he opened the door, and we walked in. Rayna and P were in the living room watching TV. Neither of them said anything, but I was glad she had calmed down. The rest of the night was a blur; I remember sitting on the opposite sofa from P and Rayna and laying my head down on the arm of the sofa, and that was it. I fell asleep.

When I woke up, it was around 5:30 AM The living room was dark, but I could see the sun starting to peek up. I lay on the sofa and looked at my aching knuckles. They were no longer red, but bruised with a few cuts. Everything in me wanted to go back to sleep, but it was a school day. So, I sat up, stretched, and folded the blanket that had been over me. I headed to the bathroom to clean up a bit before heading home. Miss Chyna always kept a spare toiletry kit for me, so I washed my face, brushed my teeth, and fixed my hair. I felt refreshed and ready to go home to finish getting ready. When I opened the bathroom door and turned off the light, I almost ran into Donte. He was already dressed for work and headed toward the living room.

"Hey," I whispered, trying not to wake anyone else.

"Sup! You good?" he asked, looking at my face, then at my hands.

I'd almost forgotten about last night just that quickly. My face was fine, but my hands looked rough. I nodded.

"Yeah," I was about to walk away.

"You about to head out?" he asked.

"Yeah, I need to go get ready for school, I guess."

He nodded. "Okay, cool, I'll walk you out."

I nodded, and we headed toward the front door. I waited for Donte to lock the door, but before we headed down the steps, I tried to think of something smart to say, but my quick wit failed me. So, I said something different.

"Thank you for last night… I appreciate it."

He stood emotionless and just nodded. I wanted to say more but didn't have the words. So, I headed down the stairs.

As we reached the front door, we ran into Regina, who was obviously just coming in.

"Sooo, looks like I wasn't the only one in them streets last night, huh?"

She reeked of alcohol and whatever else she'd done the night before. She looked like hell but tried to play it off terribly. I was so ashamed in that moment; I was about to say something when she looked at my hands.

"What the fuck happened, Sharnel?" she asked, slightly annoyed while pointing at my hands.

I took a breath. "Eric hit me, so I hit him back."

She touched my chin and surveyed my face. Regina shook her head.

"I bet it was that mouth." Her insinuation that I deserved it crushed me; however, she wasn't finished. "You never know when to shut it, and you're always doing something to run men away," she scolded. "You need to go apologize and hope he takes you back!" she mumbled.

I couldn't believe she had the audacity to say that to me. Drunk, high, or whatever she was, no good mother should ever say that about their child. I was stunned. After her rant, Regina walked down the steps to unlock the apartment and went inside. I was completely crushed. In shock, I forgot Donte was even standing behind me. When he put his hand on my shoulder, tears began to fall. I tried to wipe them quickly off my face, but it was no use. I headed toward the steps to the apartment, but he stopped me.

Still emotionless in his face but stern in his voice, he spoke, "Nah man, let's go!" We headed outside; the coolness of the air was amazing, but my tears were cold. Taking in the air, I tried to find new life, energy, or something to replace the verbal gut punch Regina had given me. We walked to his car just as Miss Chyna pulled up from her overnight shift. I tried to get myself together and put on a normal face, but she read me like a book.

"Hey, Miss Chyna," I said with a weak smile.

"Hey, babies," she said. I could tell she wanted to know what was wrong but didn't ask. She looked at Donte and just nodded. "Why don't y'all go get some breakfast for the house?" she said, smiling. "Take my car, and Donte, put some gas in it for me," she instructed.

He nodded, and she handed him the keys. Miss Chyna came over and gave me a big hug, then looked at my hands.

"No need to be ashamed; you stood on your two feet. James taking up for you doesn't mean you're weak… he did what a man was supposed to do," she said before walking away.

No surprise that she had heard about the incident with Eric. People couldn't keep secrets in this neighborhood. Miss Chyna headed inside, and Donte and I got into her car. Once we saw her enter the apartment from afar, thanks to the lights in the building, we headed to get breakfast and fill up her car.

Donte turned on the radio, and it was just a bunch of talking.

"You mind if I put on some music?" I asked.

Donte looked at me and frowned. "So when you're in this car, you ask, but in my car, you just touch shit?" He shook his head. "Go ahead, man, but I don't wanna hear no girly shit," he fussed.

I shook my head and rolled my eyes. I decided to put on my *Vibin'* playlist, which was a mix of rap/hip-hop and trap music. Before the song started, I turned the volume up. Donte glanced at me from the side of his eye, frowning. When *Outkast's "Liberation"* played, his attitude changed. He smiled slightly, turned up the music, and nodded his head. Guess my music choice wasn't so bad after all. As we drove along, I wanted to enjoy the breeze.

"You mind if I crack the window a bit?"

Donte never stopped nodding his head; he just let down all the windows enough to enjoy the breeze. It was the perfect scenario: music, relaxation, and the sunrise. I almost regretted it when we pulled up to the local diner. Donte parked, and I turned down the music.

"I can call in the order, and we can just wait here… or we can go in," I said.

"Okay, cool, let's call it in," Donte replied, rattling off the order as I called it in.

"They said about 15 minutes," I said after hanging up the phone.

Donte nodded and turned the music slightly up.

I was still feeling slightly weird about my interaction and reaction with Regina. When I turned the music down a bit, he looked at me. Feeling uncomfortable, I finally spoke.

"Look, about Regina, I'm sorry…"

He put his hand up. "No explanation needed. Don't even take that shit to heart. Just 'cause she ain't shit don't mean you are."

Wait, did he just pay me a compliment? I looked at Donte, confused, but he just turned the music back up and pulled out his phone. I faced forward, still baffled. His comment made me feel good; it soothed me, and I almost wanted to cry. However, I had enough of that and didn't want him to see that, especially not because of him.

He was right, though; I didn't have to be a reflection of Regina. While looking at his phone, I kept glancing over at him. Who was this, and why was he so damn nice now on multiple occasions? I guess my glances were too frequent.

"What, Shar?" he said, never looking up, just waiting for a response.

"Don't take this the wrong way, but who are you right now?" Now looking at him, he closed his phone and shrugged to indicate he didn't understand.

"Donte, you ain't never been this nice to me."

He gave me the *really?* face, so I continued, "Don't get me wrong, I appreciate it, but it's just… I don't know," searching for the words I mumbled, "different."

He cleared his throat. "I ain't a complete asshole, Shar, despite being emotionless, as you described."

Wait, was that what he got from my comments that night? I acted quickly to clear it up. He was about to get out, but I locked the doors and touched his arm. Donte was surprised by my actions, further surprised by my touching him. I urgently rushed the words out.

"Donte, that's not what I meant at all that night! What I meant was…"

He immediately started laughing; it was then I realized he was joking. His hysterical laugh made me laugh slightly.

"Got your ass, Shar; was about to have a *Lifetime* moment thinking I misunderstood you."

Now I wanted him to get out as my embarrassment settled in. After he contained himself, he spoke up. "But for real, though, you good, man?"

Now I couldn't look at him; it was too much. He just nodded and chuckled.

"Yo, I'm about to go get this food."

When Donte returned, we continued to vibe in silence. He filled up Miss Chyna's car, and we headed home.

As he drove, I thought about his words regarding Regina. As I pondered his words again, I smiled and sat a little taller in the seat, stepping into my confidence. I was literally having a therapy session with myself, hyping and assuring myself I was going to be fine. I was so in my head I didn't realize Donte was staring at me, wondering what just happened. What I didn't factor in was the head movements and finger pointing that took place. Nor did I realize we were already back home.

Laughing yet looking concerned, Donte asked, "You good? Having a *Fix My Life* moment?"

"Yep, sure was." Fuck it; he'd seen me cry already; might as well be honest.

As we sat in the car, Regina and Uncle of the Week were headed toward the parking lot but didn't see us, thankfully. Part of me felt a little sad, but I shook it off. I just shook my head and smiled; unaffected, I had a new mindset.

"Let's go before everything gets cold," I said. We both opened the door and got out.

As we walked toward the building, Donte mumbled the last song we heard on my playlist. "Cash rules everything around me."

I couldn't resist and finished the line, "CREAM, get the money, dolla dolla bills, y'all," laughing and smiling.

Impressed I didn't just listen to the music but knew the words, he nodded and smiled. On the way upstairs, we talked about the *Mics of Men* documentary on the *Wu-Tang Clan* and argued about who was the best lyricist.

"It's Deck or Meth," I said, standing my ground. He waved me off.

"Man, it's Rae, Ghost, or GZA." I stopped him before we reached the last few steps.

"So, you're telling me neither one of my picks is in the conversation?"

He thought about it. "Aight, aight, they are."

Satisfied, I was about to walk away. "Hold up; you saying mine ain't?" he asked, looking for confirmation.

I pulled one of Keith's numbers, putting my hand on my chin while I pondered and hummed. "Okay, okay, you got a point... but we also gotta include Cap." He nodded, and then I went up the remaining stairs.

As I waited for him to open the door, he looked over at me. "Let me find out you got taste in music, at least."

At least? What the hell did that mean? I scowled. "I got taste in a lot, thank you. Too bad you're just getting hip."

Donte opened the door, and I walked in. I knew I was well-rounded and versed in a lot; he needed to wake up. By the time we got inside, everyone was up and ready for the day. We all ate, and then everyone dispersed. P announced last night he was going to give Rayna and me a ride to school, "in case Eric's bitch ass decided to show up," so I headed home to get dressed.

"Aight, y'all, I'm out," I said. "Thank y'all again for everything," I said, looking at Donte.

He nodded, and Rayna frowned her face, then walked me to the door. She whispered, "Ewww, what's going on with that?" leaning her head toward Donte.

I didn't even respond and was about to walk away, but she stopped me. "Umm, I don't know what happened, but something changed." She gave me the eye and laughed.

I just brushed off her comment, still not responding. As I headed downstairs, I realized something did happen… Donte and I found common ground that didn't involve fighting, which changed everything.

CHAPTER 4

After everything that happened, things between Donte and me went back to normal. We hurled sarcastic insults at each other, cussed each other out, and purposely pushed each other just because. He called me "Big Head," and I referred to him as "Him," as if he didn't have a name. So, it appeared as if nothing had changed between us. I tried to ignore what Rayna said, but I couldn't. Internally, I was having different feelings. I found myself looking for him and wanting to be in his space. Although I'd never admit it, he was always on my mind.

As I walked around the neighborhood, like I often did when Regina pissed me off, I needed to clear my mind of her latest rant. She complained I was home "too much," meaning she was about to have company, and I was fucking it up. Not unusual for her, but it meant I'd spend my evening in the laundry room until morning or when the coast was clear. This wasn't a problem for me; I was used to it. At least I'd get some peace.

As I made my way back toward the parking lot, I saw Donte with Trina, of all people. He leaned against his car, looking at his phone, and she was standing in front of him, ranting and pointing, as usual. There she goes again, not paying attention to his disinterest. It surprised me how she didn't realize he didn't give two shits about her rants or angry outbursts. Usually, I would have made a face or drawn attention to piss Trina off. But after recognizing how he dismissed her, it was no longer worth my time or interest. If anything, I hoped she would wise up, but if that's how she wanted to keep a man, she could have it. I walked but kept my eyes on him.

"Why can't she see he's not interested in her and his interests lie somewhere else?" I said aloud, almost shocking myself with the comment.

"Oh yeah, and who has his attention, Shar?" Rayna said, snapping me out of my thoughts. She waited for a response, looking me up and down. I had no response and shrugged my shoulders.

"Dang, Shar, you like Donte." Rayna scrunched up her face while acting like she was throwing up. I didn't acknowledge her words; I just kept walking.

In that moment, I had an epiphany. What if I was standing in front of Donte? What would be different? *He'd be leaning against his car; only his phone would be in his pocket. His hands would be around my waist, and I would have my hands around his neck. We'd smile at each other right before we…* As I smiled, Rayna waved her hands in front of my face.

"Shar, are you listening to me or nah?" I rolled my eyes and then looked at her. She busted out laughing so loudly that both Donte and Trina looked in our direction. He put his phone away, and we made eye contact. His expression was emotionless as usual, but his eyes said something different. I wondered if he was thinking of me the way I thought of him.

Almost simultaneously, Rayna and Trina started waving their hands in front of our faces, and we both looked away. "What did you say?" I finally acknowledged her.

"I said, earth to Shar! I've been talking for the last few minutes, and you ain't heard shit I said!" she complained.

When I looked at Donte, he looked in my direction as Trina was now pointing at me and yelling. "What the fuck you looking at, Donte? Why that young bitch got you in a trance?" she yelled.

Usually, I would have stepped to her, but it was no point. Donte didn't do outbursts, and her jealous rant would only piss him off, and he'd walk away. True to form, he stood up and walked away from his car and Trina. Of course, she followed him, re-asking her questions again.

They were about 30 feet closer to us when he turned and finally acknowledged her. "If I was interested in shorty, you just showed she got the upper hand!"

What did he mean, if? His words stung a bit, but I didn't reply; I just kept walking toward the building. Rayna was also on repeat with her questions, so I finally stopped walking and listened to her.

"So, Shar, do you like him or something?" Rayna waited for a response, but I honestly didn't know. I felt something, but I wasn't sure if it was because I was vulnerable, wanted to piss off Trina, or if it was because it was real. I smiled and said anything to get her to move on.

"Girl, please! I only entertain him to piss Trina off! The fact that she acts all jealous is fucking hilarious." Right as I finished my words, Donte walked up. I immediately regretted them and prayed he didn't hear them. He didn't say a word; he just looked at me, then nodded.

"Where's your hood booger?" Rayna said as we walked toward the building.

"Man, ain't nobody thinking about Trina's ass!" he said.

"Urgh, why you deal with her anyway?" Rayna said. "She ain't even your type; she must have some bomb head or pussy!"

I was curious and wanted to hear his answer, so I turned my head towards him to hear his response. Donte looked at me, but before he could answer, Rayna's phone rang, and she answered it.

"Hold up, y'all! I gotta meet P real quick… I'll be right back!" She walked in the opposite direction, leaving Donte and me standing. We watched her walk toward the parking lot as P pulled up.

I looked back at him. "So what's your answer?" I said flatly.

Donte dropped his head and chuckled a bit as he shook it. Then he looked up and stood closer to me. "What difference does it make? You only entertain me to piss Trina off, right?"

The words from his mouth made my heart drop. I guess my face showed my reaction; then he whispered, "Keep feeding yourself that bullshit; we both know it ain't true!"

Bullshit or not, I knew I wasn't alone in my potential feelings… at least I hoped not. He was about to walk away, but I stopped him by putting my hand on his chest. He looked at my hand, but I didn't move it, then whispered, "Bullshit or not, what difference does it make? You still entertain her, and you ain't checking for me!" Donte didn't say a word, but his face softened a bit.

I was surprised by his reaction; usually, he would say something smart, but he didn't. "Wait, do you…?" Just as I was about to finish, Rayna walked up with P. Donte stepped back and turned his attention to P.

"What up, brotha Dee!" P said, giving him a brotherly handshake. "What's up, Sister Shar!" he added while giving me a side hug.

"I'm coolin', P! What's up with you?" I said, looking at Donte but talking to P.

"Ain't shit! Hoping my man Dee's gonna slide out to the pool hall with me a little later!" Donte nodded at P, then glanced at me. We all walked toward the building.

"We wanna go!" Rayna yelled. She was always trying to get P to take us out with him and Donte. She knew we weren't of age to get in anywhere, so it was pointless. Donte always reminded her of that.

"Man, y'all young asses can't get in nowhere," he snapped. Rayna folded her arms, and P laughed but tried to soothe her with a kiss on the cheek and put his arm around her as we walked.

"Hate to say it, babe, but he's right!" P said. When we reached the building, P opened the door, and we all walked in.

I headed toward my steps, needing air and space to myself. Rayna said, "Shar, where you going? You're supposed to be having dinner with us!"

Of course, she would say that. Everyone looked at me, including Donte, so I made up a quick lie. "I need to go home and grab some stuff to put in the wash, and then I'll be there," I said. I needed to do laundry, but I also needed a moment. She nodded, and then I headed home. When I entered my apartment, I closed the door and leaned against it. "What the fuck, man!" I said out loud. "Of all the shit for him to hear… why that? Further, he didn't answer my question—what kind of bullshit was that? Was I tripping, thinking he showed some reaction?"

Just as the words came out, my phone chimed. I reached into my purse to check the message, and it was from him:

Him: *Mommy said can you bring her some season salt… dinner at 7!*

Big Head (as it appeared in his phone): *Sure, I'll bring it up shortly!*

I wanted to say more but didn't. I wanted him to know I lied to Rayna, but he already knew it, right? This was all becoming too confusing, and I wanted to stop it before it got worse.

I took my time going upstairs and decided to freshen up and change. When I got upstairs and opened the door to Miss Chyna's house, I could smell the food. My stomach instantly growled as I closed the door.

"Hungry ass!" Donte said as he took his seat at the table.

"Shut up!" I snapped. Now I knew things were back to normal. Of course, he hurled an insult as soon as he saw me. Good, no need to even think about that other shit. I made my way from the platform to the kitchen where Miss Chyna was.

"Oh, thank you, baby! I asked my daughter weeks ago to get some, and you see she followed directions!" she said.

"You can keep that; ain't like Regina's using it." I laughed.

Miss Chyna smiled and put her arm around me. "Well, you know I'ma cook for you anytime you're hungry! Go wash your hands so we can eat!"

I smiled and headed toward the bathroom. Donte was looking at his phone while at the table, which was against the rules. "Miss Chyna! Donte's got his phone at the table!" I yelled.

He looked up and snarled at me.

"Donte, you know I don't allow no phones at my table!" his mother snapped.

"Yep, you sure don't!" I said and laughed as I headed toward the bathroom. I heard Donte get up from the table, so I hurried to the bathroom as I laughed. As I finished up, I opened the door just as he was coming out of his room.

"Ole snitchin' ass!" he mumbled.

"Whatever, you know the rules!" I said, laughing as I walked down the hall with him behind me.

"Don't be salty because I ain't entertaining you!" he mumbled.

There it was again; why were we even discussing this? I stopped short, and he ran into the back of me. I turned around, and he didn't back up. "Ain't like you're interested anyway!" I said, glaring at him.

He didn't respond but looked down at me. "Man, take your young ass on, Shar; keep moving!" I kept moving, and we headed toward the table.

Donte sat down, and I headed into the kitchen. Once I entered, Miss Chyna handed me a plate. "Shar, make Donte's plate," she instructed. I nodded. "Remember he don't eat…"

Before she could finish her sentence, I said, "pork, collard greens, baked beans, and he likes his cornbread or roll on a separate plate so they don't get soggy."

She was impressed and raised her hands as if to say she surrendered. I made his plate, then walked back to the dining room. I set the plate in front of him, and he inspected it and nodded. "You can say thank you!" I snapped.

He shook his head. "Yeah, I could!" he replied.

"Donte, where are your manners! Thank that girl!" his mother snapped.

"Nah, it's okay, Miss Chyna; next time he can have his hood booger make his plate! Since that's what he likes! Oops, she ain't allowed in the house!" I said, making eye contact with him as he glared before I headed back into the kitchen.

Miss Chyna did not like Trina and had banned her from the house after she showed her ass. *When Donte first started dating Trina, he didn't tell anyone. As a matter of fact, we found out by accident when she showed up unannounced one day. The family (including P, Paul, Tonya, and myself) had just come back from dinner.*

We were sitting in front of the building talking shit as usual. Miss Chyna, who normally went inside, decided to stay outside to allow a then three-year-old Keith to tire himself out since he was riled up from the dessert she now regretted giving him. The fellas were engaged in a sidebar conversation, while Rayna and Tonya did the same, and I entertained Keith. Keith and I were engaged in a repetitive game of tag, which consisted of him running a few paces and me scooping him up.

Miss Chyna stood next to Donte; they leaned against the brick wall that lined the handrails of the front steps of the building. Miss Chyna was on her phone, and no one paid attention to Trina walking up until she was right on us. Trina, in her typical ratchet fashion, assumed first and asked questions last. She rolled up on Donte's alleged woman and stood toe to toe with her. "Umm, who the fuck are you? And why are you standing so close to my nigga, bitch!"

Miss Chyna didn't flinch or even show any emotion. Donte was about to say something, but Miss Chyna put her hand in front of him while still looking at her phone.

"Oh, so you don't hear me?" Trina yelled again.

Miss Chyna looked up at her, then smiled before she stepped closer. "Oh, you must be her!" Trina nodded confidently to confirm the statement.

Miss Chyna looked Trina up and down, then continued. "Son, you should really pick a better caliber of woman! You've seen and know of better!" She said, side-eyeing Donte and then looking back at Trina. Trina's mouth fell open as Miss Chyna nodded and smiled.

Miss Chyna took her hand slightly and closed Trina's mouth. However, she didn't drop her hand but used it to clinch Trina's cheeks. "Now, I'ma give you a pass because you obviously didn't know who I was. Plus, I respect a bitch protecting who she THINKS is her man."

Donte just shook his head, knowing Trina had utterly fucked up. Trina tried to look at him, but Miss Chyna wasn't having it. She directed Trina's eyes back toward her. "In case it's not clear, Donte is my son, honey, and I am his mother! Nice to meet you, I'm Chyna," she said, smiling. We thought she was finished, but she wasn't. "Let me give you a word of advice. Don't ever roll up on any woman and disrespect her the way you did to me… you never know what type of day someone is having." Miss Chyna moved Trina's face to help her nod in agreement. "Had I been about the age of my daughters there, I'd mop your ass up and down this sidewalk on sight. And I still might, or let my daughters do it on the wrong day; you got me?" Trina nodded, and Miss Chyna let her face go. Trina tried to get the feeling back into her face. Miss Chyna shook her head and stepped in front of Donte. "I hope she's a plaything because I know I raised you better than that!" He didn't say anything, just stood with a straight face.

She came to me and took Keith, not before winking and heading inside. We had never seen Miss Chyna boss up on someone, so we just stood silent and stunned when she left. Trina walked off, still rubbing her face, and Donte didn't even follow her or ask if she was okay. A few minutes later, we all finally made it upstairs. Miss Chyna let Donte and everyone know Trina *was not allowed in her house, let alone her space, or she'd make good on her bad day promise. That's all we needed to hear.*

When I finally fixed my plate and sat down across from Donte, we were ready to pray and eat. We all joined hands, and Miss Chyna prayed, then we ate. "So, ladies, are y'all ready for graduation?" Miss Chyna asked. I nodded.

"Yep… we're even more ready for this party!" Rayna said.

I smiled. "Yep, gonna be bomb AF!" I chimed.

Miss Chyna beamed. "Well, y'all deserve it!" She was right; we finally made it through high school.

"Miss Chyna, did Regina send you the last of the money?" I knew my mother was irresponsible when it came to things, but I hoped she wasn't with this.

"You know your mama is last minute, baby! But don't worry about it… she will catch up! She always does!" Miss Chyna said while smiling. In that moment, I felt embarrassed and ashamed. Why was I always an afterthought with Regina? It was bad enough I was here all the time and Miss Chyna practically took care of me. The least she could do was be on time with the money and show appreciation.

"It's alright, Shar! Nothing to worry about!" Miss Chyna said, snapping me out of my thoughts. I knew my face reflected my feelings, but I couldn't help it.

Rayna put her hand on my leg and said, "It's still gonna be lit, bestie! So, don't even let it get to you. You know Miss Regina's gonna come through at the last minute."

I half-smiled and knew I had to get the rest of the money to Miss Chyna ASAP. I made a note to call Regina and remind her until she actually did it. When dinner was over, Rayna was on Keith duty while I cleaned up the kitchen.

My mind was still on the money; why did she have to be so irresponsible? As I cleaned the counter, I heard P and Donte talking in the living room. They were about to head to the pool hall. Rayna, in her typical fashion, was whining about P leaving her out. It was the same song and dance, so I tuned her out. I was so wrapped up in cleaning that I didn't see Donte standing in the doorway.

"You good?"

I didn't say a word; I just nodded yes. Not believing me, he inquired further.

"I know you ain't still thinking about the money," he said, then looked for confirmation.

I just shrugged and turned my back toward him as I felt tears form in my eyes. I was tired of Regina embarrassing me. Every time she came around or something involving her happened, I hid my head in shame.

"Shar, man, you heard Mommy… everything is good!" he said, then he walked over and touched my shoulder, and I nodded.

I felt a few tears fall from my eyes, and I prayed he didn't see them.

"Aye Dee, you ready!" P yelled from the living room.

"You good either way, man… we gonna make sure you're straight, aight?"

I nodded, and he removed his hand from my shoulder. When I heard him leave the kitchen, I wiped my face and shook off my feelings. When I was sure I was good, I went to the dining room to put the placemats back on the table. Donte and P were headed toward the door; he looked at me, but I just stared down, and then they left.

When I finished cleaning the kitchen, Rayna and I decided to sit outside at the front of the building. Tonya's mom said she could chill a bit before her curfew of 11:30 PM. We sat outside and talked about graduation and, of course, the party. I really didn't want to think about the party anymore, but that wasn't an option with these two.

"My daddy and cousin Tammy are coming into town!" Rayna said proudly.

I loved Mr. Tony, but Tammy I'd pass on! She didn't care for me, and I didn't care for her.

"Well, all my people are here!" Tonya said, not to be outdone. "What about you, Shar? Anyone coming in from your family?"

I shook my head no. "Nope, other than Regina and Uncle of the Week (maybe), that's it."

Rayna nudged Tonya; it was a stupid question because she knew the answer, but that was Tonya. Messy was her MO! I didn't pay it any mind or even care; my life was no secret. Plus, if I reacted to every messy comment, I'd be constantly whooping her ass.

My Papa and Granny would attend if they hadn't died, but I knew they'd be there in spirit, so that worked for me.

"Well, what about Eric?" Tonya said.

Right then, Rayna and I looked at her.

"Really, bitch? That's all you could muster up!" Rayna said, "dumbass!"

Tonya wasn't outside the night Eric and I got into it. She had to go home early for one reason or another. However, she heard the replay the next day as a few people attempted to recount what happened according to Eric, of course. Still, she knew Eric and I were completely done, so that question was uncalled for. Tonya immediately felt bad and tried to apologize, but I put my hand up. I was over her and the conversation.

"Well, her undiscovered boo will be there!" Rayna said as she nudged me.

I frowned and wondered why she would say that in front of Tonya. We told her things but not everything. Tonya looked at me, and I rolled my eyes.

"Umm, Shar, who is Rayna speaking of?" Tonya said while smiling and waiting for the "undiscovered" tea.

Rayna was too happy as she responded, "her boo Donte!"

I shook my head and rolled my eyes. The mention of Donte caused Tonya to lean in as if she misunderstood.

"Wait, doesn't he belong to Trina?" Tonya asked, as if this was news to me.

I took a breath and wondered why my friends couldn't just shut the fuck up.

When I didn't reply, Tonya continued, "Well, hell, if he's free…I'd date him! He's cute in a scary way!" She blushed and smiled while flipping her hair.

Both Rayna and I looked at her. "You joking, right?" Rayna said, thinking she was playing.

When Tonya didn't back down, I inquired, "Since when did you become so interested in him?" Rayna and I looked at her, waiting for a response.

"What you mean? I've always thought he was cute…I mean, he is closer to my age than y'all!" Tonya said with sass.

Now, it was true Tonya had stayed back two grades, so she was slightly older than us. I shook my head because I knew she was only interested in him because she thought I was. Which pissed me off; I knew Donte would never consider Tonya. Not to be mean, but she was almost equivalent to Trina in terms of her need for attention. I knew it was messy, but I called her bluff.

"If you like him so much, shoot your shot!" I said sarcastically.

Tonya waved me off. "I'm serious! Who knows? He might be the one boo!"

There was no way in hell he would say yes, but she acted like it, so I wanted to see her try.

Rayna chuckled and looked at Tonya for a response. I had to give it to Tonya; she didn't back down. Rayna looked towards the parking lot.

"Oh, look who's coming, Tonya! Here's your chance!" she said.

I stood up and leaned against the wall so I could get a front-row seat to the foolishness. As Donte and P walked up, they talked. Rayna laughed and shook her head, knowing Tonya would not back down. When they finally made it to us, Rayna spoke while trying to control her laughter.

"Hey, y'all!"

Donte nodded, and P hugged her while she continued laughing.

Donte was about to go in, but Rayna stopped him.

"Wait, Dee…hang out with us for a few minutes!" Rayna said, smiling, then nodded her head towards Tonya, giving her the green light.

Donte must have peeped the game; he stood at the bottom of the steps and looked at Rayna. Rayna and I both looked at Tonya; she took a breath.

"What's up, Donte!" she said slyly, then walked down the stairs to stand next to him.

His face immediately dropped, and he frowned. "Man, Tonya, get your ass on somewhere!"

She tried to get closer, and he held up his hand. "Not gonna happen!"

She was annoyed and put her hands on her hips. "Why not? What, you can't handle a real woman?" she said while snapping her fingers.

This was becoming funnier by the minute. Just as the words came out, Tonya's little brother appeared in the front door of the building.

"Mama said it's after 11:30; it's time for you to come in!"

We all died laughing as the building door closed. Tonya was fuming and made her way back up the steps to the front door. "That shit couldn't have been timed better," P laughed while holding on to Rayna, who also laughed.

The only person who didn't laugh was Donte; he looked disgusted at her attempt. "Grown women don't have a curfew!" Donte said, shaking his head.

We all laughed again, and Tonya became enraged. She opened the door and was about to go in but not before addressing Donte.

"Whatever, Donte! I don't want no GED-ass nigga anyway!"

I know this bitch didn't! Before my mind could process her comment, I hopped up the stairs and stood toe-to-toe with Tonya. Everyone was silent, including myself. However, my face displayed my frustration that she even had the audacity to say such a comment. My expression dared her to say something else, and I would break loose on her. She'd seen me do it to others—never her or Rayna, but this time I would definitely make an exception. My fists were at my side balled up and ready. Tonya stood confused and hurt at the same time.

"Damn, Shar, it's like that!" she said, almost in tears.

I didn't say anything but moved closer to her to show her I meant it. Rayna came up the steps and stepped to the side of Tonya and me. Without acknowledging Tonya, she searched my face and put her hand on my chest. I looked at her hand, then at her, with the same glare I had for Tonya.

"Come on, Shar! You good?"

I nodded, and Rayna moved me so she could switch places with me, and I faced the glass, staring into the building. As I needed a moment to get it together.

"Tonya, man, just go!" Rayna urged.

I wasn't sure if Tonya acknowledged her, but I did hear the door close.

"Dammmn!" P mumbled. "Dee, Shar jumped up them damn steps!" He laughed. "Shorty was about to give it to her! That's what she gets for always popping off at the mouth…bout to be an ass whooping long overdue!" he added while still laughing.

P was being messy, but he was right about the last part. Only, I wasn't going to fight Tonya over the bullshit she said to me but about Donte.

When I finally turned around and looked down at Donte, he looked skeptical about what had just happened. However, my scowl was confirmation of my reaction. I just looked away and nodded. I felt a myriad of emotions: frustration, shock, and awkwardness. I needed to walk off whatever I was feeling, so I headed down the steps without saying anything to anyone.

"Sister Shar, where you going, man!" P yelled.

"I need a minute, P; I'll be back!" I yelled, increasing my pace.

"Wait up, Shar!" Rayna yelled.

I just waved her off and didn't acknowledge her, just kept walking.

It was dark, but I didn't care. I needed a moment, but I also knew Rayna would follow me. So, I wasn't surprised when I heard footsteps behind me. I didn't even turn around; I just started talking.

"Tonya crossed the line twice tonight! She was lucky her curfew saved her ass; P was right—that was about to be an ass whooping long overdue! What the fuck is wrong with her, Ray?" I shouted in frustration.

"I dunno; shorty's on one tonight, I guess!"

My face dropped immediately when I realized Donte responded and not Rayna. I turned around and stopped as he was about ten paces behind me.

When he caught up, he just stood there emotionlessly, and I matched his expression. Eventually, we started walking in silence. I started to feel embarrassed about my reaction and wished he wasn't there.

"You don't have to..." I said, hoping he would turn and leave. However, I knew he wouldn't.

"I ain't about to let you walk out here by yourself, man."

I shook my head and tried again. "I'm not scared! This ain't my first time...I'm good!"

Donte was now frustrated. "Man, Sharnel, keep fuckin' walking, man." I knew he wasn't leaving, so I just let it go.

We walked in silence, then he finally spoke up. "Why y'all set shorty up like that?" he said bluntly.

It was a good icebreaker as I was still coming down from my emotions. So, I responded in frustration. "She thought she was hot shit, so we called her bluff!"

He shook his head, so I continued. "Tonya is my girl, and I love her like a sister, but she be doing too much!"

I filled him in on Tonya's previous comment about graduation. From his facial expression, he understood why I was pissed in that regard.

"Yeah, she was tripping with that fuckin' question!"

I gave him the *I know right* face as we walked along.

"She was so bent on the fact that she could pull you," I said, still annoyed. "Then folded like a damn chair when she didn't get her way! What the fuck did she even try for?"

Donte looked at me with his eyebrow raised. "Yeah, she does do too much...but what bothered you more?"

I looked at him confused, so he stopped me and finished, "Was it that she thought she could pull me? 'Cause that shit wasn't gonna happen regardless, or that she acted on it?"

The question stumped me. I didn't have an answer, or one that I wanted to reveal. But I knew he was waiting for me to answer.

Donte nodded, then continued. "Let me put it to you this way...I done seen Trina talk shit to and about you. But you only entertain her ass 'cause you petty as fuck! Plus, you know she gonna act out just because."

Donte stopped us both from walking. I looked away, but when he got closer to me, I looked at him again.

"But with Tonya, you were about to knock her block off for saying something disrespectful to me. Y'all been friends since the sandbox! So, what made you madder?"

I didn't know how to answer the question, and answering would be a mirror I wasn't sure I was ready to face yet. As a children Rayna and I had smacked around a few chicks for disrespecting Donte. However, I knew this was different, Rayna didn't even get a chance to react before I stepped to Tonya.

Donte just nodded. I looked away, then back at him. "I don't even know...but what I do know is I don't allow anyone to disrespect my people." I knew he could understand; hell, it was in his brotherly mantra. "After all y'all have done for me," I could feel the tears forming, so I took a breath. "It would be a slap in the mothafuckin' face to let anyone say anything slick against y'all!"

The response was partially bullshit, but it did have some truth. I was going to walk away, but Donte grabbed my hand to stop me.

"But she said that shit about me! You know I don't give a fuck, and you know I never would...but you reacted anyway!"

I looked into his eyes as he looked into mine. Right as I was about to say something else, his phone rang.

He ignored the call. "What's up, Shar? Say your peace, man," he said, touching my shoulder.

I looked at his hand, then at him, then his phone rang again. This time he looked at it, and it was Trina. I looked back at him and eased back to walk away. Of course, she would call right now. I couldn't even be mad he answered, that was his woman or whatever. I just walked slowly, and he eventually caught up to me while he was on the phone. He didn't say anything, just looked over at me. I tried not to make eye contact and kept walking.

He hung up the phone as we made it back to the parking lot near P's building. The same car from last time, with dark tints, pulled up right as we stood in front of P's building. I looked at Donte and shook my head, then walked toward our building. Donte went toward Trina, who was getting out of the passenger seat. Before he could approach her, she began ranting. The only thing I heard was, "Why the fuck you out here in the dark with her? This the second damn time, Donte!" I didn't even catch his reaction. I just kept walking and thought about his question...what made me madder?

P and Rayna were gone, so I decided to go get some laundry and go to my favorite place. Once I got into the apartment, I went to my room and loaded everything I needed into the basket. I grabbed my journal, pen, something to drink, then opened the door to the apartment. Once I locked the door, I made it up the four steps to the platform of the front of the building. I set the basket down to adjust my grip and tie my shoe. When I finished, the front door opened, and Donte picked up my basket. I was not in the mood for this now. I rolled my eyes and stood up.

"I got it!" I said plainly.

He looked at me and proceeded to the laundry room anyway. As he held the door open, I walked in.

He set the basket on the table. I removed my journal with pen, my bottle containing my pineapple and ginger drink, my phone, and ear pods. I thought he was leaving, but Donte sat down at the table. So, I grabbed the basket to start my loads.

"Why you always be in here late at night?"

I turned around. "'Cause it's quiet, and I can kill two birds with one stone!" My tone displayed my frustration, but he didn't care; he just kept talking.

"You got a whole apartment to yourself, so that don't make sense!"

I came back to the table and sat on the opposite side of him. His face was scrunched up in reference to his unanswered question. He had a point. I sighed and replied in a calmer tone.

"Sometimes that apartment is too loud, even when it's silent."

He nodded. "One of those nights!"

I was surprised he remembered, so I nodded he was correct.

He picked up my journal and acted like he was going to flip through it. I was about to snatch it back, but he moved it out of my reach.

"What you be writing in this?" he asked. He never opened it completely, but didn't give it back either.

"Whatever, I think or feel…it's my escape."

He nodded, "You think you will write a book one day?" He placed the journal back on the table and slid it towards me.

I shrugged plainly, I thought about it, I wanted to—but I knew my writing wasn't exactly academically proficient. Funny how constant correction can ruin or impede your passion. "Maybe…I hope! Just need to work on it more though. Especially since it don't meet always 'industry' or 'academic' standards."

He frowned, "Why? this your shit—fuck what everyone else gotta say!"

I half smiled and nodded. "Yeah, true that! Who knows, I could be a New York Times top seller one day!" I said jokingly.

Donte didn't laugh, "You could if you believe that shit!"

I laughed a little. "Dang look at you being all encouraging and shit! I'm going to dedicate my first book to you"

He just shook his head.

Trying to break the ice, I said a snide remark "Guess I should almost slap a bitch more often!"

Donte frowned and laughed, "You ain't do that shit for me…that was all for you!"

His words made me uncomfortable, and I eased up. Seeing my reaction, he continued

"I don't give energy to bullshit like that."

His words shifted my mood. He was right but, at the same time, I was confused. I didn't know if he was judging me or trying to get a reaction, so I asked.

"So, what I was supposed to laugh or some shit?"

He shook his head, "Nah, but you ain't supposed to show all your cards either."

There it was. He wasn't judging—but apparently, I'd revealed more than I meant.

"If Tonya was your enemy, you just left yourself wide open...She knows your pressure point. It's one thing if Rayna had said something—that's my sister. Her reaction was expected. But yours? That was a surprise...to some."

He made a lot of sense. I respected what he said. It was chess, not checkers. I reacted emotionally instead of logically. Good job, Shar.

"Well, she lucky it was me and not the real hood booger herself," I said, chuckling.

"Well, she aint gotta worry about her anymore." Donte looked at me with a straight face.

I gave him the *oh really* face. "So, you done with Trina, huh?" I said rolling my eyes.

He leaned closer and whispered, "Showing your cards again!"

I nodded as we stared at each other. I wanted to know how and why things ended, but truthfully it didn't matter. He was single now. That was that.

I reached for my bottle but he snatched it away. I sucked my teeth, "Really dude?"

He inspected the bottle, shaking it while eyeing me suspiciously. "Better not be not alcohol, your ass ain't grown enough!"

I gave him the *really?* face as he sniffed it. When I reached for it again, he put it to his lips and took a big gulp. Epic fail—he instantly started choking.

I chuckled, "that's what your ass gets for being nosey!" I got up and grabbed a napkin for him and handed it to him.

"Whatever man!" he muttered, took the napkins to wipe his mouth then he took smaller sips.

"I take it you like it!"

He just looked at me, then motioned the cup back towards me as if to give it back.

"I don't know where your mouth been…better yet, I know where it hasn't!" I slightly laughed and he did too, then took another sip.

"Don't matter anyway—you aint getting this back."

I rolled my eyes.

"Your eyes gonna get stuck one day!"

I smiled and crossed them. "Would you still talk to me if I looked like this?"

Donte frowned, "hell nah, I don't trust no one who can't see what's straight in front of them!"

I knew it was a joke—or maybe not. Maybe it meant something else. I shook my head and got up to put the clothes in the dryer. "You don't have to sit here the whole time," I said.

He was scrolling through his phone. "Man calm your ass down…you was struggling trying to bring this basket up here."

I rolled my eyes, "Whatever, I would have made it."

Donte closed his phone and looked at me. "Learn how to accept help for once in your life Shar. You always talking about me being nice then when I do you always got some shit to say!"

"Whatever Donte…thank you. I appreciate it!" I said sincerely.

He nodded and pulled out his phone again. We didn't say much else, before I knew it the clothes were dry. I folded them as I put them into the basket.

When I finished, Donte didn't say a word. He just grabbed the basket, and we headed to my apartment. I unlocked the door and turned on the lights. I thought he was gonna hand me the basket, but he continued inside.

"Where you want this?"

"Umm you can set it on the sofa, I'll take it to my room."

Donte shook his head, "Is it the first or the second room?"

I looked at him confused. "It's the second one."

He took the basket and placed it inside the room, then walked into the guest bathroom. I headed into the kitchen. When he walked back to the living room, I was just coming out.

"You good?"

I smiled at him. "Yeah," I said, handing him a container.

He looked at it, shook it and he looked at me puzzled.

"It's the ginger drink you seem to enjoy," I said sarcastically. He nodded, clearly pleased. "That has extra ginger, so it's kinda extra spicy."

He took a sip. It must've been good—he actually smiled. "Thanks, Shar. Appreciate it."

We were quiet again. Then he spoke. "You sure you good?"

I nodded. "Yeah. I'm probably going to get some sleep—it's like 2:30 a.m."

He nodded and headed towards the door.

"Thank you for staying with me. I needed the company after everything that happened tonight."

A lot happened that night—but maybe it happened for a reason.

"You're welcome," I said, walking closer so I could lock up behind him. But then Donte leaned in and hugged me.

It wasn't a side hug—it was a real hug. I put my arms around him and inhaled his cologne. Trying not to be obvious, I was about to ease up, but Donte held me a little tighter. Body to body, chest to chest—or at least my head on his chest since he was taller. I leaned into the hug more, returning the squeeze. He rubbed my back up and down, so I rubbed his as much as I could reach. We held on for a few more seconds, then pulled back and looked at each other.

Keeping straight faces, we held each other's gaze. But something had softened in both our eyes. He broke our embrace, opened the door and stepped outside. As he made his way up the stairs, I called, "Donte!"

He turned around. I glanced at him.

"Now who's showing their cards?"

He winked, smirked, and kept going up the stairs. When I heard his door close, I closed mine. I didn't know what the hug meant—but we both had shown our cards tonight. Now, it was time to see who deals the next one.

CHAPTER 5

After finally contacting Regina, I was able to get Miss Chyna the rest of her money. I texted Miss Chyna, and she said to give the money to Donte whenever I saw him. So, when Regina and Uncle of the Week went on their "weekend getaway," she left me her car with the promise to get an oil change. We were off school on Friday, so I decided to get up early and head to the shop where he worked. I could give him the money, get the oil change, and hit the streets later with Rayna and Tonya. Tonya and I had worked things out a couple of days after her comment about Donte. She did apologize, and I accepted it; we were girls, and of course, this wasn't our first spat. I didn't feel like she owed me an apology because I wasn't extending one back. The person she needed to apologize to was Rayna and Donte, if they cared. When she attempted to apologize to Rayna, she didn't care, especially since our party was coming up soon.

When I got to the shop at 9 a.m., it had just opened. The building itself wasn't too big, enough room for a small waiting room, a reception desk, and an office. The garage attached was large enough for at least four cars and plenty of tools. The great thing about the shop was it had a wraparound parking lot with plenty of space to park cars. Also, it was attached to retail space with more parking and provided additional entrances/exits. Mr. Charles planned to purchase the additional space so he could expand the shop and garage.

I parked Regina's BMW and headed inside. When I entered the shop, the receptionist was behind the desk. She had on a blue uniform shirt that displayed her name, but it wasn't buttoned up and exposed her white low-cut spaghetti strap undershirt. Her hair was straight and parted down the middle. I had to admit she was pretty, but she was definitely a hood booger. I wondered if she knew Trina; she could definitely be her cousin.

When I got to the counter, I waited for her to acknowledge me. However, she didn't speak and continued popping her gum and flipping through her magazine. Not in the mood for her antics,

I cleared my throat, and she continued to ignore me. I smiled and took a breath.

"Excuse me!" I said a little too loudly. The rude receptionist's name was Kim; she grunted and finally looked at me.

"Can I help you?" then looked back down.

"Actually, you can't…is Donte or Mr. Charles here?" I said as I looked her up and down.

"Umm, actually, I'm the one you need to deal with, so how can I help you?" I laughed at her.

"I just told you what I needed, so…" she frowned and closed her magazine as if I crossed a line or something.

"Look, I don't know who…" Before she could finish, the office door opened.

"There's my baby girl! Where you been hiding?" Mr. Charles said.

Mr. Charles was the shop owner; 60 years old, average height but stocky. He stood on the motto "health is wealth." So, he didn't allow anyone to smoke or drink on the shop's premises. Mr. Charles had a face that reflected he played no games. However, he was the sweetest, softest man. He always treated me like his daughter, very protective of me. So, when I saw him, I knew Kim was about to change her tune.

I smiled at her and rolled my eyes. "I'm good, Mr. Charles! How you been?"

He came from the office and gave me a big hug. As I hugged him, Kim was now in her feelings.

"I been good, been good! Finally, got back in them dating streets," Mr. Charles said as he pulled out his phone to show me a picture of his lady, Pam. She was beautiful, brown-skinned with a salt-and-pepper bob. She definitely took care of herself. The picture was of Mr. Charles and her at dinner; they looked so happy. Nothing but smiles and positive energy radiated from the photo and Mr. Charles.

"Ok, ok! I see you, OG! You gotta bring her around soon; I want to meet her!" I said, excited at the opportunity.

"Definitely, I need my daughter's approval, ya know!" he said, smiling.

"And I'm glad to give it to ya, Papa!" I said, looking at Kim, who was now over our interaction.

"So, what brings you to see me?" Mr. Charles said.

"I need an oil change and just an overall inspection!" I spoke. "Oh, and I'm looking for your boy!" I grunted while rolling my eyes.

The mentioning of Donte caused Kim to boss up as if something was going on with her and Donte. Just then, the front door opened.

"Well, speak of the devil!" Mr. Charles said.

Donte walked in and didn't say anything, just headed towards Mr. Charles. While they exchanged handshakes, I looked at the receptionist, who was now beaming. Oh, I see; she showed her cards, and now I was going to use it to my advantage. I was about to fuck her all the way up—smiling at the thought. Donte nodded towards her and then turned his attention to me.

"Sup, big head! What you doing here?" he said and gave me a hug.

He initially gave me a side hug, but I put my arms around him, so it became a full hug. I purposely squeezed him for too long. Mr. Charles shook his head while Donte looked down at me confused once we broke our embrace.

I smiled, then continued while looking at Kim, "Your mama asked me to give you something, and I need an oil change."

I sighed. Mr. Charles chuckled and headed towards the side door, which led to the garage. When he finally put everything together, he looked at me, then at her, and gave me the *really* face then shook his head.

"Man, come on," he said as he opened the office door and I walked inside, purposely switching too hard in my sundress.

I sat down in the chair in front of the desk as he closed the door, and then he leaned against the desk.

"What was all that?" Donte pointed out at the door.

"Oh, that was a pressure point!" I said, slightly laughing.

He shook his head. "More like a fuck you, bitch!" He shook his head and smirked.

"Look, anyway, I got the last of the money for the party."

Donte nodded. "Cool."

I handed him $750 in cash.

"Shar, you could have sent this to my account."

He was right; I had his information and the money plus more on my account for some other things I needed to purchase. I honestly hadn't thought of that. But I also had to admit I wanted to see him again.

I nodded. "Fine, I'll transfer it now and I'll put this in the bank." I pulled out my phone and made the transfer.

Donte looked at his phone and nodded once he got the transfer. Returning his phone to his pocket, he urged, "Make sure you do it as soon as you leave, Sharnel!"

I rolled my eyes. "Oh, you worried about me?" I said jokingly.

Donte gave me the *really* face, got up, and mumbled, "Man, you heard what I said, Sharnel!"

I nodded. "Fine, your highness."

Donte put his keys on the desk, and we headed out of the office. "Aye, Kim, you got my schedule for today?" Donte said.

She smiled a little too hard. "Yep, here you go!"

He took the paper without even paying attention to her. I chuckled as she glared in my direction.

As I was about to sit down in the waiting area, Donte chimed in. "Oh, nah, bring your ass on!" He said as he grabbed a folding chair. "Your ass gonna sit outside!"

Donte opened the door, and I smiled. "Whatever you say, love!"

I turned back toward Kim, who was fuming. I walked out the door, purposely swaying my hips and Donte just shook his head. When Donte opened the chair, I sat down.

"Sit your trouble-making ass down, man!" He said as he walked into the garage.

"What you mean? I tried to be nice to ole girl; she bucked at me!"

He looked like he didn't believe me, so I explained what happened. When I finished, he nodded. "It might not have been you for once!"

I waved off his comment. I wanted to say something else, but I left it alone.

Donte got to work, and I put in my earbuds to listen to music while I enjoyed the sun beaming down. It was the kind of spring morning that made you want to just sit outside for as long as you could. I watched as he maneuvered around the car, checking different things. I loved that he worked with his hands and was passionate about his craft. Although we didn't talk about cars, I witnessed him and P discuss them. He knew everything there was to know about how the engines worked and a whole bunch of other stuff I didn't understand.

As I listened to my music, I couldn't help but groove and smile. Plus, I saw him glancing at me a couple of times. Even though he shook his head and looked away, I knew he was watching me. I felt like everything was right in the world. When he was almost finished, another guy who worked at the shop arrived.

"Sup, Dee! Sorry I'm late, man!"

The guy looked in my direction. Donte looked up slightly while still under the hood in time to see the guy turn his attention toward me. When I noticed his hand, I just looked at it and took out my earbud.

"You was grooving, momma. I'm Jus. What's your name?"

Jus was cute, tall, rocked a low cut, had blue-black skin, and beautiful white teeth. From his accent, I could tell he was from the South, which I liked. However, I knew better than to mix pleasure and business at the shop. If we were somewhere else, I might have considered him.

Donte immediately broke up the interaction. "Aye, forget all that; you already 30 mins late, brah. Clock in and let's get it!"

Jus backed up and winked at me, then replied, "Aight, man, my bad. I just wanted to speak to the pretty lady!"

Donte stood up, and Jus headed into the shop. I would have usually said something smart to Donte, but from his expression, I knew now was not a good time. He looked at me, then went back to work. After another 10 minutes, Donte was done. In a calmer tone, he spoke.

"Aight, Shar!" I took out my earbud and waited for him to continue.

"Oil change is done; tell your mom she's gonna need some brakes soon!" I nodded.

Donte closed the hood and wiped his hands. "Now can you go inside and check out like a grown-up?"

I rolled my eyes and didn't respond. I wasn't the problem, and he knew it, so there was no need to even indulge the comment. So, I got up and walked into the shop. When I got inside, Kim was behind the counter but with a different attitude. When I approached the counter, she smiled and was professional. Mr. Charles must have gotten in that ass! With a pleasant tone, she spoke, "So how did everything go? Did we meet your needs today?"

I smiled and thought about saying something smart but didn't. "Yeah, everything went well."

She rang me up and handed me a receipt to sign.

As I was signing, Jus came into the reception area from the back office and made his way to the counter. He was trouble and definitely wanted whatever smoke was coming to him. I shook my head and smiled at the thought.

"You ain't tell me what your name was?" He said smoothly.

Don't even think about it, Shar! You already know Mr. Charles and Donte would lose their shit. I signed the receipt, handed it back to Kim, smiled at her, and then shook my head at Jus.

"Oh, so you ain't got nothing to say? You worried about Donte, huh?"

I laughed out loud at the comment. He was really trying it. I looked at Kim, who just observed, shaking her head as well.

I knew Mr. Charles had a no fraternization policy at the shop, and the employees respected it. However, Jus had his own policy and plans. Jus stepped closer to me and was about to say something else when Mr. Charles and Donte entered from two separate doors. I looked at Donte, who looked pissed. He rushed toward us, stepping between Jus and me. Jus took a few steps back.

"Aye, what the fuck you doing? She's still in fucking high school. Back the fuck up!" He barked as he pointed at me.

I know he really ain't just say that! HIGH SCHOOL! I was pissed he put me out there like that. Graduation was next week; he didn't have to announce it like that.

When he saw my face, he knew I was pissed, but he didn't care. I looked at Kim, who smiled, almost laughed.

"Oh my gosh, that is so cute! When do you graduate, boo?"

I grabbed my receipt from the counter and headed toward the front door, being sure to hit Donte with my arm in irritation. Donte looked at me and followed behind me, while Kim got her last verbal jab in.

"Bye, Sharnel. Congrats on graduating high school, boo!" she said sarcastically.

I looked at her and shook my head; however, Jus nodded his head and smiled since he now knew my name. Donte opened the front door and held it as I walked past him. As the door closed, I heard Mr. Charles fussing.

Donte walked me to the car, which was in the parking space. He handed me the keys, and I snatched them. He just looked at me; he obviously didn't care I was mad, which pissed me off more. When we got to the car, I reached for the door handle before he could. He pushed my hand out of the way. I didn't want or need his help; I just wanted to leave. So, when he reached for the handle, I pushed his hand away.

"Man, Sharnel!" he grunted.

"Why you have to do that in there?" I said, pissed. He almost laughed as he responded, "Oh, so you wanted ole boy!"

I shook my head. "Fuck that nigga. I ain't even thinking or talking about him! But obviously, you are!" I snapped.

Insulted, Donte backed up a bit, tightened his lips, and spoke through his teeth. "Man, get the fuck outta here with that bullshit. I'm trying to help you out…"

Fuck his annoyance; he was wrong as fuck, and he needed to know it. "Yeah, well, all you did was help embarrass the shit outta me in there!"

He didn't say anything else, just looked at me, then looked away.

He reached for the door handle again, and I let him open it. However, I made sure to slam it shut while he stood outside.

As I started the car, he knocked on the glass. I acted like I didn't hear him but then barely cracked the window.

"Let the fuckin window down, man!" He barked.

I let it all the way down and didn't look at him. He leaned in the window. "Go and put that money in the bank!"

I rolled my eyes. "Sharnel, man, stop being stubborn for once and just do what I said, shit!"

I looked at him blankly as if to say anything else. "Then text me when it's done!"

I looked away and turned up the music. Donte backed up from the car, and I drove off. I rolled up the window and texted Rayna and Tonya to tell them I was heading back.

I got a half mile down the street when my phone chimed. I was stopped at the traffic light, so I checked the message from Donte.

Him: *Don't take that long to get to the bank. You there yet?* URGH! I grunted.

Big Head: *I gotta make a stop first!* I lied, as I was now in the drive-through line at the bank. But he didn't know that!

Him: *Sharnel, stop playing and do what I said!*

Big Head: *Damn, relax. I'm in line!* he sent a thumbs up to my message and I closed the phone. Once the money was deposited, I sent him a picture of the receipt, which he liked.

Later that day, Rayna, Tonya, and I went to the mall to pick out outfits for our graduation party. Everyone knew I hated shopping, so it was no surprise that I found what I was looking for in one store and was ready to go. As Tonya and Rayna went from store to store, I sat on the bench as usual. When I heard my phone chime, I checked the message, and it was from the *family* group text (Miss Chyna, Donte, Rayna, P, and myself) from Miss Chyna: *Dinner is at 7 pm; make sure y'all are on time!* Everyone liked the message except me. Just seeing Donte's name pissed me off again. Why did he have to do that? Is that all he saw me as? I pondered the question and wondered if that was all he would see me as. Yeah, I was 17 ½, but my birthday was soon. I might have been young, but my maturity level was not equivalent to my age. I know it sounds cliché, but it was true. I'd been through enough experiences to have to grow up sooner than most.

As I thought about it, it didn't matter what anyone in that shop thought. With Kim's attitude, she wouldn't last very long there anyway. Based on Jus's scorecard (from what I saw), he wouldn't last either. I really could care less, but when it came to Donte, it mattered…a whole lot, and that is what pissed me off. As I sat on the bench in my thoughts, I didn't recognize that someone had sat down next to me.

"Miss Sharnel!"

I shook my head and looked to the right, and there he was, smiling and showing all his pretty white teeth.

I looked uninterested but responded, "What's up, Jus?"

He smiled more. "Oh, so you do know my name!" Jus said, as if he was surprised.

How corny can this guy be? I didn't say anything, just waited for him to finish.

"Look, when you gonna let me take you out?"

I frowned, confused.

"Oh, you think this morning turned me off? Ain't no one thinking about Donte! Besides, I heard you graduating next week, so…"

The fact that he knew the graduation date (since I didn't mention it) meant he asked around. I raised my eyebrow, still unimpressed.

"Dang, you still ain't got nothing for me! You a tough one, woman!"

I slightly laughed.

"Besides, that's the least you could do!"

I straightened my face and got up to leave, but he touched my arm. I snatched away and glared at him.

"Wait, hold up…relax! What I meant…is I no longer work at the shop!"

I was still unbothered. "You know Mr. Charles' policy!" I said, annoyed.

Jus nodded. "Yeah, I know, and that was my fault! I knew better, but I couldn't not speak to you!"

I was still standing, so he stood up.

"Look, can we at least go to dinner or something? I am unemployed because I wanted to say hi to a beautiful lady!"

His corny lines didn't sell me, but the mention of the word dinner got me. I was intrigued by the idea, plus I wanted my lick back on Donte, and this was how to get it.

"Fine, Jus, let's go to dinner tonight!"

Jus smiled. "Aight, give me your number, and I'll pick the place!"

I nodded and gave him my number. Just as we exchanged numbers, Rayna and Tonya came out of the store. They both looked at Jus; Tonya looked intrigued, and Rayna was trying to place where she knew him.

"Aight, see you tonight!" Jus said as he gave me a side hug and then left.

"Ummm, so you won't be joining us for dinner then, huh?" Rayna asked.

I smiled, "Yep, I've got plans. Let me respond to the group text now." Shar: *Sorry, Miss Chyna! I got a date tonight! But I will catch up with y'all tomorrow!*

I sent the message, and Rayna looked at her phone and laughed, "You had to throw the date in there, huh, Shar?"

I smiled, "Yep, sure did!" We all laughed and then headed to the car.

When we arrived back at the apartment building, everyone went home except Tonya, who decided to take my place at dinner—surprise, surprise. I went home and took a shower in preparation for my date. Jus and I decided to go to a local spot where they played music. We agreed to meet there by 7:30 PM so I wouldn't get carded. I chose to wear a strapless romper with gold accessories and high heels. I put my hair in a bun with a swooped bang in the front to keep it off my shoulders, giving me an even sexier look. As I admired myself, I felt damn good. I no longer saw high school Shar but a grown woman who was definitely about to turn some heads. I applied my makeup, and Rayna agreed to meet me out front with the shoes I had lent her.

As I headed out of the building, I started the car while walking toward it. I heard the building door open behind me and turned to see Rayna coming out.

"DAAMMMNNN! Look at Shar all grown and sexy and shit!"

I stopped to let her catch up. "Well, ya know, motha tries!" I laughed, popping my booty a bit.

"Fuck a try, bitch, you're doing it!" Rayna said as she hyped me up. I laughed.

"Girl, if ya boy saw you, he'd definitely be looking!"

I knew Rayna was talking about Donte. I waved her off, and we continued walking to the car. The mention of Donte pissed me off, especially since I was still mad about this morning. I mumbled, "If he knew who I was going out with, he'd definitely feel something."

Rayna looked at me curiously, waiting for me to respond, but I didn't. She didn't say anything else, but I knew she wanted to know more.

When we got to the car, I leaned on Rayna to change my shoes, then kneeled to buckle them up as a car pulled up, blaring music. I was still fumbling with my shoes when the occupants got out.

"What's up, babe?" P said.

"Fuck," I mumbled. I knew if P was there, then Donte was not far behind. I almost didn't want to stand up, but I bit the bullet, stood up straight and tall with a straight face, then partially smiled. Both P and Donte did a double take. I purposely didn't look at Donte, who leaned against the car parked next to Regina's, displaying his usual emotionless glare. P then stood behind Rayna, who leaned against the front of Regina's car. After placing his hands on her waist, P immediately went into big brother mode.

"Yooo, YOUNG girl Shar, where you going?" P asked.

Usually, it was Sister Shar, but the emphasis on "young" let me know he was about to start his 21 questions rant.

"Oh, Shar got a date!" Rayna said as she leaned against P.

P nodded and pondered the response. "Oh yeah, do we know him?"

I looked at Donte, and he waited for me to respond. I tried to laugh it off, but I didn't answer. P noticed I didn't answer his previous question and nodded.

So, he asked his next one, "Where you going, Shar?"

Rayna just stared at me and shook her head. We both knew I wasn't going to get out of this anytime soon if I didn't start talking.

"Some local place that plays music," I said.

I didn't want to give too much information, but apparently what I said was enough. Both P and Donte nodded but didn't say another word. I hoped they were satisfied with that tidbit of information because I was now running late.

"Aight! Look, I gotta go, y'all! Ray, I'll text you when I get home," she smiled.

"Have fun, boo…don't be staring at that JUS chocolate too hard!" she yelled.

I dropped my head, what the entire FUCK! P didn't know what just happened, but Donte did. He flared his nostrils and tightened his lips, then flashed me the *oh really now* look! Rayna was also in the dark, so she just smiled at me, and then they started to walk toward the building. I got in the car and immediately texted Rayna.

Shar: *Really, Ray! I'm gonna kill you!*

Rayna: *My bad, Shar! His name just slipped out! I just realized that's ole boy from the shop! Bitch are you crazy! Donte is going to kill you!* I just closed my phone and backed out of the space.

"Fuck Donte and his feelings; he didn't care about mine this morning," I mumbled.

When I arrived at the lounge, it was around 7:45 PM, and happy hour was just about to end.

"Pretty girl Shar! What's up, love!"

I smiled and gave Jus a side hug. However, he pulled me closer and squeezed me a little too tightly for my comfort.

I eased up and gave a weak smile, "Hey, Jus!"

He unhooked his arms from around me. Jus didn't seem fazed; he grabbed my hand, and we walked into the lounge. Jus was dressed in an all-black button-down and pants, which matched my romper. The hostess showed us to the dining room, and he pulled out my chair. As we were seated, I caught the eye of a gentleman in the back of the room. He was about three tables away. We made eye contact as I sat down and he talked on his phone. There was nothing special about him, but for some reason, I felt like he was watching me. I was already on edge enough, so I kept my back to him and hoped my feeling was wrong.

Once we were seated, we talked as a band set up to play. I'd never been on a real date, let alone with an older guy. My nerves were all over the place. So, I sat up straight and kept my hands under the table, trying to keep them from shaking. My mind was telling me I was in over my head and should leave, but I composed myself. Shar, relax. Enjoy yourself; you look too good to go home. Plus, you have a plan.

As I finished my mental pep talk, I took a breath and rested my elbows on the table.

"You look good tonight, momma!" Jus said as he admired me.

I just smiled and replied, "Thanks, you look nice as well!"

Jus smiled and scooted closer to me. "Wanted to make a good impression tonight!" he said as he rubbed my arm.

I leaned up and slid away from him and the table, not feeling comfortable with him touching my arm. However, Jus smiled and winked. I rolled my eyes and hoped he would move on.

I heard my phone chime, but I didn't answer it. If it was an angry message from Donte, I'd let him stew rather than react. When the waitress came, we ordered drinks.

"Can I get a Hennessy and Coke? What do you want, babe?" Not feeling the nickname, I shot Jus a look, but he didn't care.

"Can I have a pineapple sunrise mocktail?"

When the waitress left, Jus leaned closer to me and whispered, "You could have ordered a real drink, babe."

My face dropped. I knew he didn't think he was gonna get me drunk and then get some. Urgh, this was a becoming a disaster already.

"I don't drink!" I snapped, and at that moment, I thought about Donte. He would have been proud of me for not drinking or at least nodded his head with approval. I smiled at the thought.

Jus thought it was for him and smiled back and winked, "Ok, cool!"

Jus and I continued with small talk, but the more he talked, the more I realized he was a chauvinistic idiot.

"So, Sharnel, what you doing out in these streets single?"

I frowned in annoyance.

"As a high-value man, I can show you how to handle yourself. You women out here trying to be independent, but y'all ain't got the rules to the handbook. You're only looking at the cheat sheet, and half of y'all are reading it wrong."

Was he serious? What the hell did he think he could teach me? The only interest I had in any book he was reading was to ensure I burned a copy to save someone else from spewing the bullshit he did. Jus continued to piss me off. Although I didn't say it verbally, my facial expression showed it.

However, he was unmoved and kept talking. "I mean, you're cute, got a nice body, but you need to be smart too."

Da Fuck! At this point, I wished I did drink; then maybe I wouldn't have to listen to this shit any longer. If I hadn't wanted to see the band, plus stay out as long as possible to get my lick back on Donte, I would have already left—before I shared a few choice words with Jus. To calm myself, I sipped my drink and tried to zone out.

Jus continued to quote the ignorance he heard online or that someone else he knew said. When the waitress returned for our food order, I wasn't interested, but Jus ordered another drink. I was mentally exhausted and excused myself to the bathroom. As I was about to walk away, he smacked my ass then smiled. I turned around to show him my displeasure and fury.

"Keep your mothafucking hands to yourself, or I'll break them bitches off!"

Jus blew a kiss toward me. "Why the fuck did I do this!" I mumbled as I walked to the bathroom.

I stared in the mirror, pissed at myself. "Fuck, Shar! I hope this dumb shit was worth it!" I didn't need to use the bathroom; I just needed a moment. I heard my phone chime as I washed my hands, but I didn't check it. There was no rush; whatever awaited on the other side could wait until this sham of a date was over. As I walked back to the table I was not excited but sucked it up.

When I walked around the corner and looked at the table, Jus was getting the number of our waitress. "Good for her; maybe he will leave my ass alone!" I shook my head as I walked up just as they finished exchanging numbers.

"Aight, I'ma hit you later, ok?" he said with no regard for my presence—not that I cared at all.

The waitress looked uncomfortable, but I just smiled to assure her it was cool. I was no longer interested in him; she could have him now if she wanted.

"That was just business, babe," Jus attempted to say as he tried to touch me again, and I slapped his hand away.

He laughed as if I was playing. "My bad, boo boo upset!" He thought this behavior was okay, and I allowed it long enough.

"Look, one, stop with the pet names; it's annoying as fuck; two, I'll never be jealous of something that don't belong to me; and three, stop making advances…I'm not interested!" I snarled.

However, Jus smiled. "Ok, Shar, that's cool…but let's keep it a buck! I saw you lose your cool this morning, and last I checked, ole boy didn't belong to you! Unless you on some make believe shit too? Better yet on some get back or some creep shit?"

What the fuck was he talking about? Yet another person speaking on something they knew nothing about. "Jus, why don't you just leave, huh? This date, or whatever this is, is obviously over!"

Jus didn't move but said plainly as he sipped his drink, "Nah, I'm good, Shar…but I'll cool out! I promise."

It was complete bullshit, and my gut told me so, but I still didn't leave—like an idiot.

Jus attempted to talk to me, but I acted like I couldn't hear him since the band was doing a sound check.

"Oh, so you don't hear me now? Look, boo…I mean Sharnel, I'm sorry; don't be mad!"

Jus attempted to lean in and touch me again. What the fuck was his problem? Was he hard of hearing? I grunted and inched away, but Jus moved closer and attempted to kiss me.

I had enough and immediately stood up, slapped him, and yelled, "Oh, I know you done lost your goddamn mind!"

Jus looked infuriated and grabbed my arm. My mind immediately went back to the incident with Eric, and I saw red as my fist balled up, ready to strike if Jus was bold enough to test me.

Before I could react, three guards surrounded the table.

"You good?" one asked.

"Yeah, thanks," I said, then slightly smiled. A security guard put his hand on Jus's shoulder.

"Yoo, my man, let's get it!"

As Jus stood up to leave, the same security guard looked at me and nodded. I returned the nod, glad to see him but confused by his actions. I mentally hoped they didn't throw me out too. The night and the outfit would have been a waste if I couldn't at least enjoy the music. The guards escorted Jus to the bar, and after he paid the tab, they put him out.

"Excuse me, don't mean to bother you…you sure you're good?"

It was the guy from earlier at the other table. Urgh, yet another man. He was only being nice, so I replied politely, "Yeah, I'm good, thanks!"

He nodded and returned to his table. I thought that was nice of him. However, I still felt like he was watching me, and I caught him looking again when I came back from the bathroom and when I turned around a few times. When I looked at him again momentarily, he was still on his phone looking in my direction. "What the hell is he looking at?"

Shaking off the feeling, I decided to pick up my phone. I had five missed messages: three from Rayna and one from Donte.

The lounge was now playing music over the speaker, so I grooved while opening my phone to finally read them.

Him: *Really Sharnel! Da fuck is you doing!*

Rayna: *Girl!!! You good?! Donte is not happy…who is this guy?*
Rayna: *Shar! I haven't heard from you…let me know you good!*
Rayna: *SHAR!!! Why you not answering!!!*
Rayna: *Bitch you done did it now…you got some company coming your way!*

"Da fuck!"I mumbled. When I looked up again, I saw Rayna headed toward me. I smiled, glad to see a familiar face, but she looked pissed.

"Bitch, I'm glad you ok!" she said as I stood up and hugged her.

"Of course I'm okay. What's wrong with you?" We sat down.

"Shar, you just disappeared!" Rayna said, concerned.

Seeing her face, I regretted not answering my phone. "Sorry, Ray…Jus was pissing me off, and then they threw him out," I said, shaking my head.

"Oh, I know!" Rayna said, still annoyed. How did she know? Did she pass him on the way out, or did she see it?

I was about to ask her how, but the band began to play, and I got distracted. If you knew anything about me, you knew I loved music, especially Go-Go music. If you were from where I was from, you were raised on it. So, when the music started, the conversation turned to radio silence, and Rayna and I fell into the groove. It was all good until I began to process things.

I grabbed Rayna's arm and gave her the eye, "Wait! How did you know where I was?" I thought again and then laughed. "Further, how did your ass get in here?"

Rayna started laughing, causing me to laugh as we continued to groove.

"We were worried about you!" Rayna pouted.

"We?" I said, confused.

Rayna pointed to the bar. Not seeing anything, I waited for her to finish. Rayna continued, "Well, P and Donte are here!"

My face dropped, and I motioned for her to explain immediately.

"Well, see, what happened was…when I didn't hear from you, I got worried. Since I have your location, I told them we should go check on you!" Rayna gave me a sad face.

But she was full of shit! I knew Rayna better than that. "Bitch, you just wanted to get out!" we laughed.

"Well, they don't have to know that! Plus, I heard them talking about this place, and I wanted to come see it…so I got my way!"

I looked back at the bar but still didn't see P or Donte.

"Oh, they're probably putting their name on a pool table!"

I nodded and continued grooving. Rayna cleared her throat and then spoke hesitantly.

"But umm, Shar…ya boy is on fire!"

I rolled my eyes. I knew I'd hear an earful from him later, so I would enjoy myself now. Seeing me unphased, Rayna grabbed my hand to get my attention.

"Nah Shar, he is pissed for real! I heard him tell P that Jus aint want nothing but some pussy and to piss Donte off!"

It was then I felt bad and hoped Donte would give me a chance to explain or at least apologize. However, when he and P came to the table, I got a front-row seat to their foul mood. They both looked at me and sat down. Then Donte turned his back to me and faced the stage.

P eased his mood some and at least spoke to me, "you good, Sister Shar! We saw what happened with ole boy!"

I nodded, yes, but again was perplexed. "Damn, how long have y'all been here?" I felt a little weird that they saw the interaction.

"Long enough to know your ass shouldn't have been here in the first place! Bet your ass will listen next time!" Donte grunted, still not looking in my direction.

"We ain't been here too long, but that's my man…" P said, then pointed to the guy from earlier. "He kept us updated!"

The guy raised his glass to P and nodded. I turned around to see the guy from earlier; now my feelings made sense. I frowned and crossed my arms.

"Don't nobody care about your attitude; keep that shit to yourself!" Donte mumbled.

What the hell, did he have eyes in the back of his head? I looked at Rayna, and she mouthed, *I told you*! Then she shook her head. Donte turned toward the table and picked up my drink, sniffing it.

"Really, dude!" I said, snatching the glass out of his hand.

"You're ass out here being grown! Already had to save your ass once tonight!"

I was over his attitude and the fact that he thought he could talk to me any kind of way.

"Although I appreciate you coming out and all the little spies and shit, I'm good! Further, I didn't ask you to come play superhero, Donte! So, keep your little attitude to your damn self!"

He couldn't believe I had the audacity to buck back at him. As he glared at me, I continued, "Besides, what do you care anyway? Don't you got other business to attend to?" I snapped.

He was about to say something, but P chimed in, "Yo, Dee, let's go, man! Cool off a bit!" he said as he got up from the table.

Donte didn't move, just looked at me as I looked at him. P and Rayna observed our exchange and shook their heads. Eventually, Donte got up and then walked off, mumbling something.

"The fuck is his problem, Ray! Why he gotta act like that?" I whined.

Rayna put her hands up in defeat and shook her head. "Look, Shar, don't pay him any mind! Let's just enjoy the music and being grown tonight!"

I smiled. "Yeah, you're right, fuck him and his attitude…we're in these streets tonight!" We high-fived and continued to groove at the table. Since P apparently had the hookup (hence the nodding security guard), we were able to sit at an empty booth closer to the stage.

When the band took a break, Rayna suggested we go check on the fellas.

"Do we have to?" I said as I rolled my eyes.

She nodded, "Yep, suck it up!"

I rolled my eyes again, and we walked to the pool area. When we entered the room, we surveyed it for the guys. When Rayna pointed them out, I decided to go to the bathroom since it would give me more time before I had to encounter Donte's angry ass. When I headed out of the bathroom and walked toward the room with the pool tables, I felt a tap on my shoulder. I turned around.

"Sup, sexy! How are you?" It was some random guy trying to talk to me.

Not again; I was over the attention for tonight. I smiled weakly, then tried to walk away, but he put his hand up to block me as I tried to enter the room.

Frustration immediately rose. I put my hand up to give the guy a piece of my mind, but Donte walked up.

"Aye, shorty, with me!"

The guy turned around. "Oh, shit, Dee! My bad, I meant no disrespect!"

I looked at Donte as he dapped the guy up.

"You good, brah! Bring your car next week; I'll hook you up!"

The guy nodded and bowed in apology toward me, then went on about his way. Donte stood in front of me but didn't say a word. I just looked at him with a remorseful look. He put his arm out to lead me into the pool table room. We walked in silence to where Rayna and P were.

"Damn, Shar! You pulling em tonight!" she joked.

I sat on the nearest bar stool and looked at Donte, who put chalk on his pool stick. He looked over at me, then went back to playing pool. Rayna and I decided to stay in the room, talking as we grooved to the music, ordered chicken wings, and just continued our own little party. By 11:30 p.m., the fellas were ready to go. When we walked out, I said my goodbyes to everyone and headed toward Regina's car. When I realized Donte was following me, I was a bit confused.

"I'm good to drive!"

He ignored me and kept walking. "Give me the keys, man!" I was about to protest, but he cut me off.

"Man, I'm not in the mood, Sharnel! It's too late for you to be driving by yourself; I saw your ass yawning…so you're going to get in the passenger seat and leave it alone!"

I reluctantly handed him the keys. He opened my door and then went to the other side. Donte pulled off; I turned on the radio, and we listened to whatever came on. We didn't say much, but eventually, he turned down the volume and spoke.

"Why couldn't you just listen!" he said, frustrated. I looked over at him but didn't reply, so he continued, "What were you that salty about what I said? Thought you were gonna get your lick back or something?"

He read me like a book.

"What, did he slip you his number at the shop or something?"

I was speechless; he knew everything, so what was the point of responding? I didn't want to respond, but I knew I had to say something. I thought about lying, but if I denied the truth, he would know I was lying for sure.

So, regretfully, I said, "Look, he approached me in the mall, I guess after y'all fired him. Yeah, I was mad, and I did it to spite you. It was wrong, and I should have listened…I apologize!"

Donte just looked over at me, then back at the road. In a calmer tone, he said, "Shar, man! I knew he was trash, which is why I reacted the way I did." He got quiet, then finished, "Glad I fired his ass because it would be a problem tomorrow."

After hearing that, I too was glad Jus was gone. I didn't want Donte to act out and lose his job. I didn't think Mr. Charles would fire him, but I also didn't want to be the cause either. My plan backfired hard; I regretted the whole thing, especially not listening to Donte.

"I know that now," I mumbled.

"You should have listened when I said it the first time. If he was decent, I wouldn't stand in his way."

Wait, did I hear that right? He would be okay with me dating someone else? My heart sank; maybe he wasn't interested in me. The words stung; I felt like he dealt his last card while I was still holding onto mine. When he looked over at me, he could tell.

I looked sad, almost lost in the moment; how did we get here? I wanted to leave it alone, but I couldn't. I needed to know how he felt, so I gathered the courage to ask.

"So, you would be okay with me dating someone else?"

My words revealed my disappointment. Donte looked at me. I wasn't ready for that answer, so I changed it and hurried the rest, "...you know, if you thought they were decent?"

Although I really only meant the first part of the question. He didn't respond at first. However, when Donte burst into hysterical laughter, it confused and hurt me.

"Shar, ain't nobody I know dating your young ass…"

Before he could finish, I got mad. "Why you always gotta do that shit!" Donte frowned in confusion.

"Keep telling me I'm young…putting my age as a barrier or something! What the fuck is that shit, Donte!"

He relaxed his face and looked annoyed.

"I know how old I fucking am! But in case you haven't noticed, I'm quite mature for my age."

We had reached the parking lot for our complex, and he put the car into park, then looked in my direction.

"I've had to grow up fast and experience a little more life than most my age. Plus, you don't say shit about P and Rayna…if I'm not mistaken, P is your age and Rayna is close to my age. So, what the fuck is your problem? I ain't like Tonya, spreading myself to every nigga who blinks my way. Everyone else can see me except you; it's like you see me as Shar in the fucking sandbox!"

I could tell Donte was considering my words as I spoke. "Open up your eyes! See the woman in front of you!"

Donte chuckled again, "Woman, Shar, please, you're barely of age!"

Frustrated, I got out of the car and slammed the door. Donte turned off the car and got out.

He was still chuckling right before he said, "...and a barrier? Please, ain't nobody holding back from your underage ass!"

He hadn't heard a damn word I said. I was so pissed, I could barely breathe. Rayna and P were standing outside the car.

"You good, Shar?" Rayna asked, concerned. I nodded as I leaned back on the passenger door, keeping my back to Donte.

"Dee, I'm going to P's for an hour…can you cover for me, please?" Rayna whined.

He shook his head, "One hour, Rayna!" he mumbled.

She smiled, and they walked toward P's building. Donte walked to the passenger side of the car and handed me the keys. I was about to walk away, but he stopped me.

"Let me ask you something," I looked at him and waited for him to finish. "Why do you care so much what I think?"

Was he serious? It was a valid question, but I wasn't ready to answer it, so I deflected.

"Why do you see me as a little girl? How can you see Rayna as a woman but not me?"

He looked confused. He couldn't be this slow; he had to be pretending. At least, I hoped.

"Really, Donte! You just gave your sister the green light to go get some dick!" Donte looked disgusted, so I continued, "They damn sure ain't going to play fucking video games at midnight!"

He looked like he was about to throw up. "Why you had to say that shit, Shar? I mean, I knew that shit, but I don't wanna think about it."

I waved him off. "Well, answer my question!" I could tell he didn't have a response.

"I don't know, Shar! Just how it is!"

I was over him and the conversation. "How is that fair?" I yelled.

"Didn't say it was!" he said as if it was nothing.

"So, that's how it is, huh? Shar is just the little girl in your eyes!"

Donte was now over the conversation as well. "What the fuck are we even talking about? Why are we discussing this? It don't even matter!"

I nodded, annoyed, in defeat. I stepped closer to him. "You're right; it don't matter! So, fuck it, right?"

Donte kept a straight face, and I walked away, cutting across the grass to get to the sidewalk. I was home when I realized

I had left my purse in the car. "Fuck!" I yelled, knowing I had to walk back. My feet were tired, and I was over everything. Plus, I wasn't in the mood for round three with Donte. I gathered my composure and walked back to the car.

As I walked back, I didn't see Donte in the parking lot. When I made it to the car, I grabbed my purse and decided to change into my flat sandals. I sat in the driver's seat and bent down to unbuckle my shoe when I heard someone walk up on me. It scared the shit out of me.

"What you doing back out here?" he mumbled.

Out of breath, I replied, "You scared the shit outta me! I left my purse in the car, so I decided to change my shoes before I head back in."

Donte leaned against the front of Regina's car and didn't say a word. I changed my shoes, then got out and closed the door.

I stood in front of him. "Still waiting for Rayna?"

He nodded yes. I was about to walk away, but he grabbed my hand. I looked at his hand, then at him.

"I heard you, Shar! I meant no disrespect!"

I nodded. "But you still ain't answered my question!" I knew I hadn't, and the truth was I didn't know what to say. So, I answered, still displaying my frustration.

"I'm gonna be honest…I don't know how or why it matters! I don't know why it pisses me off! I don't know why we even talking about it!"

He raised his eyebrow.

"You see what you see, and everyone knows what you see is what you get with you. So, all that fussing I just did was pointless because there ain't no changing your mind!"

He slightly smiled. "That's what you think or what you know?"

I looked up and saw Rayna and P coming our direction. I looked back at him. "It's what I know!"

Donte nodded and let my hand go. I walked past him toward Rayna and P. He stood up and followed me; they stopped so we could walk to our building together.

"What's up, Ricky and Lucy? Y'all still arguing?" Rayna joked as she put her arm around me.

"Nope, pointless anyway!" I said, looking at Donte, who just walked up. When I moved, Rayna walked with me while Donte and P walked together.

When we got to the building, P opened the door, and we all walked in.

"Shar! Get some rest, love! I'm gonna call you tomorrow!" Rayna said as she hugged my neck.

I smiled and nodded. "Good night, y'all!" I said, then went back toward the front door.

"Where you going?" she said, concerned.

"I just need a minute. I'm gonna go inside in a bit!"

Rayna nodded. "Aight, well text me when you get inside, okay?"

P walked behind Rayna; Donte looked at me as I walked out the door. I sat on the wall and just put in my earbuds. I needed a break from everything that happened tonight.

After an hour or so, P came out of the building. When I saw him, I took my earbuds out.

"Sister Shar! What you still doing out here?"

I smiled. "Just need a break before I go in, P!"

P nodded. "I hear that…tonight was a lot, huh?"

I nodded.

"You know we was worried about you! I hope you ain't take us rolling up on you the wrong way."

I shook my head no and replied, "Nah, not at all…glad y'all had my back!"

P nodded. "Yeah, when Dee started telling us about that dude, he was pissed! Glad Rayna knew where you was and we went together. If my guy went alone, it would have gone differently, especially when ole touched you, and you checked him, but he did it again…my G was not pleased!"

I looked confused; that was early on—what else did they see?

"Damn, how long were y'all there?"

P thought about it. "Truthfully…probably an hour after y'all got there! My guy was not gonna have it any other way!"

I felt a little bad about what I said to Donte, but I still meant what I said.

"Look, Shar, I probably shouldn't tell you this, but fuck it!" I waited for P to finish. "Dee really cares about you, man! He gives you a hard time, I know, always ragging on you, but that's just him being him. Don't mistake it, though; my guy cares!"

I thought hearing that would make me feel better, but I wasn't sold.

I just shrugged. "Thanks, P," I said flatly.

He could tell I wasn't convinced. "I'm gonna say this one last thing…then I'm taking you home, and I'm out!"

I rolled my eyes.

"What, Shar? I can't leave you out here alone; it's 1:30 a.m.! But anyway, think about this…what guy you know crashes someone else's date to make sure they're safe? Huh? What guy you know willing to go above and beyond for a 'childhood friend'? Huh? What guy you know takin' up for another female in front of his main thing?"

P made some valid points, and I could see his point, but I needed to hear Donte say it to me. It would validate what I hoped we both already knew.

We were quiet, and he continued. "So, before you write him off…think about that shit! He might not be ready now, but he's showing you something."

I nodded at P, then he held the door open and escorted me downstairs. We said goodbye, and he left. I heard my phone chime, and I knew it was Rayna. I shook my head and pulled it out as I walked toward my room.

Him: *You in the house?*

Big Head: *Yeah, just got in!*

He replied with a thumbs-up. I texted Rayna I was home and decided to get in the shower before bed. When I finally laid down, I looked at the ceiling and considered the evening's events. I heard P, but I couldn't make heads or tails of Donte. The only conclusion I had was I was done trying. The next move was his or not…either way, I had to focus on me.

CHAPTER 6

The last day of school, the day before graduation, was finally here. I was glad and decided not to go to school because it didn't matter. I already got clearance for graduation, so fuck those people. I decided to just chill out until I got my hair done later with Rayna and Tonya. After the outing with Jus, I was a little quieter. Between Jus's foolishness, Donte, and everything else that seemed to follow me, I stayed to myself and tried to figure out what was next for me. Everyone seemed to have plans and goals but me, and I didn't like it. Among the other things lingered in my mind.

Surprisingly, I hadn't directly encountered Donte after everything with Jus. Technically, I had, but I made my exit as soon as he entered the room or space. For instance, Miss Chyna asked me to watch Keith while she went grocery shopping. As soon as she came back, he came home. I immediately grabbed my things, nodded at him, and left. Another time, I saw him leave the building as I was headed up the sidewalk. I couldn't turn around, so when we got close enough to pass each other, I pulled out my phone and acted like I had a call. As he passed me, I nodded again and kept going. Donte shook his head and kept walking as well. With all I had roaming around in my head, I couldn't make space for Donte or thoughts about him. When I did, I found something to distract myself, but mostly I avoided being in his presence. As far as I was concerned, I was doing great and getting him out of my system. Maybe one day soon, I'd gain enough strength to be around him and not want to run…maybe.

Earlier that week, Rayna had asked me to go out with her and Tonya to the movies. However, I passed; I wasn't in the mood for any gossip or any other potential foolishness. The previous week, she asked me if I wanted to hit the city just to get out, and I declined again. Rayna complained I was becoming too much of a recluse, so I knew canceling today was out of the question. Plus, I also wanted to get my hair done, so I wasn't going to cancel anyway. I was ready to finish getting glammed up with the girls. Since Rayna and Tonya already had their nails done, I went alone so we could all be together today. Rayna and I had appointments at a local hairdresser, and Tonya tagged along.

I had Ms. Kena sew in a weave for me, but I needed it to be styled. Tonya and Rayna had braids, but Rayna wanted hers styled in a certain way. P agreed to drop us off and pick us up so we didn't have to take an Uber, which worked because I wasn't in the mood to deal with some rando today.

"Can y'all believe we finally done?" Tonya said for the hundredth time today.

I smiled, and Rayna ignored her. "What I can't believe is that our party is almost here! It's about to be lit!" Rayna said as she took a selfie of her new hairstyle.

"Yep, all the cuties will be there!" Tonya replied. I didn't say anything, just looked at my phone while the stylist worked on my head.

"Damn, Shar! Can you act a little excited for once?" Rayna whined. She leaned closer to me and whispered, "Your ass ain't been right since that night!"

I side-eyed her and didn't say anything. We agreed we wouldn't tell Tonya about that night with Jus since she didn't go. She was supposed to take my place at dinner, but at the last minute, her mother made her stay home. So, Tonya would have been salty, and we wouldn't hear the last of it if we said anything.

"Let that shit go, Ray, please!" I mumbled.

"I will, if you will!" she replied and leaned back into her sitting position. She had a point; I needed to swallow the pill between me and Donte. Although I heard what P said that night, the proof was still in the pudding. Donte saw me as a child, and I was no longer interested in trying to help him see me as more.

When the stylist finished, I marveled at her work. My hair looked amazing; the style consisted of a part down the middle and loose waves that went past my shoulders. It gave me the confidence boost I needed. As the stylist added volume to the style, I loved it even more. I rotated the chair back and forth so I could admire her work.

"Yess! That's my girl!" Rayna said happily, then I posed as she snapped a picture. Then she and Tonya joined me for one.

Once we finished, she looked at her phone. "Cool, let's go! Our ride is here, ladies!"

We gathered our things, paid at the front, and headed out of the shop.

I hadn't felt that good in a while; the hairstyle provided some much-needed new energy that I craved. As we walked out of the shop, I was all smiles until I saw whose car we were getting in. My smile faded into a blank stare as I looked at Rayna, who gave me a pouty face.

"Sorry, boo; he was the only one available."

For a second, I thought about finding another ride, but that would make things worse, so I decided against it. We all got into Donte's car, and I didn't say a word nor did I bother to look in his direction. Of course, Rayna got in the front seat; I sat behind her and looked out the window.

"Sup, Dee!" Rayna said as she buckled in.

He nodded and pulled off. No one said much until Tonya chimed in.

"Ray, what time do Tammy and Mr. Tony get in?" Rayna turned toward Tonya.

"Umm, I think about 4:30 p.m. Then once they get settled, we're going to dinner!" She adjusted her posture again and turned her attention to me. "Shar, you coming, right?"

I looked at her, shook my head no, then turned back to the window.

"Damn, Shar! You ain't been wanting to do nothing lately. What the fuck! Don't be like that…c'mon, man! PLEEAASSEE!!!!" she begged.

Without looking at her, I replied, "I'm good, Ray; I got some things to prepare for tomorrow." I lied but wasn't in the mood to be around Tammy or Donte.

"Whatever you need to do, I promise I'll help you. Come on, man!" There was no need to reply, knowing Rayna wouldn't give up. "You can ride with me and P!"

I looked at her, then at the rearview mirror at Donte, who was looking at me. I looked back at her. "Ray…" Before I finished, she cut me off.

"Nah, I'm not taking no for an answer, so suck that shit up! You know I'm gonna be leaving soon; hell, we both are, so we need to kick it as much as possible." I didn't respond; I just looked out the window again.

When we finally made it to the parking lot of our apartment complex, I didn't hesitate to get out of the car, leaving everyone behind. I made my way across the grass toward the building.

"We leaving at 6:00 PM, Shar!" Rayna yelled. I put up my hand and gave her a thumbs up. When I finally got to my apartment, I was relieved! I leaned against the door and caught my breath. I went to my room, tied my hair back and decided to head to the living room to watch TV on the sofa, but I ended up falling asleep instead.

Around 5:00 PM, there was a knock on the door. I yawned and stumbled to open it. I knew it was Rayna; she wasn't going to let me miss dinner. As I walked, I mentally prepared for her antics as I told her I wasn't going in a firmer tone.

However, when I partially opened the door, it wasn't her but Donte. I shouldn't have been surprised he showed up; we hadn't spoken since our last encounter. I didn't even bother to say hello, just waited for him to get to the point. I wanted even more to send him on his way, just as I planned to do if it were Rayna in front of me.

"You busy?" he asked.

"Nope!" I said flatly.

"Can we talk for a minute?" I opened the door completely so he could come in. Whatever he had to say, I hoped it was quick. I had enough back and forth for one day. I closed and locked the door, and Donte sat on the sofa in the living room. Taking my time, I sat on the opposite end. After curling up, I placed a blanket over my legs and waited for him to speak.

However, he didn't, so I started the conversation. "So, what's up?"

He took a breath, then spoke. "Why you been MIA?" he asked, looking at me.

"Just needed a minute, figuring some stuff out."

"Like what, Shar?"

What did he expect from this conversation? It didn't matter; it was what it was, in my opinion. He just needed to get to the point and get out. To move things along, I decided to keep my answers short and to the point. I hoped my lack of emotion and conversation said what I didn't.

"Just stuff…"

Donte picked up on my mood and gave me the same energy back. "That's what we doing now?"

I shook my head. "Look, what do you want me to say… I just need time to figure out what I'm going to do after graduation. This summer, everyone else has a plan and I don't, so…" I shrugged my shoulders and lifted my hands in defeat.

Donte nodded. "You will figure out something."

No, he wasn't trying to be supportive—ugh, too late, brah!

"Yep, I will." My lack of appreciation for his "assuring" response pissed him off, but I didn't care.

"You ain't gonna figure that shit out tonight, so you coming to dinner, right?"

Was he serious? I knew he didn't just ask/tell me to come to dinner. I was over the dinner conversation and even more frustrated.

"Nah, y'all enjoy." I adjusted my position on the sofa as an indication that I wasn't leaving it tonight.

Donte shook his head. "Man, stop whatever this shit is… you know Mommy's gonna be looking for you and Rayna! Don't…" Before he could finish, I cut him off.

"I'll see everyone tomorrow. Plus, I'm flat…" Donte gave me the *really* face. Before he could respond, the front door was unlocking, and I shook my head.

"Da fuck is my life right now! URGH!" I grunted as Regina walked in with Uncle of the Week. I'd seen him before but didn't know his name. He was a tall, stocky dude who looked like he played football at some point. He rocked a bald head and a neat goatee. I could tell he smoked—not only because of his lips but because he reeked of it and cologne. Regina smiled brightly when she saw Donte. She always liked him and seemed to be extra nice when he was around. I rolled my eyes and waited for the shitshow about to unfold.

"What's up, y'all!" Regina said as they entered the living room. She was dressed like she had been rummaging through my closet again. Although I knew the dress that was two sizes too small for her wasn't mine. Uncle of the Week didn't speak; he just looked at Donte and me.

"Donte, how you doing, baby?" Regina asked, all perky and extra, as they sat opposite us on the other sofa.

"I'm good, Ms. Regina! How you been?" he said, smiling slightly.

"I been good, baby!" Regina fawned over Uncle of the Week as she rubbed his arm and head, but he was too busy with his phone to notice.

"You know I'd be better if my daughter would do something other than sit on her ass." Regina's sarcastic comment caused me to roll my eyes. She turned her attention back to Donte. "Anyway, baby, how's your mom?" she asked, showing all her teeth.

"She's good." he replied. Regina smiled.

"I know she's excited about tomorrow, seeing her baby graduate. I know I am! I hear Tony is coming tomorrow; it's been a while since I've seen him."

Regina was obviously fishing for some tea, but she had the wrong one. Donte was a vault for the most part. I was over the small talk and got up to leave.

"Ummm… where you going?" Regina said with an attitude. I stopped to look at her but didn't respond. "Can you please find somewhere else to be than here?" she said, annoyed.

What the fuck was everyone on today? Why couldn't I just stay home in peace? "I'm flat, so no!" I snapped back. Before I could walk away, Uncle of the Week reached into his pocket and held up $200. I looked at the money and at him; he didn't even acknowledge me, just looked at his phone.

"Take the damn money, Sharnel!" Regina said, as if I was tripping. When I didn't take it, she grabbed it and then handed it to me. I snatched the money from her and was about to walk away.

"Wait, you can't say thank you!" Regina barked. She was really tripping, so I walked back to the sofa.

"I took it because you told me to get out, so you thank that nigga!" Uncle of the Week looked in my direction. He didn't react, but I could tell he was sizing me up.

Donte looked at me as well; this was a normal reaction for Regina, so I was sure he wasn't surprised. I was about to walk away again but decided to add more. "Oh, and when you thank him, be sure to do it well!"

Regina looked insulted, but Uncle of the Week smiled and nodded, as if to say "good response." I didn't give a fuck what he thought. I was giving Regina what she wanted and getting the hell out.

"Sharnel, don't get smart!" Regina yelled. I waved her off and headed to my room to change. "See what I gotta deal with, Donte! I swear!"

I heard her say before I slammed my bedroom door. Regina got what she wanted; now all I had to do was get what I wanted. "How the fuck can I avoid dinner and get rid of Donte's ass?" I mumbled to myself. I couldn't think of anything at the moment, so I focused on getting dressed. I decided to throw on a black sundress, flat sandals, and a jean jacket. I untied my hair and put on a little makeup and perfume.

When I came back into the living room, Regina was still talking to Donte. When I walked in, he glanced at me and then returned his attention to Regina. She was still talking, and he didn't seem to mind it, but I was over it all. Uncle of the Week continued with his phone. When I walked toward the platform to the front door, Donte stood up. Regina turned her head and sized me up.

"Look who decided to look all cute for her man!" Regina said. Uncle of the Week turned his head to survey me while Donte looked at him. He nodded his head with approval, as if I needed or wanted it. Then he went back to his phone.

Donte walked toward me. Still reeling from Regina's comment, I frowned at her. "Man? What are you even talking about?" I said, annoyed. I was about to let Regina have it, but she waved me off.

"Sharnel, please… y'all make a cute couple! Plus, I know Donte can handle that mouth of yours!"

Was she serious? Why did I always need someone to handle me and my mouth in her opinion? What the hell was she saying, or better yet, what did she really think about me?

I was about to respond, but Donte gently grabbed my arm and guided me toward the door.

"See what I mean?" Regina said, as if he proved her point. I looked up at him, annoyed, but he kept walking toward the door. "Y'all have fun! Don't be in a rush to get home… Momma's got plans tonight!"

I almost threw up in my mouth.

"Bye, Donte baby! Take care of my girl!" Regina said as I slammed and locked the door.

"Urgh! She gets on my damn nerves!" I mumbled as I walked up the steps. Donte didn't say anything, so I added, "and your little escape plan didn't help!"

He just grunted but didn't say anything. When we got to the front door of the building, I stopped. "Look, I ain't in the mood for dinner, so y'all go ahead, please!" I yelled, hoping he would just leave me alone.

A frustrated Donte looked at me. "What now, Shar? Every time I turn around, you got a fuckin attitude! What is it now, huh? I'm over this shit!"

As the frustration built, I could feel tears forming in my eyes, but I refused to let them fall. So, I just folded my arms and looked away.

I didn't say anything, so he continued, "You got the bread… not like that was even an issue! So, what is it?" He was pissed but waited for my response, then he continued. "You know everyone's gonna be looking for you!"

I knew it was true, but I didn't give a fuck at that moment. I looked at him, showing him I was pissed off. Donte was perplexed; he asked all the right questions but still had no answers. When I didn't move, he asked more questions.

"Is it Tammy?"

I gave him an annoyed look, reflecting my displeasure in even mentioning that as an option. How could he even think that was a factor? I looked away and gripped my arms tighter. Donte had yet to ask one question he knew he should.

"Is it me?" he asked, empathy in his voice.

Fuck. As much as I didn't want to react, I did. I loosened my stance a bit and dropped my arms but didn't look at him. *Fucking showing your cards, Shar!* I thought as I mentally kicked myself.

He moved his head in my direction, so I had to look at him. "Is it me, Sharnel?"

I didn't have an answer and wasn't sure how to respond.

"So, it is me!" he said, then nodded. He reached for my hand, and I looked at him. He stared, then got a little closer to me. "Shar!" he whispered, smiled, then got serious and yelled, "Get over that shit, man, and bring your ass on! I'm tired of this shit!" He barked and pulled me toward the door.

Such an asshole! I snatched my hand away as he opened the door. He motioned with his head for me to go, and I folded my arms and walked out. We didn't say a word as we walked to the car. Donte started the car as we walked. I stopped and was about to turn around.

"Man, Sharnel, don't even do it! I aint in the mood to run after your ass!"

I rolled my eyes and kept walking.

"I don't care about you rolling your eyes either… that shit is gonna get stuck one day, and you're gonna be mad!" he mumbled.

When we got to the car, he opened the door, and I got in. Once he got in, I adjusted the seat. "Always touching shit!" I didn't even bother to say anything.

Donte turned on some music and pulled out of the space. We rode in silence for a bit before he spoke. "Aye!" He turned down the music, and I finally looked in his direction.

"So, what you gonna avoid me forever? What type of sense does that make?"

I didn't respond. I wasn't interested in having this conversation or its outcome.

"You can't ice everyone else out because of me!"

I laughed; here we go with the bullshit! He wanted me to indulge him, so I did. I turned my body toward Donte and finally spoke up. "Funny how everything surrounds you!"

Donte gave me a side-eye.

"So you're saying it doesn't?" When I didn't respond, he nodded. "I don't know what my plan is, Donte! But this bullshit," I said, motioning between him and me, "is getting old!"

He nodded in agreement. "Well, figure that shit out soon… I'm tired of everyone looking for you, whining to me, and asking me to do something about it… I got other shit to do!"

Now I was beyond pissed off; he just showed his cards, and they read complete bullshit! I folded my arms and began yelling. "So, you came to see me for everyone else?"

Donte didn't reply; he glanced over at me and kept driving.

"Yo, let me out this fuckin car, dude!" I undid my seatbelt and tried to unlock the door while the car still moved, but he locked them again.

"What the fuck are you doing, man? The car is still moving! Sharnel, calm the fuck down! That's your problem—always so fuckin' ready to run!"

Was he really trying to pin this shit on me? "For once, this one ain't on me, Donte! You say that shit and then turn it around on me! Get the fuck outta here! Now pull the hell over!" I was angry but mostly hurt. He didn't care about my feelings; his concern was getting everyone off his back.

"Here I was thinking that maybe you wanted to make things right, but you only came to me for your benefit!" I yelled.

"Make things right? What the fuck do you mean? What are we even talking about, Sharnel? I'm tired of this shit!" he yelled back.

Now I was officially done. Donte acted as if I made everything up, and he was oblivious to it all. When he stopped at the light, I went to open the door, but he locked it again.

"Stop doing that shit, Sharnel!" he barked.

"I'm over this, and you, Donte! Forever wasting my damn time with your bullshit…"

Donte looked at me and flared his nostrils. "Man, chill the hell out! We're almost there! Then you can gladly get the fuck out!"

I was tired of holding it all in, so I gave him a piece of my mind. "I swear you start these arguments by acting fuckin' clueless all the time. You see me as some little girl. Maybe you should see yourself as a little fuckin' boy because that's how you act! But you know what…it don't fuckin' matter. See me or don't! I'm over this bullshit and you!"

Donte didn't say a word; he just drove. When he finally pulled into the parking lot of the restaurant, I unlocked the door and opened it.

"I'm not going in that fuckin' restaurant. If anyone asks where I am, you be sure to tell them your sympathy-ass talk didn't work!"

I got out and slammed the door. This time, Donte didn't follow or even respond. I walked to the mall, which was a few yards back.

I didn't want to be at the mall, but I knew I couldn't go home. I heard my phone chime, but I decided to put it on silent. I sat on a bench in the mall to cool down a bit. What is my life? Every day, I'm pissed, angry, or just exhausted because of some bullshit! I needed a break—a serious one! After a few more minutes, I decided to eat at a restaurant in the mall. I was thankful when the waiter sat me at a booth in the back. I ordered a drink and an appetizer, then decided to look at my phone. I had three missed messages from Rayna, Tonya, and Donte, respectively.

Rayna: *What happened, Shar? I thought you was coming tonight!*

Tonya: *Girl, what happened? We saw you, then we didn't! Donte came in, whispered something to Miss Chyna, and left! Lover's quarrel?*

Donte: *Where you go? I know you ain't walk home!*

I left all the messages on read, turned off my location, and closed my phone.

I knew my hair was a mess, so I texted Miss Kena and asked her if she would fix it. Of course, she said yes. I told her I'd be at her house tomorrow morning at 7:00 a.m. since graduation wasn't until 10:00 a.m. I enjoyed the quiet while I ate dinner. The place was dimly lit, and I could have fallen asleep. When I got the check, I realized I only had cash. "Fuck! I need to get home!" I mumbled. I knew I had to text Rayna.

Shar: *Ray, can you send me $50? I'll give it back to you tonight. I only have cash!*

She responded immediately. Rayna: *Say less!* She sent me the money, and I requested an Uber.

When the Uber arrived, I settled in and hoped the driver saw my message about wanting a quiet ride. He followed directions, and I looked out the window as I rode. I was exhausted mentally and hoped he would get me home soon. I wanted to go home and go to bed, but I knew that wasn't possible. I settled into the fact that I'd spend the night in the laundry room before I went to Miss Chyna's house. When the Uber made it to the complex, I had him stop at the front. I decided I would walk the rest of the way to the building. As I walked, I took in the warm air and listened to my music on low.

My thoughts drifted to all the interactions I had lately—everything was a shit show that kept growing. Maybe it's me; obviously, I keep attracting bullshit. I had to be the cause. Something had to change, and that something was me. When I made it to the corner, I could see P's building and people sitting on the steps. "Not tonight, please! Not tonight!" I mumbled. I shook my head and headed towards my building, hoping the group didn't see me.

"Shar!" Rayna yelled.

I stopped and waited as she came my way. She looked concerned when she saw me.

"Where you been? I thought you were taking an Uber!" She grabbed my arm, and we walked slowly.

"I did; I had it drop me off at the front. Look, Ray, I'm really just tired! I wanna go home…" I was on the verge of tears as I spoke.

Rayna just nodded. "I know, Shar…I know you are! Look, why don't you come…"

Not wanting to be near the groups of people, I shook my head. "Nah, I'm good. I just wanna go somewhere and sleep! Please!"

She nodded. "Okay, Shar, but look, I need to get my stuff from P's house, so just walk with me, and then we can head home!"

I wasn't in the mood to argue, and I hated the idea of going to Miss Chyna's, but I didn't argue but filled her in on Regina's rant from earlier. We cut across the grass and headed toward P's building. I could see P and others sitting on the stoop talking.

"Sup, Sister Shar!" P examined my appearance and looked concerned. I could only imagine what he was thinking.

"Sup, P!" I said, yawning.

The rest of the guys just looked. Rayna whispered something to P; he nodded, and then she guided me inside the building. No one lived in P's apartment but him. He had two bedrooms, two baths, a small kitchen, a dining room, and a living room. Once inside, I stood and waited for Rayna to grab her stuff. However, she had a different plan.

"Look, let's just hang out here a bit!" I didn't protest; I just sat on the sofa with Rayna, and she turned on the TV. Rayna found something to watch, and the next thing I knew, I was asleep. This wasn't the first time we'd hung out at P's house. In fact, we'd spent the night a few times. Of course, Rayna spent time entertaining P, but when I woke up, she was always back on the sofa with me. So, I felt safe at his house, knowing neither of them would let anything happen to me.

When I woke up, I was covered with a blanket, and a pillow was under my head. I looked at the other end of the sofa, and Rayna was gone. I immediately sat up and almost panicked. But then I saw Donte in the chair with the ottoman, sleeping. I laid my head back down and looked at the ceiling. While I slept, I vaguely remembered waking up and hearing his voice as he talked to Rayna and P.

"What y'all doing here?" Donte asked her.

"Shar was exhausted and couldn't go home…so we came here." I was sure he nodded.

"Yoo, what happened to her tonight? Sis is looking more than tired," P asked. No one responded verbally.

"Well, I'm not leaving her, Dee." I was sure he nodded again.

"Aight, well I'll hang out with her if y'all want to get some sleep."

I felt safe knowing Rayna wasn't going far and would stay at P's tonight. I felt her get up and kiss my cheek. The thought of being alone with Donte made me more exhausted. In my mind, all the feelings and thoughts I had about him rushed over me. However, that changed when I felt him put the pillow under my head and cover me with the blanket, then he kissed my cheek. I was sure I dreamed it, but when I saw the evidence, I knew I hadn't. That was the last thing I remembered.

Donte purposely angled himself so I had to step over him to leave the sofa. I checked my phone, and it was 5:30 a.m. I wanted to go home and prepare to see Miss Kena. But I knew it wasn't gonna be that simple; yet I had to try. I quietly folded up the blanket and placed the pillow on top of it on the sofa. I stood and watched him sleep for a second. He seemed peaceful despite being the menace he was. It had been a while since we'd been in the same room without arguing. Maybe it was time to set it all aside, even if it was just for today—not that I had any interest in continuing our ever-growing argument.

I pulled up my dress a bit so I could step over Donte. I placed one foot on the other side of him and was about to step over him again when he grabbed my arm.

"Where you going, Shar?" he mumbled, slightly opening his eyes.

"I'm going home." I whispered.

He opened his eyes more but still held my arm. "Let's talk before you head out."

I nodded okay, and he let go of my arm. He took his feet down and sat up, then I sat on the ottoman. I took a sip of my water that I had before I fell asleep. I set the bottle down, and he picked it up and drank the rest.

"Look, Shar, my bad for last night…for everything!"

I nodded, too tired to argue or even respond. However, I mustered up a response: "You good, it is what it is!" My response wasn't what he was expecting; he looked a little disappointed. But he didn't say anything else. So, I continued, "I'm tired, Donte." I said, shaking my head. "I'm tired of arguing, being frustrated—all of it…so I give up! Everything in my life right now seems stressful. I don't have the energy anymore to fight…especially not with you." After taking a breath, I continued, "You made a point about not icing everyone out, so I'm gonna figure it out."

Donte nodded. "Look, man, I hear you, and I don't want what happened to ruin your day. You earned this shit! Enjoy it! Look, if you need me to…"

I knew what he was about to say, so I put my hand up to stop him. I didn't need him to back off. It wouldn't change anything anyway. "Let's just move forward…cool?"

He nodded. I was done talking, so I got up, but he motioned for me to sit again putting his hand on my shoulder. "Look, Shar, it's a lot of shit I wanna say…but can't. I know you wanna know why, but I don't have the answers right now…just know…it ain't because I don't care. I do."

I nodded; at this point, I didn't want answers. They didn't matter—none of it did. My focus was getting through the day and praying Regina or Uncle of the Week didn't do anything to embarrass me.

"Look, Donte, let's just put a pin in all that. Let's try to get back to the way things were before they got…whatever this is!" I said the words, but in my mind, none of this made any sense. Donte and I were always this way, constantly pissing each other off for one reason or another. Only this time, there were untapped feelings on his end and an overflow on my end.

Donte didn't react; he just pondered my statement. When I attempted to stand up again, he did the same.

"Give me a hug, man!" He put his arms around me and held me. "I'm proud of you, Shar! You did this shit! You accomplished something I didn't!"

I pulled back a bit to see his face. "You didn't need a piece of paper to solidify your success! You did it the right way, your way. That's something to be proud of."

He acted like he was wiping a fake tear—typical Donte! I let go, and so did he, then we headed out the door. When we reached the front of the building, the sun was blaring. I was ready to take on whatever the day held. "It's a beautiful morning!" I said as we walked toward our building.

"Yeah, it is!" Donte said as he looked down at me. I smiled slightly, and we kept walking.

When we got to the front door, he opened it, and I headed down the stairs and he headed upstairs. He was halfway up on the first flight, and I was halfway down.

"Aye!" he yelled over the rail, looking down. I looked up, waiting for him to respond. "Do something to that mop on your head!" he said, smiling.

"Whatever, Donte! You're gonna regret those words later!" I snapped. He shook his head and headed upstairs. I headed inside so I could get ready to see Miss Kena.

CHAPTER 7

The graduation ceremony was boring; we were outside, and the heat was melting us all. I was glad that I wore all white. Rayna, Tonya, and I all managed to sit together. We spent the entire ceremony taking pics and talking to each other and those around us. When it was time to walk across the stage, I immediately felt nervous. When Rayna walked across the stage, I heard a loud roar, which included Tonya and me. The same thing happened when Tonya walked across the stage. When it was my turn, I felt like I would throw up, but I earned this diploma. Throw up or not, I was walking across this stage.

"Sharnel Raeshawn Grace!" I heard a loud cheer as I walked across the stage. I could hear various voices chanting as I walked: "That's my sista! That's my baby! Shar Shar! That's what's up, Shar!"

I smiled as I glanced at the family with Regina and Uncle of the Week as I exited the stage.

Regina snapped pictures while I walked to my seat. I posed, smiled, and waved as I walked.

Donte was still standing and cheering me on, "Hell yeah! Shar!" I was glad we resolved things or at least were cordial for today.

I saw Tammy; she clapped for me but looked salty. It was no secret—Tammy didn't like me. However, the bigger issue was that Tammy wanted Donte, and bad! She had convinced herself that I wanted him. Therefore, she would come for me and any woman who got in her way. Tammy was Mr. Tony's niece, so she and Donte were not blood related. Even when we were kids, she attempted to flirt with him and entice him. However, Donte made it clear he wanted no parts of her. I'm sure his loud cheers and claps for me pissed her off. I didn't care; I looked at Tammy like I did Trina. Her annoyance only caused me to poke the bear more, and today I was time enough for it.

Everyone met up after the ceremony. We took some quick pictures, then Donte and Uncle of the Week walked off in different directions just as P came back. He handed Rayna a beautiful bouquet of long-stem red roses. She smiled from ear to ear; I was happy for her. I knew the family, along with P, was going to lunch. Miss Chyna invited me (of course), but part of me hoped Regina had something planned for a celebration. I was sure she would say the party was my gift. However, I hoped she would act differently, at least today.

In true Regina fashion, she acted proud and celebratory for 2.5 seconds. After we took pictures, she started fluffing my hair. I knew the bullshit was coming as Uncle of the Week, Roy, waited for her in the car.

Regina tried to whisper poorly in my ear, "Umm, Shar! I need to go; you think you can get a ride with Rayna or Tonya?"

My face dropped. Everyone witnessed Regina's fake proud antics but now her dismissiveness. I wasn't surprised; if anything, I expected it. But that didn't stop it from hurting deep inside.

Before I could respond, Miss Chyna approached us with a smile. "Shar, you still coming to lunch, right? I mean, we need to celebrate with both our girls before the big celebration!" Miss Chyna gave an urging nod as if this was the plan all along.

I sprang into action. "Yep, wouldn't miss it!" I smiled back, not wanting to give Regina the satisfaction of seeing me upset.

Regina was ecstatic. "Oh cool, you got your own plans! Y'all enjoy!" She handed me $200, kissed my cheek, and left.

I watched her hurry off as she ditched me for her "man." I tried to hide my disappointment, but it showed.

Miss Chyna put her arm around my shoulder. "Don't even worry about it, Shar! Better to be around people who want to celebrate with you, right?"

I nodded, and she kissed my cheek. Miss Chyna kept her arm around me as we walked toward the car. As we walked, we saw Donte coming toward us with a paper tote bag. When he looked around and didn't see Regina, I knew he put two and two together. He just looked at my face as if to confirm I was okay. Once he caught up to us, Tammy put on her best act. She stopped and turned toward me.

"Aww, poor Shar!" she said sympathetically. "Dang girl, Rayna got flowers, is getting a free lunch, and she's getting a party… but you didn't get nothing!" Tammy chuckled a little.

The bitch in Tammy couldn't help herself but "kick me," thinking I would fall apart. I'd never give her that satisfaction!

Miss Chyna never got in between Tammy and me because she knew I could handle myself. So, I smiled slightly and just nodded. I stepped up to Tammy and was about to give her a piece of my mind, but I was interrupted.

"I got her some flowers," Donte said as he reached in the bag and handed me a bouquet of pink peonies—my favorite. I immediately smiled. "Plus, I'm giving her a ride and buying her lunch!"

Tammy shrugged as if it was nothing, but then he grabbed my hand, which shocked everyone since Donte was not one for PDA. Jackpot, pick up your face, BITCH! To make matters worse, Donte's touch pissed off another Wright man, and he was not shy about it.

"That's my Shar Shar, Donte!" Keith fussed.

Donte gave him the *really* face, and Keith pouted.

I just smiled and bent down to kiss Keith's cheek. He smiled and hugged me. I felt like a million bucks—two Wright men vied for my attention while Tammy stewed that no one checked for her.

When I stood back up, I purposely picked up Keith and grabbed Donte's arm, and we all walked together. I made sure to put some extra sway in my hips because I knew she was behind me.

"You just gonna rub it in, huh?" Donte whispered as we walked.

"Yep, that bitch tried the right one," I said.

"Shar Shar, you say bad word!" Keith said.

I laughed and kissed his cheek. Donte shook his head, and I pushed my body against his arm as we walked. I could hear Mr. Tony, Miss Chyna, Rayna, and P chuckling as we walked along to their cars.

I gave Keith to Miss Chyna, and Donte walked me to the front seat of his car. He opened my door for me to get in. Tammy reached for the door to the backseat of Donte's car and he immediately responded.

"Oh nah, you can ride with Mommy and Tony," he said. I wanted to burst out laughing but contained myself. Tammy glared at me as Donte got in on the driver's side.

"Had to rub it in, huh?" I said.

He just slightly laughed, started the car, and drove us to lunch. Of course, I had to adjust my seat. "You can't ever just get in and ride!" he complained.

"Nope! If you would program my settings, we wouldn't have to go through this every time I get in!"

Donte looked over at me. "Shar, first, this is my damn car! Second, you ain't in this car enough for that ever to be an option. Third, like hell that's EVER gonna happen."

I smiled and shook my head. "You say that now."

He waved me off and kept driving. Although it hurt that Regina ditched me, I felt special that Donte did this for me. It was just what I needed.

When we finally got to the restaurant, Donte parked, and I pulled down the visor to check my hair and makeup in the mirror. Donte looked through his phone.

"See, you got that mop together!" He closed his phone and looked in my direction.

"Whatever! You know I look good, hater!" I shot back as I put on my lip gloss and then looked at him.

"Yeah, it looks nice…but don't get excited, big head!" he mumbled as he opened his door.

"If I didn't know your insults were actually compliments, I'd be hurt!" I said, rolling my eyes. He got out, closed the door, and came to the passenger side to open mine.

"Whatever, Shar, just get your ass out!" he said. I got up and stood between the door and the car.

"Tell me I'm wrong!" He looked at me and got closer to my face.

"You're wrong! Now bring your ass on!" I laughed and pushed him out of the way.

We headed to the restaurant to meet up with the family. Everyone was seated and waited for us to come to the table. Of course, there were two seats between Tammy and Rayna. As we walked, Donte pulled my arm to slow our pace and leaned close to me.

"Yo, do me a solid and sit next to Tammy, man, please!" he mumbled. I smiled and laughed.

"What's in it for me?"

Donte gave me the *really* face and shook his head. "I'm already buying you lunch, brought you flowers, and helped you make Tammy jealous…what else do you want, man?"

I acted like I was pondering the question. "I want $50 and free rides all summer!"

Donte looked at me like I called him out of his name. I really didn't want anything; however, my face said I was serious. I just wanted to see what he would agree to. He didn't respond; he just shook his head.

When we got to the table, I put my purse in the chair next to Tammy.

"Oh, I was saving this seat!" Tammy said.

"Oh for me? You're far too kind, boo, thank you!" I blew Tammy a kiss as she grunted while Donte rushed to the seat next to Rayna.

Once we were both settled and comfortable, he whispered, "Good looking, ma G!"

"Whatever!" I mumbled under my breath. Miss Chyna smiled in our direction, then continued looking at her menu. At lunch, the family had small talk about the day and plans for the summer. We all laughed and joked while Tammy sulked about sitting next to me. I think the fact that I didn't seem bothered annoyed her more.

When lunch was over, we went back to our respective cars, and I purposely waited for Donte to open my door. As I slid in, I looked at Tammy and smiled as she got into Miss Chyna's backseat.

Once Donte got in, he said, "Good looking," then reached in his pocket and pulled out $50.

"You kidding me, right? You did me a few solids today. I'll take one for the team…this time!"

He nodded and turned on the car. I went to touch the radio, and he popped my hand.

"Ouch, what the fuck!" I yelled.

"Don't touch my shit! It's like Optimus Prime all over again!"

The mention of an incident that happened when Rayna and I were eight and he was ten caused me to laugh hysterically. But Donte was serious and only glared at me. I couldn't believe he was still salty about that; shit, he was petty! The more I thought about it, I couldn't stop laughing as I tried to get it together. Fed up, Donte continued his rant as I tried to regain my composure.

"This is my car, Sharnel! MINE! I ain't listening to nothing you like, so relax your big head, or your ass can walk!"

I wasn't fazed by him or his Optimus Prime tantrum. "How soon they forget!"

Donte looked over at me and then said, "This one time, play your shit, Shar!"

I smiled, connected my phone to his car, and said, "Don't make me regret this shit!"

I paid him no mind and decided to play some *DMX*, starting with my favorite, *Get at Me Dog!* "Is this okay, your highness?" I said, annoyed. He turned up the music, and we headed home.

By the time we got to the parking lot of the complex, he was nodding his head.

"Thought you didn't like nothing I liked," I said as he parked the car. He put the car in park and continued nodding his head. I purposely changed it to *Summer Walker's CPR*; he frowned and turned the car off.

"Get your ass out, man!" I laughed at his immediate change in reaction.

"Not till you open my door! Don't be a douche now!"

Donte got out and opened my door. I saw Tammy in the distance walking in our direction, so I put on my best act!

"Thank you so much, bae! You really went all out for me today!" I said, touching his face.

Donte gave me the *what the hell* face, but when he saw Tammy, he shook his head. Tammy mumbled something, and he did the unthinkable.

"You're welcome, anything for you," then he planted a juicy kiss on my cheek. I almost lost my balance, but he grabbed my arm.

He mouthed, *you good* as he tried not to laugh.

I laughed in shock, then nodded and tried to shake it off. Donte helped me onto the sidewalk, and I walked toward Rayna and P while Tammy stormed off toward our building.

Rayna grabbed my arm and whispered, "I saw that little act you just pulled off! Bitch, you like to pass out when he kissed you!" We both laughed as we walked arm in arm.

"Ray, I was not ready!" I mumbled. She smiled as she continued to laugh.

"Bitch…if that's all it takes to make you weak…wait till your ass gets some D. It's gonna be a long summer, boo!"

I knew D stood for dick, but part of me wondered if it also stood for Donte.

CHAPTER 8

The day after graduation was our party. It was turning into a neighborhood block party; everybody was going to be there. Some of the people we graduated with already made plans to ditch their parties early and come to ours. The good thing was it started late in the evening and would go until at least 1:00 AM. We planned to have lots of food, music, decorations, and drinks all in the courtyard of the apartment buildings.

Miss Chyna, Miss Kena, Tonya's mom (Mrs. Nash), along with Rayna, Tonya, and I spent the day preparing for the party. Although, some people helped more than others. At the break of day, we began setting up and preparing things. Donte said he wouldn't help set up since he helped pay for the party, plus he had to work earlier that day. So that only left us girls, our moms, and Mr. Tony. P did offer to help when he got off, but that wouldn't be until later. When the tables were delivered at 9:00 a.m., Tonya and I stood outside to direct the movers.

"Hey, can you put a couple of tables over there?" I said, as Tonya stood around and texted on her phone. It was bad enough that Rayna disappeared and did the bare minimum. I was over them but knew nothing would get done if I stopped.

"Can you help, please?" I said to Tonya, who eventually put her phone away as one of the guys approached us.

"Umm, he's cute," Tonya said.

I looked at the guy and rolled my eyes. She was now only interested in the task because of some dude. I shook my head; she was locked in on him, and now he was too. She began smiling and drawing attention to herself, and it worked. The moving guy took the bait; he was light-skinned, full of tattoos, with wavy hair in a man bun.

As he made his way to us, I took a breath. "Ugh, here we go," I thought.

"So, what y'all got going on today?" he said, smiling and showing two gold caps on his fangs.

"Oh, it's our graduation party," Tonya said flirtatiously.

He smiled and said, "Oh, okay, where's my invite?"

I thought he was being flirty, but Tonya took him seriously.

"Let me give you my number and I'll give you the information." Tonya proceeded to pull out her phone and give her number to the delivery guy. I rolled my eyes and straightened up a table that was leaning.

"Whoa, whoa, whoa, momma, let me help you with that," the other delivery guy said. He looked similar to his partner, only he was shorter and didn't have any caps on his teeth.

I really didn't want or need his help, but I knew he wouldn't take no for an answer. When the guy came over to help me with the table, he smiled, but I ignored it. When the table was straight, I looked at it and was about to walk away when he stepped closer as if to get my attention. I backed up, giving him the indication I wasn't interested, but he didn't get the signal. Then he intentionally touched my hand, and I was pissed. My facial expression showed my anger, and I immediately went off.

"What the fuck you doing? Don't you ever put your hands on me?!" I yelled loud enough to wake the neighborhood.

Tonya and the other delivery guy looked in our direction but didn't move.

"Yo, you overreacting, momma, chill out," the guy replied while he chuckled. His lack of sincerity in his non-apology only fed my anger.

So I got in his face. "Overreacting! You don't know me; I will…"

Before I could finish, Donte used his arm to move me away from the mover. He didn't say anything but displayed his emotionless expression, which caused the mover to sing a different tune.

"My bad, I didn't mean no disrespect," he said, looking at Donte. Donte looked at me, and I was still fuming. I didn't say a word, and he never moved his arm. The mover apologized again and then backed away, and he and his partner left. I just stood still, trying to calm down, but I felt violated.

"You good?" Donte asked.

I just looked forward and nodded. He stood in the direction of my gaze, and I nodded again. "I'm good, thank you."

He looked over at Tonya, who stood at a distance and tried to act confused about what had just happened. He shook his head, then finally put his arm down. He made eye contact with me one more time, then proceeded toward his car. I watched him walk to his car and get in. As I saw him pull out, I was thankful he showed up. Who knows what would have happened if he hadn't? Seeing him drive away made me feel a bit sad, which was weird. I wished he would have stayed.

"Girl, what was that?" Tonya asked.

I couldn't believe she had the nerve to ask me that... this shit was her fault. I walked away from Tonya; I needed a breather before I blew up on her. I decided to head home and relax since we didn't need to do anything else until later. Rayna entertained Tammy, who was leaving right before the party started. Thank goodness! So, I'd update her on the antics from this morning later. When I got to my apartment, no one was home, and I was glad! I turned on the TV but pulled out my phone.

Big Head: *Thank you for earlier! I appreciate it!*

I was surprised when he responded quickly.

Him: *You're welcome! What the hell was Tonya doing? Why she ain't help?*

Big Head: *Being fuckin' thirsty! Damn, you would swear she's a bum ass chick...*

Him: *Crazy shit! When I saw them roll up, I knew it was about to be a problem!*

I smiled.

Big Head: *Oh, so you was watching me, huh?*

Him: (thumbs down emoji)

Big Head: *Funny how you always happen to be right there when I need some help!* (heart eyes emoji)

Him: *Stop needing help so much!*

Big Head: (crying laughing emoji) *Where's the fun in that, especially if you can't save me?*

Him: *SMDH! Shar, take your ass somewhere...I got work to do, man!*

As I read it, I could hear you saying it.

Big Head: *LOL! Yeah, get back to work! Don't be late tonight!*

Later that day, the party was underway. I had completely decompressed since earlier, but I still steered clear of Tonya. Rayna and I made our rounds, dancing and mingling with people. Everyone was having a good time. The music was loud, the food was amazing, and the drinks were flowing. Everyone covered the courtyard, even Donte, who arrived an hour late. I saw him come in and shook my head; I knew he was late out of spite—petty ass. He nodded in my direction and then went to sit off to the side with P and some other guys.

As things got underway, I realized I was hungry. With all the preparations, I hadn't eaten all day, so I decided to make myself a plate for later. I grabbed a plate and stood in the line, which seemed to be constantly growing. But it didn't matter; I just grooved to the music while I waited. As I got closer, I was a few people away from the food table Donte approached me.

"Sup?" Donte stood next to me.

"Hey," I said without looking at him.

"You good?" he said while staring at me.

I finally looked at him. "Yeah, I'm cool. Running late or something?" I said nonchalantly.

"You was looking for me, huh?" I rolled my eyes, and he just nodded.

He didn't say anything else; we just moved along with the line.

I continued to groove with the music, then it hit me. "Wait?!?" I said.

"What?" he said, confused.

"Your ass ain't come to check on me; you came to cut in this long ass line," I said, motioning to the line behind us.

He dropped his head and then looked up and smirked. I laughed.

"C'mon, Shar, man! I've been working all day, and I ain't ate today, man!" he whined.

"Ohhh, you raggedy as shit for this one!" I cracked up laughing. When I got to the front of the line, he gave me a sad face. I acted like I didn't see it.

He nodded and said, "Aight, at least hold this, let me tie my shoe!"

I took his plate, and he backed up. When I looked down, I noticed he had on slides.

"Yoo, what the fuc…" I stopped when I saw Miss Chyna, who was shaking her head and laughing.

Donte gave me praying hands and mouthed, *Plleeaassee* as he continued to back away, but not before he yelled, "You know what I like, Shar, man, and don't put no pork on my plate. Aye, and don't forget to put some foil on it."

Was he serious? I should have put his plate in the trash. But I knew I wouldn't; not only would I make it, but it'd be how he liked it. Granny taught me very early on that you don't play with people's food! That was a sure way they'd never trust you again. He smiled at me once he returned to his seat. I just shook my head and made our plates.

"He got you good, Shar!" Miss Chyna said as she bumped my arm and then handed me one more plate. "You know only a wife makes her husband's plate."

I looked at her, shocked by her words. "What?!? I mean, you would make a great daughter-in-love," she said before she walked away, leaving me to ponder her words.

I ended up making two plates for both me and Donte. When I finished, I walked over to where everyone was sitting, including Donte. I scrunched my face at him, and he winked as I made my way toward him.

"Shar, you bring me a plate?" Rayna whined.

I looked at Donte as I handed him two of the plates. "I would have, but my hands were full."

He inspected the plates and gave me a nod of approval. Rayna, however, gave me the *really* face, but then I handed her one of my plates. She smiled and started to eat as I sat down to join everyone.

P, Fat Mane, Donte, and Paul played dominos, while Rayna, Tonya, Trav, and I sat at a nearby table. The fellas talked mess to each other while they played until Fat Mane spoke up.

"So, Sharnel, where your boo at tonight?"

Fat Mane was typically soft-spoken, a gentle soul who would give you the shirt off his back, but don't cross him. He also lived in the neighborhood in the next complex, so we met him on the bus to school. He was only 5'7", almost 250 lbs, but solid in his stature, with a bright future. He would graduate next year and had already received a scholarship to wrestle at college in the Midwest.

I knew Fat Mane was being flirtatious and had a crush on me, so I wasn't mad or surprised by his comment. I smiled, and just as I was about to respond, Trav chimed in.

"Shar's sensitive ass ran him off this morning, apparently just like she did Er…" Before he could finish, both P and Donte shot him a look that let him know he crossed the line.

Trav was cute, but he wasn't my type physically, mentally, or emotionally. He was tall, light-skinned, a star basketball player in high school on his way to college; he just did too much. It boggled my mind that he and Fat Mane were cousins—talk about complete opposites. He wanted to be seen; he put himself on a metaphorical throne. Trav lived in the wealthy part of town but was always trying to chill with us in the neighborhood. I was not interested in being his trophy piece nor feeding his ego.

I wasn't in the mood to entertain bullshit, but I would indulge him this one time. I now needed to address two people at once, and both needed to know it directly. I took a breath and looked at Tonya, who was on the other side of the table.

"Sorry, I thought it was kinda funny…but guess not!"

I rolled my eyes and wondered what would make her think any of that was funny. I made a mental note to check her ass again later. "First of all, mind your fuckin' business, because whatever you were told happened was likely exaggerated!" I said as I looked in Tonya's direction. "Second, I don't have a man, but if I did, I wouldn't be flaunting him around like some little girl trying to get attention."

Donte turned his head in my direction. We made eye contact momentarily, then he looked back at his dominos.

Not to be outdone, Trav replied, "Maybe you should try women since dick ain't your flavor!"

I smiled as I stood up and leaned across the table to get closer to Trav. "Yeah, tell your mama to come around; she can come taste this virgin pussy! I heard her head game is fire! Oh, make sure she brings the pillow she uses for her knees when she's sucking off that dude she's messing with that ain't your daddy!"

Everyone laughed, including Fat Mane, while Trav saw red! I leaned up and smiled while Trav glared at me, displaying his anger. It was well known that his mother was having an affair. So, I didn't care if he was mad; he came for the right one on the right day.

Since I had enough fun, I got up and walked away from the table. Rayna followed me. "Damn, Shar! That was funny but cold as fuck!"

I waved her off as we headed back toward the crowd of people. "Please, he deserved it for minding business that ain't his…"

As we made our way past Donte, he looked at me, and I looked at him as I responded to Rayna. "His mama got more of a chance than he does, and I don't even like girls. Besides, I like a man who doesn't need to be seen or heard!" Donte just looked back at the dominos, and we walked back toward the people.

We partied until 2 a.m., and no one in the neighborhood complained because they were all there. Plus, we agreed to clean up the next day and end everything at a respectable time. But of course, Miss Chyna had the after-party at her house until 5 a.m., so we kept going. It was truly a night to remember. Of course, Rayna had her spotlight moment when P brought her some lavish gifts that made everyone go "ohhh" and "ahhh" over her. Tonya had to have her moment, so when her daddy presented her with the keys to a car (used but nice), she acted like she was going to pass out. Always on team too much, but I was happy for my girls.

As for me, I preferred my gifts in private, and I actually got one. Regina asked me what I wanted, and I said I wanted a few days away from the neighborhood. She said she would send me to the beach for a few days, which worked for me. It didn't matter if it was Ocean City, Myrtle Beach, VA Beach, or even Atlantic City; I just wanted to be near the water. However, when everyone asked me what I got, I just said the party and handed them a drink so I could move on.

I needed to take a break from the party, so I snuck inside to freshen up. On my way to the building, Miss Chyna asked me to check in on Keith. He had passed out after running around and dancing at the party. She had the video monitor, but I told her I didn't mind. So, I headed upstairs to see if he was okay. No one was in the house but me, so I used the bathroom and then crept into Miss Chyna's room. He was knocked out, drooling and snoring. I just watched him for a second; he was the perfect little guy. If I ever had a son, I hoped he would be as smart and cute as Keith.

I closed the door and made my way down the hall to the guest bathroom, which had all the hair products. I fixed my hair and washed my hands, then exited the bathroom. As I came out, Donte had just come in through the front door and walked toward me. Before I reached the end of the hall, he blocked my way. I put my hands on my hips and acted annoyed with a smile, then waited for him to move.

"Excuse you," I said, but he didn't budge.

"You lit Trav up out there!" he said plainly.

"His ass deserved it!" I replied.

"You know his ass likes you, so why even respond?" I acted like I was about to throw up.

"I don't give a fuck; I would never consider his ass! If he would keep his nose out of my business and stop running his mouth about shit he knows nothing about, there would be no problem."

Donte nodded, looking at me with a straight face.

I thought the conversation was over, so I walked forward and he put his hand up. "I got you something." I did a double take and smiled.

"You got me something!" I laughed loudly. "What, an empty box or a mouse so I can feed Tony? Very funny, Donte!" I laughed him off and rolled my eyes.

"Damn, I can tell you ain't used to getting shit," he said. Then it hit me—OMG, he really might have gotten me something. Inside, I was excited but still doubtful. I tried to hide my expression, but he called my bluff. "Don't get all excited now." I moved aside so he could pass.

He walked toward his room, and I leaned against the inside of his door and looked around. There wasn't much to it other than the black paint and posters on the wall, a queen-size bed, a nightstand, drawers, his shoe collection, a desk, a chair, and a stand that held his pet snake, Tony, which gave me the creeps. He sat on the bed, opened the nightstand, then handed me a box. I reached for the box and sat down beside him. Still skeptical, I shook it and heard something rattle inside.

"Really, man!" he said, annoyed. "Urgh, you're always doing the most."

I laughed. "Nah, doing the most is Tonya almost passing out earlier." He slightly smiled and shook his head.

He handed me a ring box, but I knew there was no ring inside. However, it could be anything, knowing Donte. I looked at the box and then searched his emotionless face for a reaction.

"Just open it, man." I obliged his request and was completely floored by what I found. All I could muster up was, "You remembered…"

He was quiet and eventually said, "Yeah."

"It's beautiful," I whispered, still looking at the necklace. In the box, I found a dragonfly necklace. It was silver, with onyx and rhinestones in the wings and spine. It was beautiful. I just stared at the necklace, then at his face, which had softened. I was still stuck on the necklace. "You know…" I tried to finish, but I couldn't get my words together.

When I was about 12, my Granny had given me a birthday gift: a sterling silver dragonfly necklace. I loved it; I wore it every day. I knew it didn't cost much—Granny likely got it from a yard sale—but I loved her, so it was priceless.

One day on the playground, it slipped off my neck, and I didn't realize it was gone until after dark. I was devastated. Rayna helped me look for a while, but we didn't find it. Night after night, when no one was home, I was back on the playground looking for it. I couldn't find it. I searched for the next three weeks, both days and nights, but I had no hope.

After the third week, I had just given up. After every unsuccessful search, I walked back to the building and just sat on the steps and cried. I felt hopeless. To make matters worse, my Granny died not long after I lost it. She was my person; she saw me well before I knew my worth. I felt like I failed her.

I remember one of our last conversations; she said, "Shar baby, don't forget your wings and who made them. You miss your blessing trying to stay low to the ground." There was not a day I hadn't wished she was here now. I could use some wisdom to push me forward or at least let me know what was next.

After shaking off my thoughts, I felt Donte's face slowly coming close to mine. As he got closer, my face turned up to meet him. Was this dude about to kiss me? Whatever was about to happen, I was ready. I wanted it and reached my hand up to touch his face. My whole body was weak at the thought.

As he got in proximity, the front door opened, and Rayna's voice boomed throughout the apartment, "Girl, did you see Terry's ole punk-self trying to push up on me?" Damn it! This girl always shows up at the most opportune times.

"Ugh, yeah, but his friend is fire. Is he single?" replied Tonya.

Donte eased up slowly as if our window had closed. He kept his eyes on me, and I grabbed his hand and squeezed it.

"Dee!" I managed to say while trying to hold back my tears, still moved by the gift.

"You're welcome, Shar!" he said, then just half-smiled and got up and left the room. I closed the box and quickly put it in my pocket as if to conceal our moment and almost-kiss, or whatever that was supposed to be.

Everything in me wanted to move, but my body was stuck, like I couldn't wake it the hell up. When it sounded like Rayna and Tonya were getting closer, I acted quickly. I needed a reason to be in Donte's room. So, I got up, grabbed the lotion, and put some on my hands. We always went to Donte's room for lotion, which sat right on the edge of his door, so this wouldn't be unusual. I left the room to join the ladies and Donte in the living room.

"Girl, don't let P see that mess! You know he don't play about you," I said as if I was always in the conversation.

"Yeah, I love it though. At least I know he cares about his woman," Rayna said, flipping her braids to one side. Funny how I knew how she felt despite not having a man. I smiled at the thought. Both Tonya and Rayna looked at me.

"Umm, what you smiling at, Shar?" Rayna said, giving me the eye.

I shook my head, saying it was nothing, and hoped she would move on. Donte walked into the kitchen while we continued to talk amongst ourselves. As Tonya and Rayna continued their dialogue, I walked to the kitchen and stood in front of him. I mouthed the words *thank you so much, I love it.*

He stood before me and looked down at my 5'3" from his 6'3" height. As I inched closer to him, I reached to touch him, but Miss Chyna entered the front door. Regretfully, I backed up and just looked at him. He nodded, then I walked out of the kitchen.

Donte stayed in the kitchen and finished his drink while I sat back on the sofa, disappointed at yet another opportunity missed.

"How's my baby? He's still asleep?" Miss Chyna said without giving me a look.

"Yes, ma'am, knocked out!" she replied good, but this time she looked at me with the *what did I almost walk in on?* expression.

I joined back in the conversation between Tonya and Rayna, but my mind was all over the place. I didn't want to read too much into the necklace, but it was hard not to. It meant something; obviously, he was finally putting his feelings out there, or so I hoped.

I was so wrapped up in my thoughts that I didn't hear Rayna talking to me. "Earth to Shar," she said, waving her hand in my face.

"What you say, Ray?" I finally acknowledged her. She just laughed, and so did Miss Chyna and Tonya.

"I said, what has gotten into you? I know you ain't thinking about Trav's bitch ass!"

I frowned at Rayna but looked in Donte's direction as he stood in the kitchen doorway before heading toward his room.

"Nah, that gets no mental! I was thinking about something else," I said as I followed him with my eyes, "...but I'm back!"

Rayna nodded, confused, but Miss Chyna wasn't; she smiled.

"Well, since you're back...let's go back outside!"

We went back to the party; however, it was almost over. I started cleaning up to get a moment of peace, plus it would save us some time later. Donte came back outside for a bit, but I purposely avoided him. He didn't come to talk to me either, but I think we both knew our conversation was far from over. Eventually, he went back inside. I heard Rayna say he decided to stay home in case Keith woke up. When the party was officially over, most people went home, but the crew—Rayna, Tonya, P, Paul, Fat Mane, and Trav—plus some of the neighborhood people went back to Miss Chyna's. I didn't want to be anywhere near Trav, but I needed another moment with Donte.

When I went back upstairs, I didn't see him anywhere among the people, so I sought him out. I went to the kitchen and ran straight into Miss Chyna.

She smiled and laughed. "Umm, can I help you, Sharnel?"

I blushed. "No, Miss Chyna, I'm good!" She knew I was bullshitting and laughed harder.

"Well, since you are good, if you're looking to be better...it may be in a room across from the guest bathroom! If you catch my drift!"

I blushed harder and laughed. She winked and nudged my arm before leaving the kitchen.

Someone started a spades game, turned on some music, and it was on and poppin' again. Even Mr. James and Miss Kena came up for a bit. When everyone seemed distracted and since I knew where he was, I made a beeline to his room. I knocked on the door and waited for him to answer. The music was loud, so I wasn't sure if he would hear me. I was about to knock again but was relieved when he opened the door. It was slightly ajar.

"Hey…can we—" As I was about to finish, he opened the door wider, and I saw P sitting at the desk. I was disappointed but smiled at P and nodded.

"Umm…I'll catch up with you later!" Not giving Donte a chance to speak, I made my way down the hall toward the living room with everyone else.

I thought I heard P and Donte behind me but never turned around. When I reentered the living room and saw Regina and Uncle of the Week among the people, I no longer wanted any part of the gathering. I hurried past everyone and out the door. Miss Chyna tried to make her way to me, but I was already gone. Standing outside the apartment door, I wanted to get away immediately. I wasn't ready to go home yet, but I wasn't too sure about walking the neighborhood alone so early in the morning. So, I went to my hiding spot, the laundry room. I let out a breath and just soaked in being alone for the first time since earlier that day.

I sat down at the folding table, which was a metal picnic bench, and took the box back out. "I can't believe this!" I smiled at the necklace. It really was beautiful and thoughtful; it was like he gave me a piece of Granny and him to carry with me always. Man, how could he remember? We were so young…he knows me so well… My mind continued to race with thoughts when I heard someone coming toward the door. I quickly put the box away and hoped no one would come to the laundry room. I just needed a moment. I wasn't really in the mood for anyone's company. However, when I looked through the small plate of glass, I saw it was Donte, and I was glad it was him.

He opened the door and came in. "Figured I'd find you in here!"

I didn't respond; he just came to sit across from me at the table. "What's up, Shar?" he said.

I was a bit confused, and it must have shown. "You came to my room earlier?" he said inquisitively.

I nodded. "Yeah, I just wanted to thank you again," I said. Honestly, I didn't want to say thank you. I wanted to know what was about to happen before Rayna and Tonya came in. But I was too shy to ask, so I lied.

Donte didn't buy my story but nodded anyway. "You know you can actually wear it!"

I smiled at the thought of the necklace. "I know…I will on special occasions."

He looked confused and shook his head. "Whatever, man; it's yours. Do what you please!" I could tell he was a bit disappointed.

"Donte, I really love it! I just don't want to mess it up."

He shook his head, confused. "Give it to me, man!"

Was he serious? Was he taking it back because he thought I insulted him? I frowned at the request.

"Hand me the box, Sharnel!" he said more sternly. I reached into my pocket and regretfully slapped the box into his hand. I hadn't meant to hurt his feelings.

Donte opened the box and took the chain out. He got up and walked to my side of the table. I heard him open the clasp. "Lift your mop, man!"

I immediately turned around and looked at him. He laughed, "Lift your hair up, man!"

I rolled my eyes and lifted my hair. He slid the necklace around my neck and fastened it. Then he sat down next to me. I looked at him as he adjusted the charm so it lay perfectly on my chest.

He half-smiled, and I smiled back. I pulled out my phone so I could see it in my camera. I held the camera back. "It's gorgeous!" I smiled.

"Yeah, it is!" he said, looking at me.

"Take a picture with me!"

Donte's face dropped. "Man, Sharnel, you know that ain't me!"

I smiled. "Yeah, I know, but today is special, so suck it up!" I leaned closer to him, and he leaned in. I made sure to get the charm, then counted down, "Okay, 1…2…3!" I snapped the picture, which consisted of me smiling and him partially smiling. "I'm going to save this as your face card! So every time you call or message me, it will come up!"

Donte shook his head and backed up. "How much longer you plan on hanging out in here, man?"

I took a breath. "I don't know… but I'm not in the mood to go home where I know Regina and Uncle of the Week will be."

He nodded. "I hear that! But you know I'm not gonna leave you in here alone, Shar!"

I smiled. "It's safe here! I've spent many nights here! The door locks and only people who live here have a key."

He frowned. "Why you ain't just come upstairs?"

I shrugged. "I don't know, maybe it was too late, or I didn't want to bother anyone!" I waved him off.

"Yoo, don't do that shit no more! You got a key for a reason, man!" he fussed.

"I promise!" I said, making the cross-my-heart sign.

Donte's phone chimed, and he responded to a text. I decided to take a few more pictures. I posed while he looked down and texted.

"You finished, paparazzi? Put that shit away!" he said without looking up. "Mommy just making sure you're good!" he said, closing his phone.

I loved Miss Chyna; she was always looking out for me. He nodded his head then reached to lower my phone which was still in my hand as I was about to take another picture.

"Okay, okay! One more… just look straight ahead!" Donte looked forward, and I repositioned the camera upward. "1…2…3!" Then I snapped the picture as I kissed his cheek. Surprisingly, he smiled, showing his pretty white teeth.

"Now your ass is done!" he said as he got up. I laughed as I admired our picture. "Shar, I better not see that shit on nobody's…"

I got up and followed him to the door. "In the words of the great Nia Long… this is just for my own personal collection," I said and winked.

"Bring your ass on, man!" he said as he shook his head and opened the laundry room door.

We headed downstairs to my apartment. I opened the door and then turned to him.

"You sure you're good?" he asked as he leaned against the wall.

"Yep, I'm good!"

He nodded. "Aight, I'll see you later!" he said and made his way to the steps. As he walked up the stairs, I sent him a text with the pictures we took.

Big Head: *So you can keep these in your personal collection too!*

Him: *I don't do girlie shit like that!*

Then he hearted both pictures! Replying to the picture of me kissing his cheek and him smiling.

Big Head: *Make this one my face card!*

Him: *Not a fuckin chance. Take your ass to bed, Shar!* (laughing crying emoji)

It was now 4:30 a.m., so I prepared myself for bed, thinking about Donte the whole time. I wondered if he was thinking about me too; those were the last words I thought before I fell asleep.

CHAPTER 9

Later that morning, I was up and outside around 10:30 a.m. to finish cleaning up from our party. Tonya was still asleep but promised to be outside by 11:30 a.m., and Rayna was hungover, so I was on my own.

"Hey, little girl, them heifers done left you to clean up that mess," Mr. James yelled from his balcony.

"Yes, sir, only for a bit; they will be up soon."

He laughed and shook his head as if he knew I was lying to myself too. I decided to put in my earbuds and zone out while I picked up any remaining trash. Next, I decided to collapse the remaining tables before the workers arrived. I was almost done when I saw Donte coming toward me. He'd just walked out of the building in his uniform, heading to work, which was unusual for Sunday unless they were backed up.

As I folded the last table, it got stuck, and he stepped right in to close it for me. Then he placed it with the other tables.

"Good morning, and thank you," I replied. I tried to straighten my maxi dress as if it had something on it. But it was just nervous energy; there were so many things I wanted to say and address but didn't know where to start.

"Good morning, and you're welcome," he replied. Then he just stood there with his emotionless expression. He looked at my face, then away, then at me again. It was then I finally realized he looked for my necklace. I touched my neck, and my face dropped. I had taken off the necklace to shower that morning and forgot to put it back on.

Donte nodded and walked off, but I ran after him to stop him. I grabbed his hand so he could see the sincerity in my face. "I took it off to shower this morning and forgot to put it back on," I said quickly, hoping to soothe him.

However, his face displayed the opposite, and he shook his head, annoyed. "The shit ain't fake, Shar!"

I nodded in assurance, which was the wrong reaction because he then said, "You can shower or do anything with it on! It ain't gonna turn green or some shit! Da fuck!"

He took his hand back and walked away as he mumbled under his breath toward his car.

I immediately felt panic, regret, and agony. I wanted to yell, "Wait, I didn't know!" But I thought that would make it worse.

Further, I wasn't sure if I should tell people who asked that he brought it for me! As I processed my mistake, I hurled a bunch of words out loud. "Why didn't I just remember to put it on? He thinks I don't like it! What if he thinks I don't like him… wait, do I? Fuck! Fuck! Fuck! Fuck!" I was lost in my thoughts and hadn't noticed Tonya come out, still reeking of this morning's foolishness.

"Girl, what's wrong? What you need help with?" she yawned. I just shook my head and handed her the trash bag, then walked away.

I have to make it up to him; I want him to know I care… I'll never be without it from this day forward. The rest of the day, I tried to put myself in a position to run into Donte. I was outside, at Miss Chyna's, and whenever I was home, every time I heard a door, I went to see if it was him. However, I didn't have any luck. I wasn't going to outright ask Rayna when he was going to be home, so I gave up. I wanted to text him but didn't know what to say.

When I didn't run into him all day, I decided to bite the bullet and text him at almost midnight. I kept writing and erasing my words, so I decided to send him a picture. I had on my scarf and cute PJs, consisting of a button-down and shorts, with the necklace on. After three or four attempts, I got the perfect one. I sent him the picture and waited. I checked my phone every 5 to 10 minutes, but nothing. I finally gave up; however, when I heard the phone chime, I looked, and he responded. I opened the message, and he thumbs-upped the picture.

"Is he fuckin' kidding me?!" I yelled. I was pissed and closed the phone. I wasn't even going to dignify his bullshit with a response. I went to bed and cussed him out in my mind until I fell asleep.

CHAPTER 10

Looking for a job was a daunting process for me; I just didn't know what I wanted to do. College life ain't for me; I barely made it out of high school cause that shit was boring. Going to college didn't sound any less boring, besides I just like what I like, and I'm not interested in anything else. I don't want to go into the military; someone barking orders at me doesn't seem fun. Plus, I only fight my battles and those I care about… that's it. So, I had to get a job, I guess, but hell if I knew what kind. Hell, I can tell you what I don't want to do… cashier, fast food, janitor—not that these are not respectable positions, but I'm more of the administrative type.

Someone asked me one day what my hobbies were. I like to write, listen to music, and just be creative. I started writing a long time ago when life was crazy. Regina was into Uncle of the Week, Thomas, and I just needed an outlet, so I started writing. I wrote mostly poems and short stories. I started letting some of my classmates read them, and they loved them. I remember one of my friends at the time had my notebook, and my teacher confiscated it. When she gave it back to me, she mentioned how good the writing was and said I should pursue a journalism career. That sounded good, but again, I like what I like. Plus, in the words of the great Badu, "I'm an artist; I'm sensitive about my shit."

In addition to writing, I enjoy putting together collages of random things. I have boxes of pictures and old magazines. Regina kept trying to get me to throw them out, but I use them to put together ideas and other products. I have posters and scrapbooks of all kinds of things, but I keep those to myself. I just do it when I need a break from life. I put on my noise-canceling earphones and zone out. I love all types of music, so whatever mood I'm in, I just select a genre and let it carry me. Currently, I haven't had much time for it, but every now and again, I sneak off to my spot and just let the silence or music guide the pen.

Anyway, enough about my hobbies. Regina gave me the summer off, paid, so I'm good for now. I settled on thinking about it when it got closer to the end of the summer. Until then, I was going to do me. Usually, Rayna, Tonya, and I spent the summer all over the city and beyond, but everyone was going their separate ways for at least the first month. Tonya's mother was sending her and her siblings to Memphis to visit family. Rayna was going to visit Mr. Tony in Florida for two weeks. I was gonna miss my crew this summer, but I still had my week at the beach to look forward to. Plus, I knew how to keep myself occupied; I always did.

Miss Chyna asked me if I would watch Keith for a week since his babysitter was going out of town. Of course, I said yeah; Keith was my baby, and I'd do anything for him. I was excited to kick it with him; plus, I could make a few dollars in the process. I was saving up to buy a car; I couldn't wait to get one. My first trip once I got my car was to ride around with the windows down, music blaring, and not have a care in the world. I always envisioned riding around at night, going where I wanted to and doing whatever. I could do that now, but it was different since I didn't have a car unless Regina left me hers.

Since today was one of the last few days before everyone left, the crew and I had chosen to hang out. I decided to wear a yellow babydoll top with white capris and some wedges just to feel light and airy. Plus, it would mask the bit of sadness I felt about everyone leaving. Dang, what will I do? I shook off the thought; there was plenty to do while they were still here. Time was of the essence. I'd start the day with Tonya; she was leaving tomorrow. So, I decided I'd help her pack for her trip. She was pissed because she and Paul started hanging tough, so now she was "in love." Whatever.

When I arrived at her house, she was not in the best mood; this was going to be fun. She kept crying and whining about Paul.

"Girl, you better tell me if he cheats or if you see any chicks near him," she whined.

"Sure, girl, I'll tell you immediately," I said, knowing damn well I wouldn't. But it eased her worries, which benefited us both at the moment. I just shook my head because she knew him; he was a ladies' man. When she turned her back, he was eyeing another girl. Even when he was with her, he texted other girls because, in his eyes, they weren't committed.

For example, one day we were at school before Paul graduated. He and Tonya were "so-called" dating again. We were on our way to lunch when Paul walked down the hall with another girl. He had his arm around her and kissed her cheek. When he saw Tonya, he smiled at her and said, "What's up?" as if it was nothing. She was a wreck; I spent the rest of the day consoling her.

After school, when we were hanging out, Paul came by with some lame excuse, and she bought it and acted all happy again. Everyone knew Paul didn't consider them exclusive whenever he decided to entertain her. He had even said so in front of her, but she didn't check him. After that, I was done with Tonya's love life. I just stayed out of it.

After Tonya was done packing and whining, we went into the living room where her mother was braiding her little sister's hair. I sat down at the dining room table while Tonya tended to things in the kitchen. I admired her mom's braiding skills; she was a trooper, having all those kids with thick, long hair. I knew her fingers must have hurt.

"That looks really good, Mrs. Nash," I commented. "You've got skills."

She smiled and said, "Thank you, Sharnel, baby," as she started on the next part. "So, what do you have planned for yourself this summer?" she asked.

"Well, I'm going to babysit Keith next week and get some more writing done," I replied.

"You don't want to go to college? You've got skills—writing and your art. Those things will take you a long way, honey," she responded.

"College is not for me. I just like what I like… just not sure what to do with it," I replied, feeling a bit lost.

She nodded and then said, "You will figure it out it, my dear. Don't you worry. You are smart, beautiful, respectable, and a child of the Most High; that's all you need, love."

This was the norm with Mrs. Nash. She always made a point to talk to me. Sometimes she even prayed with me before I left. It made me feel like I had someone watching my back. I wasn't religious, but I did believe in God. My Granny took me to church a few times; I didn't always understand it, but I knew there was a God.

I smiled at Mrs. Nash's comment as I reflected on our previous conversations. Sometimes I felt like God had forgotten about me or didn't care. But she always reminded me that that's when I needed to lean even more into my belief. So, I did just that—whether it was a prayer of thanksgiving or just saying, "I still believe" out loud, at least I knew He heard me. Then I'd go about my life until He sent the next bright light into my life.

I sat quietly and reflected on Mrs. Nash's words. I felt them deep in my soul; I loved Tonya's mom. She always left me hopeful that there was always more. I think she felt bad about my living situation; most people did. That's why I was leery about letting people in. I always wondered if they felt sorry for me, and that was why they were nice to me. I was no charity case; my situation was what it was, and I wasn't ashamed. "Mom, do I have to go to Memphis? Can't I stay here with you and Dad?" Tonya whined. Her mother had obviously heard the speech before and was over it, just by the look on her face. She never answered Tonya; she just kept doing her sister's hair.

When Tonya's phone rang, we were saved by the bell. She shut up, and I could now make an exit if I needed to. She hurried to answer it, and after a quick conversation, she ended the call.

"That was Rayna. She wants us to come up and help her watch Keith until her mom comes home." Since we were finished with Tonya's packing and she assured her mom she'd be back by curfew, which was 1 a.m. since it was summer, we made our way upstairs.

Going up the two flights of stairs, we ran into P, of course. Now it made sense; she really wanted us to watch Keith while she went out with P. I thought it, but Tonya said it out loud.

"Don't be a hater because my lady loves her man," P replied. There was no love lost between him and Tonya; he thought she was jealous of his relationship with Rayna, while Tonya thought he was rude and obnoxious. I had no dog in the fight, so I never chimed in when they went back and forth. I just shook my head and kept walking. This was Rayna's business, and I wanted no part of it.

"Shut up, P! Ain't nobody thinking about you!" Tonya replied.

P knocked on the door, and Rayna looked like a deer in the headlights when she saw us together, which further confirmed her plan and our thoughts. I shook my head because I knew Rayna, and she didn't mean for us to show up together.

"Shar! Shaaaarrrrr!" Keith yelled as he pushed Rayna out of the way. He hugged my legs and then hugged Tonya's, then came back for me to pick him up. Cool, I could get out of this mess. I picked him up and brushed past Rayna into the apartment. I knew she was leaving in two days, so I had some sympathy for her. Tonya followed me and sat on the sofa, pouting. Let's see how she spins this, I thought.

Rayna decided to do a whole song and dance before she asked, "HHHeeeeyyyy y'all!" speaking to me and Tonya. "I'm glad to see my girls. Do y'all want something to eat or drink? You know Mama just went shopping..."

Tonya cut her off. "Look, heifer, if you called us up here to ditch us, I'm out! I'm over this mess!"

Here we go. I sat there and watched with Keith in my lap; this was nothing new for him either.

Rayna looked shocked yet pissed. "Ummm... what are you talking about? I just thought we could all hang since you're leaving tomorrow and I'm out the next day. Ain't nobody trying to trick you!" This was not going to end well.

"Oh yeah? So, what's the plan then, huh?"

Rayna couldn't pull a response quick enough, so she burst into laughter and just fessed up. "Okay, okay, so I do need a favor... I want to hang out with P, but I need y'all to watch Keith at least until Donte gets home, which should be in an hour or two. Pleeeaaassee."

And there it was. I just shook my head. After hearing Rayna's pleas, Keith joined in with his version of "please" while looking at me. Then he joined Rayna with a fake sad face.

Tonya was clearly pissed and got up immediately, heading toward the front door. "Nope, this ain't my child."

Now I was pissed; she didn't have to put Keith in it. I immediately gave her the *back-off* face. Although she seemed upset, she now knew I didn't play about Keith (or Donte). I immediately hugged Keith just in case he picked up on her words. "I got a man I can kick it with since I AM leaving tomorrow. Y'all got this!"

This bitch was not serious; with the man comment, she could have aborted that mission. She was better off staying here; all Paul wanted was some pussy and then he was done with her. I just shook my head as I watched her slam the door as she walked out.

"Yeah, you pissed her off, Ray. She was over the top and wrong for what she said, but you were wrong too; you need to apologize."

Rayna sucked her teeth, then looked back at me with those puppy dog eyes, awaiting my response.

"Fine, I got little man, but you better be back here before 5:30 p.m. before your mom gets back. I'm not covering for you."

"Good lookin' Sista Shar, I owe you" P said."

Rayna was overjoyed and grabbed her stuff so she and P could rush out the door.

I looked at Keith and shook my head, and he did the same. "It's me and you, kid; let's get you dressed for the day."

After getting Keith ready, I fed him and took him to the park. He insisted on bringing his tricycle and a toy with him, claiming he might get "bored." I made a stop by my apartment to grab my pen and pad in case I wanted to write. When we got to the park, no one was there, but he was cool and played by himself. So, I just sat on the bench and waited until he was ready to get on the swings. He wasn't too good at those yet. Watching him play brought me such joy; he didn't have a care in the world. I wished I could be that young again, just me and Rayna playing on the playground while Miss Chyna watched over us. Sometimes she would send Donte outside with us; he never played with us but kept us in his eyesight.

When we played at Miss Chyna's house, we used to try to get him to play Barbies, but he wouldn't. However, he would allow us to play on the floor in his room while he played video games or did something else. We'd knock on his door, and he'd open it partially, but we'd bust in with Barbie, her dream house, car, caravan, and whatever else we could carry.

However, that came to an end the day we opened his collector's edition Optimus Prime Transformer because we needed a Ken for Barbie to marry. This was after he specifically told us we couldn't use it. When Donte found out, he threw us, Barbie, and all her shit (after he broke a few things, including my Barbie 8-piece dining room set with chairs to match) into the hall and slammed the door in our faces. He didn't speak to us for two weeks. That was also the day Donte and I began our consistent bitter battle. It was then that we were banned from his room except to get lotion, which sat at the edge of his desk by the door.

Funny how he was still tight about that shit today, crybaby ass. When I looked at my watch, we'd been outside for an hour. Keith was tired and ready for a snack/nap. He was no longer interested in his tricycle or the toy, so I lugged everything back to the building while he practiced his karate moves as we walked.

As we headed back to the building, we saw Donte, who had just gotten off work, coming up the opposite sidewalk. "Doooonttteee!" Keith yelled, then he took off running to his brother. This little ninja just left me with all his stuff. Standing in front of P's building, I literally dropped everything on the ground and stopped. My arms were tired, and since Donte was here, he could carry this stuff. Donte gave Keith a high five, and they did their brotherly handshake, as always. They exchanged words, and then Keith yelled for me to join them. However, I didn't move; I just folded my arms and waited for him to come get the stuff.

Donte picked up on the cue, shook his head, and they cut across the grass toward me.

"Keithy Face, did you come back to save me?" I said when they made it over to me.

"Yep," he said on cue.

"Sup?" Donte replied.

"Hey, how was your day?" I asked, looking at him.

"Cool," he replied with that emotionless face. Donte grabbed the toy. "Aye, you're gonna need to ride that," he pointed at the tricycle.

Keith smiled and laughed, then got on his tricycle and took off.

"Learn to tell his ass no sometimes."

I rolled my eyes. He had a point, but there was no need to belabor that at the moment.

As we headed toward the building, we were quiet. When we were halfway there, we heard the ice cream man's jingle. Both Donte and I stopped and looked at each other; we knew what was about to happen next.

Keith stood up, turned his tricycle around, and bolted toward us. We both moved out of his path, and in unison, we headed toward the ice cream truck.

I mocked him and said, "Learn to tell his ass no sometimes!"

Donte gave me the *really* face and then grunted, "Spoiled ass dude."

I laughed as we walked.

"Don't laugh; this y'all fault," he said while he side-eyed me.

I couldn't argue with him; he was right. We spoiled Keith from the womb; whatever he wanted, we gave him.

When Keith got to the parking lot, he hopped off his tricycle and waited for Donte and me. When we made it to him, he was anxious and ready.

"Hold my hands," he demanded, but when I cleared my throat and waited, he thought for a second, "Plleeaassee."

I smiled and grabbed his hand.

"Donte, you gotta hold it too so I can swing."

Donte shook his head and looked at me. "See what I mean?" he said as he grabbed Keith's hand.

I just smiled, and Keith proceeded to jump and swing while we walked to the ice cream truck. Donte was over it and even more annoyed at the line. I just ignored him and continued to let Keith do his thing. When we got to the truck, I picked up Keith so he could see everything.

"Tell 'em what you want, man!" Donte said to Keith, slightly annoyed.

Keith rattled off what seemed like a four-course ice cream meal with snacks. When Keith stopped, Donte just shook his head, and I tried to put him down, but he was not having it. Donte turned his head toward me.

"What you want, man?"

I was shocked and paused for a second. Keith leaned toward my ear and whispered, "You have to get something too, Shar Shar."

I nodded and replied, "I'll have what he's having plus a water."

Donte gave me the *really* expression and tightened his lips as Keith chuckled.

While the ice cream man prepared the order, he smiled and stared at me. I guess he was looking a bit too long, so Donte slammed the money on the counter to get his attention.

I just laughed, and Keith laughed as I kissed his face while he hugged my neck. After spending $50 at the ice cream truck, we headed back to Keith's tricycle and made our way to the building. Keith was too focused on the ice cream to care about his tricycle and toy, so I carried the toy and my water while Donte carried the tricycle and the bag with everything he had just paid for.

Once we got to the building, Donte said, "I'm about to go inside."

I nodded, but Keith chimed in, "Donte, you staying outside, pleeaassee?"

Donte's face dropped as he looked at me.

"Well, he did say please," I smirked.

Donte shook his head. "Yoo, which one of these $50 items do you want? I know you ain't gonna eat this crap; you got it for him," Donte said, trying to act annoyed.

"Hmm, I'll take the cherry bomb pop," I said. He handed it to me and went inside.

When Donte came back, he had changed his clothes. He joined me and Keith on the steps while we enjoyed our ice cream, opposite us with a bottle of water in hand. He admired Keith eating his ice cream and shook his head. I continued enjoying my popsicle, which now had my entire mouth red. He didn't say anything, just looked straight ahead, so I figured I'd test him. I slowly moved the popsicle in and out of my mouth until I caught him looking. It was going well until I accidentally choked and started coughing while I laughed.

"That's what you get for trying to be grown," he said, then took a sip of his water.

"Shar Shar, you ok?" a concerned Keith tried to pat my back. I tried to get it together, but I kept laughing.

"Yep, I'm fine," I said as Donte shook his head.

"Shar Shar, where you get that?" Keith asked, a bit puzzled. He pointed to the necklace Donte had brought me. I looked at Keith and then at Donte.

"Someone special brought this for me. Why do you like it?" I returned my glance to Keith.

"Yep, it's pretty," Keith said as he reached for the charm and played with it. "…is it your boyfriend?"

His question caught me off guard, and I tried not to laugh and blush as I responded. I also noticed Donte turned his head to the side and raised his eyebrow, then awaited my response.

"Ummm…I don't know. He didn't tell me he was."

Keith pondered my response and said, "I be you boyfriend Shar Shar."

Donte shook his head and smirked.

I replied, "My one and only," and kissed his forehead while I looked at Donte. He just nodded and looked forward.

After Keith finished his ice cream, he hopped on his tricycle to ride up and down the sidewalk, leaving me and Donte alone.

"Your brother's a trip," I replied.

"Yeah, shorty be killin' us with them questions," he said.

I nodded because Keith didn't miss much. I wasn't sure about what I was about to ask, but I was curious about his response. "So, you gonna answer his question?" I asked.

With a slight frown on his face, he said, "What question is that?" Urgh, douchebag, he's gonna make me say it, so I leaned into the question and faced him.

"Are you my boyfriend?" He looked at me perplexed, but then he contemplated his response. I decided to lock in, keeping my gaze on him to hear his response.

Just as he was about to respond, we heard Keith yell, and we both looked in his direction. He'd fallen off his tricycle, and his leg was stuck underneath it. We rushed over to him; Donte helped him up and assured him he was okay, but Keith was hysterical and angry at his tricycle.

"Man, c'mon, it ain't that serious. You good!" Donte said as he wiped dirt off Keith. But his words only made him cry more and go into a full-blown tantrum.

Donte was reaching his breaking point, so I chimed in. "Keithy Face, come on, love, let's get you inside and cleaned up. You okay? I got you."

I picked him up. I knew this was just him being tired. He laid his exhausted head on my shoulder while continuing to sniffle as we walked upstairs. Donte grabbed his tricycle, and I held the toy and Keith. He followed us while mumbling a couple of other choice words as he unlocked the door.

I took Keith to the bathroom and wiped off his knees, face, and arms. Then I carried him to the living room to sit on the sofa.

"Man, you don't gotta stay; he's alright after his Academy Award acting. He's just tired," Donte said sarcastically.

I nodded, but as I put him down to leave, Keith started to cry again.

Knowing Donte was losing his patience, I decided to stay, "I'm good. Let me get him to sleep at least. If you need to do something, go ahead," I replied as I sat down on the sofa with Keith, who now wanted to lay on my lap.

Donte didn't reply; he just sat on the other end of the sofa and turned on the TV. Of course, he turned on Sports Center; what else would we watch? I rolled my eyes.

I laid Keith on the pillow and covered him with a blanket. After rubbing his head, he was out. Donte glared at his brother, then continued to watch TV.

I could care less about sports, but I just watched. I could feel myself fighting sleep. I guess it was obvious.

"Yoo, go to sleep; ain't no one gonna bother you," Donte said, still looking at the TV. Although he was being a smartass, his words soothed me because I was safe here—not just because I was at Miss Chyna's but because I was with him. I was going to say something smart, but I was too tired; I just gave in and slept.

When I opened my eyes again, Donte was asleep too. His head was on my shoulder, and I could feel his body rise and fall with each breath. I didn't mind it; I just went back to sleep. After a good hour, I opened one eye, and Miss Chyna had just snapped a picture with her phone.

"Don't they look like two worn-out parents?" she whispered and walked away.

I closed my eyes again one last time. When I opened my eyes again, which turned out to be 30 minutes later, Donte was gone, and Keith was playing with his toys while watching TV. I noticed a blanket was on me and a pillow was under my head.

"You awake now, Shar Shar?" Keith asked as if it was about time. I yawned and stretched.

"Yep, I'm awake now." I didn't move; I just enjoyed watching him play. I felt like I hadn't slept in years, so I wanted to enjoy the peace. I checked my phone, and it was almost 5:30 PM.

Rayna was attempting to sneak in, but she was busted. "It's about to go down." Before I could finish my thought, Miss Chyna was in the dining room with her hands on her hips.

"Rayna, where the hell you been?" Miss Chyna yelled. Instead of staying for the show, I decided to try to make my way out. I folded the blanket and headed toward the front door.

"Oh no, baby, you're staying for dinner. Go get yourself cleaned up; we're eating in 5," Miss Chyna instructed.

I made an about-face, then headed to the bathroom. Miss Chyna and Rayna continued their discussion. As I freshened up and reapplied my makeup, I heard a tap at the door. I knew it was Keith.

"Yes, sir," he said, almost in tears. Yelling was not his thing, so I knew he would be knocking. I sat him on the toilet while I finished up, and we knocked on Donte's door. He opened it to find us both smiling and hoping to escape WWIII. He opened the door and stepped aside; he already knew why we were there.

Once we were inside, he closed the door. Keith went straight for Tony. I hated that snake; surprisingly, Keith was not scared. I sat in the chair closest to the door to avoid the reptile.

"You scared or something?" Donte asked.

"Nope, just not my thing," I replied.

"Scared ass," he said.

"Ohhh, you say bad words, Donte," I chuckled and took a closer look at his surroundings. What else could I learn about Donte? I surveyed the room but didn't find anything out of the ordinary.

"What you looking for, nosey?" Donte said while he continued working on a car part for work. I just ignored him. Damn, was it that obvious? I thought. There was no sign of anything unusual; maybe I was overthinking him.

"I gotta go potty; I'll be back," Keith told us as he opened and closed the door.

We sat in silence while he continued working until he broke the silence. "You can say thank you for the blanket and pillow."

I rolled my eyes and, in my happiest sarcastic voice, said, "Thank you, Mr. Donte, most graciously for the fresh blanket and fluffed pillow."

He was not amused. "See, you always gotta do too much."

I was a little hurt by that comment. "At least I try to talk to you. You haven't said much to me lately. Damn, did I piss you off that much?" I snapped.

"What do you want me to say, Shar? There, I just said about eight words to you just now."

I was over him and shot back, "So, you got jokes now, huh? I'm serious."

In that moment, he stopped working, and I moved closer to him. He met my gaze. Now I was nervous; I wasn't prepared for this interaction, but forget it; I'm here, 10 toes down.

"Look, Donte, do you actually like me? Like, all jokes aside?"

His face indicated he didn't know where the question was coming from. So, I continued, "I actually like you; everyone can see that! Do you like me?"

He didn't respond, so I continued, "You realize I'm talking about more than a friend…right?"

He didn't say anything; he just looked away and then back at me, so I continued again. "I mean…it's weird; sometimes I feel you before I see you. When I'm in your presence, I feel tingly inside," I said sincerely and gently.

We sat in silence as he considered my words, never leaving my gaze. "So, you feel warm and tingly right now?" he said, then burst into laughter. "That's why your ass been acting all emo' and shit lately?" The he continued to laugh as if everything was a joke."

I was completely pissed off but not shocked. He couldn't take anything seriously. The more I looked at him as he laughed and tried to compose himself, the more I wanted to punch him in his face.

"Wow…what the hell kind of reaction was that after I just poured my heart to you? You really are a fuckin' asshole!" I got up to leave, but he grabbed my hand as he tried terribly to settle himself. I snatched it away, then reached for the doorknob. But then he grabbed my hand again, this time a bit more firmly as he stood up no longer laughing. We were now face to face (as much as we could be given the height difference), and my expression read 100 shades of pissed.

With a straight face, he said, "What you want me to do with that, Shar, huh?" He waited for me to answer. "What are you expecting? Us to run away together or some shit? I don't even know what to do with what you just said, man. You've been around since we were kids. I care about you, but that…what you said…I don't, man." Now I was really pissed. I said all that, and this was his reaction.

"You don't know what? See, for once, I expected you to act like an adult and not some little ass boy who makes jokes about how I feel! You give me this necklace; you act like you like me, but you don't want to be with me?"

His eyes got wide as if I had made all this up in my mind. "Whoa…wait, how did we get here? What are we even talking about?" He just shook his head.

"Oh, okay, this is how we gonna play it," I said. He had the right one today. "Oh, so you're just the jewelry man, giving every bitch a necklace that you know means something to them. Well, just so you know, adults who truly care about each other don't do that bullshit…they don't waste people's time, Donte!" Then I snatched my hand back, folded my arms, and stood there waiting for an answer.

When he didn't say anything, I nodded again. The more unresponsive he became, the more he was sealing the mothafucking deal with me.

"Urgh, this is irritating. What the fuck you want me to say, man? Apparently, I can't be nice to you, can't answer your questions, or meet whatever expectation you clearly have…what, man? 'Cause ain't shit I said or did good enough!"

Now I was completely done. "Nothing, Donte. FUCK you and this necklace. I can see ain't shit changed with you…you still see me as some little girl! Tell me something. Why are you so nice to me? Huh? You pity me or something? You feel like you're doing a good deed being nice to me all these years, huh?" I could tell my words were pissing him off even more, but I didn't care. "What, you racking up cool points so you can cash them in on some pussy? So, you can go brag to your friends you finally did what they couldn't? Fill me in so I can get it?"

Donte was enraged and stepped closer to me. "Do you hear your fuckin' self right now, Sharnel? What you're saying is bullshit that doesn't even make sense!" He hissed.

"Why is that, Donte? Is it because it's the truth, or you don't want to admit what you're doing or pretending not to do?" I said.

"Cause it's bullshit, and you know it!" he replied.

"Apparently, I don't know shit anymore!"

Donte backed up, smiled, and nodded. "Aight, fuck it! Don't be looking for me to do shit else for you since I'm this fucked-up dude you created in your mind! Matter of fact, get the fuck outta my room, man!"

He grabbed the doorknob and I immediately opened the clasp of the necklace and took it off then slammed it on the desk.

Donte looked at the desk, then at me, fire in his eyes. I felt my heart break in that moment, and the one thing I didn't want to happen began—I started to cry! I stared back at him, trying to hold back my tears, but one slipped.

He stood emotionless, watching two more fall, which made it worse and pissed me off even more. OMG, Shar, what the entire fuck? Pull it together, chick! Just then, Keith busted in to tell us dinner was ready. Donte acknowledged him with a nod, Keith left leaving the door opened then he looked back at me.

I wiped my face, took a breath, and walked out of the room. That was the last time this dude would see me cry. He slammed his door, and I went to the bathroom across the hall, slamming the bathroom door behind me. What the hell just happened? I washed my face and made my way to dinner. At the table, everyone sat in silence. Miss Chyna was over Rayna, I was over Donte, and Keith was over the carrots he refused to eat. After everything was done, I offered to help clean up, but Miss Chyna said I'd done enough; it was all Rayna. So, I went home to reset my mood and prepare for an evening of festivities…a night with the crew.

CHAPTER 11

I can't believe he let me cry, that sorry bastard. He got the right one! He ain't gotta worry about me no more…fuck him! I let a few more choice words flow out to calm myself down. How could he act like I made all that shit up in my mind? He's just like every other dude. But fuck him; he ain't the only dude around. I can have whoever I want, and tonight, I'd remind myself of who the fuck I really am. Tonight, I'm gonna just let everything go and be fucking free. Hate to say it, but I need to channel my inner Regina. I didn't have any rules anyway, so why not just do me? "Yep, let's have some fun tonight," I said out loud. I turned on my music and got into my zone.

I went to my closet and looked for a dress to match my mood. However, everything looked too safe, even the risqué outfits. So, I went to Regina's closet; she'd have exactly what I needed, guaranteed. After rummaging through her closet, I found a few options. However, one stood out perfectly, and it was unworn. I grabbed it and headed back to my room to finish getting ready. After a shower and completing my moisturizing routine, I finally tried on the dress. "I don't know if I'm ready for this…but fuck it, I look good." I tried to hype myself up in the mirror so I wouldn't back down, because this dress left nothing to the imagination. It was a black three-piece sexy crop top short set with a mesh see-through ruched bodycon midi dress. It stopped mid-thigh, was skin-tight, and with my gold metallic peep-toe strappy lace-up tie stiletto pumps and gold accessories, I was ready.

Miss Kena had already done my hair the week before, so I was good on that. I put my hair to one side, applied my makeup, and admired the complete look before I headed out. "Didn't need that punk-ass necklace anyway," I said out loud. "No one makes me cry, damn it!"

A night out was just what I needed to make me feel better. I told Rayna I would pick her up just so I could rub it in Donte's damn face. After a few splashes of perfume, I headed upstairs to Rayna. I made sure to use my key.

"RAYYYYYY!" I shouted her name for all to hear. I needed to be seen and recognized. When I entered, Miss Chyna stuck her head out of the kitchen.

"Ummm…excuse me, Sharnel! Babbbyyy! You look so… I've never seen you look so sexy!" Miss Chyna was unsure what to say, but she smiled and raised an eyebrow without judgment.

I giggled and modeled so she could see the entire fit. "You umm definitely look great," she nodded in approval, then whispered, "Now who done pissed you off, huh?" The statement surprised the shit out of me, and my face showed it. Damn, was she psychic or something? I couldn't say your damn son, so I just brushed it off.

"I just wanted to do something different for our last night out."

She smiled and gave me another glance over, then mumbled, "Whatever happened, he done really messed up."

Rayna came down the hallway. "OHHH MYYY GOOOSSSHHH! Girl, you are fire! Look at you! Who man you stealing tonight? Got me feeling overdressed."

I did a little dance, and we both laughed and high-fived. "Ray, you look great, baby girl! Bout to show 'em how it's done down south for real." She danced around, shaking her booty and hair. Rayna's favorite color was blue, so of course, she had on a teal strapless dress that hugged her curves, with heels to match. The dress was fire, and she looked amazing. I knew P would be all over her because of how good she looked, but she wouldn't have it any other way.

I was gonna miss her, but I was also glad for the time to refocus, especially since one particular man was no longer a distraction.

"Hey y'all, let's get a picture! Y'all are too cute for words!" yelled Miss Chyna as she grabbed her phone. She snapped a few photos, but of course, we couldn't get a picture without Keith in it. He did his best poses, and we modeled with him.

As we were about to leave, the door opened, and my heart began pounding, knowing who it was, and he wasn't alone. Donte entered the apartment with P, Paul, Fat Mane, and Trav. Before he even looked my way, I felt butterflies in my stomach. Fuck, I gotta shake that shit off; he has no power over me, not anymore.

When Donte saw me, I could feel the rage build up in his face as he looked over my outfit. I didn't care and only returned the same energy to him. When he got closer to me, he intentionally brushed past me like I was a stranger and took a seat on the sofa. Enjoy your Sports Center, asshole, I rolled my eyes. Miss Chyna looked on and nodded while she slightly chuckled.

As P approached me, he whispered, "Umm…Sister Shar, where's the rest of your dress?"

I smiled. "P, you're such a big brother!" and kissed his cheek.

He just stared at me, then at Donte. "Whatever, don't make me smack a nigga tonight because your ass is practically naked."

I rolled my eyes and went to the dining room table to sit so I could rest my feet. P and Rayna took pictures together as they complimented each other in coordinating outfits. I wondered how they would handle not seeing each other for a few weeks. They were always together or not far enough to reach each other. I silently hoped they kept it together while Rayna was gone. They were meant to be, unlike some other people I knew. I sat at the dining room table, pondering my thoughts.

"Dang, Sharnel, you're looking good, baby girl! Who knew you were hiding all that? I'm about to be your date for tonight," said Trav confidently. Then Trav tried to put his arm around me, and I smacked his arm away.

"Get the hell away from me, Trav!" He wasn't bothered; he just smiled and blew a kiss at me.

Donte didn't even look my direction; he just kept watching TV. I wanted to piss Donte off, but I wasn't that fucking desperate. There wasn't enough pettiness in my body to even consider entertaining Trav. However, I couldn't pass up the chance. Fat Mane was sitting on the steps of the platform that led to the front door. I got up and headed in his direction as he stood up.

"Fat Mane, you can be my date tonight," then I put my arms around him to give him a too-close hug.

Poor Fat Mane looked excited yet scared, he only mustered up, "Cool, I got you, boo."

He looked like he won the money pot. As I hugged him, I thought, urgh, I hope he knows this is for one night and I ain't serious. Donte didn't say a word; he shook his head.

I excused myself to the bathroom to check that everything was still in place. As I walked out of the bathroom, Donte was in his room; he looked me up and down with disgust. So, I stepped into his room.

"Is there a problem?" I asked with an attitude; he was about to let it go, but he couldn't.

"Didn't take long, huh?" I didn't know what he meant and waited for him to finish. "You ain't shit, Sharnel, hoeing yourself to the lowest nigga in that next-to-nothing ass dress," he said.

I was beyond pissed and closed the door. "Hoe! Nigga, please! Don't be mad because you ain't man enough to step up to the plate!"

He laughed, which infuriated me, then replied "Plate? Shit ain't gonna be shit left to step since your ass serving a visual and invitation to your pussy for any nigga looking. Grow the fuck up Sharnel, stop sluttin' yourself short!"

Was he serious! How dare he say that shit to me! I clapped at his failed attempt to insult me. His words were pure jealousy and bullshit, but I responded anyway. "Fuck you Donte, you actin' like a real bum ass nigga! You gonna be in this room forever with your snake and your car parts because you're too much of a bitch to express yourself."

I knew I had pushed a button because Donte got up, and we stood toe to toe. "Yoo, get the fuck out, Sharnel!" I could feel him breathing hot.

"Just what I thought," I said, laughing him off as I opened the door and walked out of the room. As I walked away, he slammed his door.

When I entered the living room, everyone was sitting around talking. Miss Chyna just nodded and looked at me, like she put the pieces together. "That's the second time today!" She went back into the kitchen. I was already over the night; he ruined my mood again.

After a few more pictures, we headed out to meet Tonya on the stoop. She didn't tell her parents the guys were hanging out with us, so she had to sneak out.

"Dang y'all could have helped a sista out with a dress or something!" Tonya fussed as she looked at Rayna and me. She had on a cute jean dress and heels, but I could see her point. After we met up with her, we were on our way—or so we thought.

From then, the night just continued to unravel. By the time we got ready to go, Tonya's car wouldn't start. Everyone couldn't fit into P's truck, which we discovered had no gas. We ended up taking two Ubers to the city, to the lounge, which turned out to be boring. I got a lot of attention from guys I was not interested in and spent the night trying to get rid of them while P watched me like a damn hawk.

I couldn't stop thinking about what Donte said. I was no one's whore. I kept reminding myself he was jealous and being spiteful, but inside it didn't matter; I was just hurt by our interaction, and although visually my plan worked, mentally and emotionally it backfired.

Poor Fat Mane tried to talk to me all night, but I just shortchanged his conversation, so finally, he just stopped. Trav couldn't help but enjoy his cousin's rejection and kept bringing it up. So, to shut him up, on the way to the bathroom, I found a pretty girl who complained about being broke and paid her $125 to talk/flirt with Fat Mane. She was more than happy to play along and even agreed to call Fat Mane for the next week. I crossed my fingers that the more she talked to him, the more she would eventually like him. The funny thing was Trav tried to talk to her earlier that night, and she rejected him. As I watched her fawn over Fat Mane and Trav sit angry, I felt like it was money well spent—mission complete.

When we were over being at the lounge the plan was to go back to P's house. Once back at our complex, everyone decided they would change their clothes and meet up there. Since Tonya was way past her curfew, we went to Rayna's house. I tried to forgo the trip to avoid another interaction with Donte, but Rayna and Tonya were not having it, so I agreed to go with them before I went home to change.

As we waited for Rayna to open the door, it felt like a death sentence, but I wasn't gonna run or hide from Donte. When we entered the apartment, it was dark, but the TV was on. Donte was on the sofa watching TV. Of course, his lonely ass had not left the house. He still looked unfazed and never looked toward us. Maybe I took it too far. I considered the thought for about 2.5 seconds, then I saw red all over again.

As we got closer, we noticed he was not alone. Trina lay across his lap on the sofa, and I could feel myself getting pissed. I wanted to curse, question, yell, throw stuff, and just completely lose it. I even considered taking a picture and sending it to Miss Chyna for permission to beat Trina's ass since she was in the house. But I let it go and just shook my head. Who's the whore now? He ran back to sloppy seconds for a bitch he don't even kiss or touch…fuckin loser!

Rayna, who wasn't a fan of Trina either, turned on the light, and we all stood there. Trina rolled her eyes when she saw me.

"Look, babe… the kids are home!" she said while getting even more comfortable on his lap. Donte looked at me with a big smile on his face. I stood there and nodded, then gave a fake hand clap and mouthed "bravo, bitch, bravo." The more I watched, the more I couldn't mask my frustration. I knew he could see it and marveled in it.

But Donte had to make it worse and take it a step further. When Trina sat up and stood, he followed suit, grabbing a handful of her ass and kissing her cheek. She seductively walked to his room while he pushed his body against hers. Now his ass wants to be all affectionate with her—such a fucking chump! When she walked into his room, he just stood in the doorframe, smiled, and mouthed "fuck you, Sharnel!" then slammed the door.

"MOTHAFUCKER," I mumbled. I had to remind myself this is not your man; y'all are not together. Not wanting to step further into the house to prevent myself from losing control or even throwing up, I decided it was time to go.

I guess my face spoke volumes because Rayna said, "Shar, why don't you go change, girl?" Then Tonya chimed in, "Yeah girl, we will catch up!"
I nodded and told them I'd just meet them outside.

As I walked down the stairs to my apartment, I mumbled, "This is it; I'm done. I'm really done now. I can't believe he would do that to me. URGH! I can't believe him." I contained myself and didn't cry despite what I felt. When I got inside, I changed my clothes. As I was about to head out, I saw Regina's car keys. It was one of those nights, and I needed a release. Not caring if she was home or not, I grabbed them and decided I'd forgo P's house and go for a drive alone. I just needed to get away.

The girls knocked on the door, ready to go to P's. I tried to put on my best "I ain't mad" attitude, but I was failing. As I locked the door, Donte rushed out the front door with Trina in tow.

"What the fuck, Donte… why?" I heard Trina whine as the door closed behind them.

"BITCH, I hope she gave him herpes… quick-pumping ass," I said out loud. Rayna and Tonya just looked at each other and didn't say a word. I knew it wasn't right and not even her fault, but I was pissed.

"Look y'all, I'm gonna give y'all some time to spend with your boos, okay? So go ahead, and I'll catch up with y'all tomorrow," I said as if I was doing them a favor when it was me who needed time. They tried to act sad, but I knew they weren't, especially Tonya's thirsty ass. After I told them I would check in on them in an hour or so, Tonya and Rayna went on their way. I felt relief—finally a moment to myself.

I started Regina's BMW, let the windows down, selected a playlist, let the music blare, and just drove. It was the perfect night; the moon was out, and it was 75 degrees. I loved summer nights. I felt like I could have driven to Florida and back, but I was beginning to get tired after an hour. No matter how much I tried, I couldn't get past my thoughts of Donte. Why did he have to do that? We weren't even together, but he was trying to make me jealous? Who's the hoe now? Thirsty for attention, momma's boy. But no matter what I said, I knew I was hurt; this pained me more than I cared to recognize. Why was this our dynamic? Why did I care so much? The thoughts kept flowing, but so did the pain in my heart. No matter how fast I drove, I couldn't outrun the obvious—I felt something for Donte.

When I finally settled my thoughts, I was finally able to enjoy my drive. I felt so good riding the wave of my drive; I almost felt drunk. It was the best feeling I had in a while. It was about 3:30 a.m. when I pulled back up to the parking lot of our building. I was tired, but hunger was taking over, and I wished I had stopped for food before I came back. But I was too tired to go anywhere else.

As I locked the car and headed toward the building, there he was, walking down the sidewalk toward our building. Where the fuck was he coming from? Damn, did he spend the night at that bitch's house? I started to get mad but shook it off and decided to purposely take my time, hoping he would just go in and go home. Just as I completed that thought, his ass just posted up on the steps.

"FUCCCCCCK!" I tried to think fast of an alternative plan but failed; the building was one way in and one way out. I straightened myself up, "fuck it. I'll show him. I'll breeze past him, and he can leave me the hell alone," I said confidently. As I got closer, I wanted to turn back, but where would I go? This is stupid; I'm no punk, and he doesn't own me! When I got closer, I could see he was sitting in the middle of the steps. What the fuck was wrong with him? "Asshole," he didn't have to move; I could go around his ass.

When I reached the steps, he didn't say a word or move but made eye contact. I tried to go left; he just looked at me. I tried to go right, and he did it again. So, I stopped and met his gaze. After a few seconds, he moved to the left so I could pass. I took a breath and began what felt like a mountain climb up the five steps. I wanted to sprint, but my body was not having it. On the first step, I kept my eyes forward; on the second step, I pulled out my keys; on the third step, he grabbed my hand. This wasn't part of the plan… damn it! I stopped and glared at his hand and him, but he never stopped looking forward. Then he guided me to stand before him. He moved up to the fourth step, putting us closer to eye level, and I didn't move; I just looked away.

I could feel him staring at me, but I refused to look or speak at first. After a few moments, he guided me closer so he could put his hands on my waist. Then he pulled me close so his face was on my left cheek.

He kissed my cheek softly, then whispered, "I'm sorry, Shar!" Fuck his sorry; too late! I didn't react or even respond, so he did it again: "I fucked up! I didn't mean any of the shit I said, I swear!" He kissed me again. Donte turned my face toward him. "Man, you were right about a lot of shit you said." His face seemed remorseful, and I finally loosened up.

He kissed my lips for the first time as he gently pressed his lips against mine. At first, it was a simple peck, but then he began massaging his lips against mine, inviting me to finally kiss him back. His lips were so soft; his kisses were gentle and seemed to overpower mine, which I didn't mind. It was the second sweetest thing I ever felt, the kiss on the cheek being the first. I felt every bit of passion as I kissed him back. Feeling as if I was about to lose my breath, I backed up.

When our kiss ended, I had a frown on my face. The kiss was nice, but he wasn't getting off that easily. Without taking his eyes off me, he reached into his hoodie and pulled out the necklace. Seeing it immediately sent frustration through me and caused me to react immediately.

"Don't you even…"

Before I finished, he gave me the *really* face. "Stop that shit, Sharnel!" I turned my cheek toward him again. "I brought it for you," he said solemnly, "no one else." He kissed my cheek again.

I looked at the necklace and then at him. He took a breath and undid the clasp. Donte put his face close to my neck, closer than necessary to put the necklace on me. He slowly backed away but not before whispering, "That was fucked up, my bad, Shar!"

I knew he was apologizing for Trina. I just looked at him, and he still had that soft look in his eyes. He gently picked up the charm and adjusted it, nodding his head.

"Don't take it off… always keep it on you, Shar." He kissed my lips again. I touched the charm with my right hand, and he put his hand on top of mine. "Forgive me, Shar!"

I was still pissed, but this felt good… it felt right. Relaxing my face a bit, I looked at him again and saw something different in his eyes. Donte put all his cards on the table; there was no hiding or mistaking how he felt. This officially changed things between us. I still had so many questions, but I knew he wasn't gonna answer them, at least not right away. That wasn't his style; he just reacted, whether you got it or not.

I didn't get this; we argued… so what was this? I stood before him, staring to see if he would indulge my apparent unspoken questions, but he didn't. He just looked away. So, I waited a few seconds and nodded my head, about to walk away. He grabbed my hand one last time and kissed me. I used my free hand to gently touch his face and rubbed it as he kissed me even more passionately than before.

Donte didn't just put his lips on mine; he opened my mouth and inched his tongue inside. The more his tongue entered, the more I welcomed it by extending my tongue and eventually began sucking on his. We fell into a rhythm; our silence turned into quiet moans as we continued to kiss. I had kissed guys before, but nothing looked or even felt like this. When I moved closer, almost putting us shoulder to shoulder, he eased up. He looked at me, then let my hand go.

"I can't answer you now, Shar… but I will!" He looked away, and I nodded my head. I was too tired to argue and too confused to stay, so I left… this was to be continued.

CHAPTER 12

With Tonya and Rayna gone, it was just me and Keith! Miss Chyna let me use her car during the day, so we were everywhere. Every day was an adventure; we went to the museum, the water park, rode the train—you name it, we hit it. His babysitter got sick after coming back from her vacation, so I ended up keeping him for two weeks. Which worked—more money for me! Miss Chyna mentioned that she needed an oil change and asked if Keith and I would take her car to get it done. I gladly agreed but was hesitant since I hadn't seen Donte the whole time I babysat for Keith.

After everything that happened with the necklace and our kiss, we just avoided each other again. No real rhyme or reason; we just didn't talk. Part of me was still a bit bothered by the thought that he'd likely fucked Trina. Although he never confirmed or denied it, he just apologized for her presence. I couldn't get past why he would show her affection now, or at least bring it to my attention— that shit hurt! Especially when I thought he was starting to feel me. The silence left us both with unanswered questions. We'd get to them sooner or later; I hoped.

When Keith and I arrived at the shop, he immediately spotted Donte from the car. "Shar Shar, there's Donte!" he yelled excitedly. As I parked the car, he quickly unbuckled his car seat. I shook my head and got out quickly so he didn't open the door. As I helped Keith out, he couldn't wait to go greet his brother. I grabbed his hand and led him across the parking lot to the garage.

"Donte!" Keith yelled, waving at his brother.

"Sup, man?" Donte said as he eased from under a car. Keith stood at the entrance of the garage and waited as Donte stood up. Donte went to the sink in the garage and cleaned off his hands. Keith continued to jump around while I held his hand as he waited for his brother.

When Miss Chyna asked me to take the car in, Keith and I made a pit stop at my apartment so I could change. In anticipation of seeing Donte today, I wanted to look extra cute and wore a peach shorts jumpsuit that almost looked like a uniform. It had a collar with a zipper down the front with peach heeled sandals to match. My hair was wavy and flowed down my back with a headband to hold it back. I looked like a cute young mom with Keith in tow. When Donte finished washing his hands, I took a breath and guided Keith to his brother. Donte and I didn't speak; we just nodded toward each other. When Keith was with Donte, I left them and headed inside the shop.

"Damn, who is that? She fine as fu…" I heard Donte's co-worker say.

Donte quickly replied, "No one of your concern."

Smiling, I retraced my steps back toward Donte and Keith and looked at his coworker, cutely saying, "My name is Sharnel."

The coworker smiled, and Donte tightened his lips as if he was about to get angry. I could have cared less about the co-worker, but I wanted to get my lick back on Donte for Trina. As his coworker continued to smile, I turned toward Donte, rolled my eyes, and then headed back toward the shop. I knew the no fraternization policy, so I had no plans of ever speaking to the guy again. However, I still made sure to put an extra switch in my hips with every step as Donte and Keith followed behind me.

When I got to the front door, I stepped aside and waited for Donte to open it. He grunted but didn't move.

However, Keith sprang into action, exclaiming, "I'll open the door for you, Shar Shar!" Poor Keith tried his hardest, but Donte still had to help him. Keith still leaned proudly against the door, so I leaned down to kiss his cheek.

"Thank you, Keithy Face, you're such a gentleman."

Keith smiled proudly, and I went through the door. When I reached the receptionist desk, I didn't see anyone, but I heard someone behind it. As I got closer, Mr. Charles stood up.

"Hey, Mr. Charles," I greeted him.

"Hey, baby girl, where you been? I haven't seen you in a month of Sundays."

I smiled, "I've been around, just living life," I said, keeping my eyes on Mr. Charles.

"Uhhh huh, so you're just living life? Does that mean you're single?"

I burst into laughter. "Mr. Charles, you're too much! Yep, I'm single, except I did see someone who may have his eyes on me," I flirted.

"Uhhh huh, well as beautiful as you are, baby girl, that doesn't surprise me."

Donte shook his head, and Keith high-fived Mr. Charles. As we stood there, Donte didn't say a word, but you could cut the tension with a knife.

Mr. Charles looked at me and then at Donte as if he were trying to figure us out. I broke the silence. "Mr. Charles, I told Keith I would take him to get lunch. About how long will this take?"

He replied, "Ahh well, baby, it may take an hour or so." That bummed me a bit. What would I do with an active Keith for a whole hour? Before I could voice my concern, Mr. Charles suggested, "How about y'all go to that Chuck E. Cheese place for a while, and I'll call you."

I immediately cringed and regretted him bringing that up. "No, he didn't just say that!" I mumbled. Keith lit up like a Christmas tree while I gave Mr. Charles a look, and he responded with a *forgive me* face. So, I acted quickly.

"Mr. Charles, I don't have a car to get there, and I don't want to put Keith in an Uber without a car seat." He pondered my dilemma and then responded, "Hey, uhhh Donte, it's about your lunchtime. Why don't you go with them? Ummm, you worked some overtime last week. I can let you off a bit so I don't have to pay you," he laughed.

What did I just walk into? Donte didn't say a word, just nodded with an annoyed expression and opened the front door. Just like that, we were trapped; we both knew there was no arguing with Mr. Charles, so we went with it. Donte got the car seat out of Miss Chyna's car, and we were off to fucking Chuck E. Cheese.

Once we arrived at Chuck E. Cheese, Keith was too excited to contain himself. He threw off his shoes and dove into the ball pit. Luckily, I was able to get a seat right near it so we could keep an eye on him. Donte sat down, didn't say anything, and just looked at his phone.

"He's gonna be hungry soon," I barked.

"What are you telling me for? You're the babysitter," he snarled back.

I just looked at him, and he stormed off. After he ordered lunch, he came back to sit at the table. His temper was a bit milder, but I didn't care; I was not happy. He faced me, but I faced the ball pit, so his stare burned a hole into the side of my face. When he cleared his throat, I ignored him. He did it again, and I rolled my eyes.

"So, you can't hear me now!" he barked, clearing his throat for a third time. I knew he was pissed, so I finally gave up and turned toward him. He still didn't say anything, and neither did I. His face softened, and so did mine. He looked sorry; maybe it was time to address the elephant in the room. He looked at my neck, and I still had the necklace on. He just nodded and stared back at me. Why does this feel so intense, but not in an angry way? I've missed that face more than I care to admit.

He was about to say something when the pizza arrived. I immediately stood up and called, "Keithy Face, come eat, love!"

However, he found a friend and sulked at the idea. "I'm still playing, Shar Shar," Keith yelled, before diving back into the ball pit, showing his lack of interest in the pizza.

"What the hell did I buy this shit for if he ain't even hungry?" Donte snarled. His reaction sent me back into a bad mood.

I rolled my eyes. "Take the shit home and he'll eat it, duh!"

Donte didn't even acknowledge my comment. We were both over each other and Chuck E. Cheese's pizza. We sat in silence for a few more minutes, then Donte cleared his throat. This time I looked at him and waited for him to speak.

"Look, I don't know if you need me to say it again so we can stop all this avoiding shit…I'm sorry about that night. That was fucked up and you didn't deserve that."

Finally, he said it—he really said it—but I didn't feel any different. I was still hurt and couldn't get past my feelings. But it was time to just be honest and put everything out on the table.

"Donte, I'm sorry too. I was wrong as well. I never intended to do anything that night; I just wanted to make you feel like I did." I told him about the girl and Fat Mane; he just shook his head and chuckled.

We were quiet again, and then I said, "After all we talked about…seeing you show Trina an ounce of affection, it…"

"Shar, I didn't even do anything with her. I don't even like her or care about her. She was just available."

I just nodded; I didn't know if I believed him, and it didn't matter. We had gotten everything out in the open, and that's what mattered. I continued, "If I'm being honest, I'm more pissed about what happened in your bedroom than that. I mean, I know you were mad, but that shit hurt for real…"

Donte nodded as if he understood. I was ready to move past the awkward phase, but I wasn't sure about anything else, so I continued. "I wish I could say let's put this past us and move forward, but I'm still hurt. I just don't know how to do that right now." I could feel myself beginning to cry, but I held it together. I needed that for me.

He nodded his head as if he understood again. "Shar…" I looked away to indicate I needed time.

Donte didn't continue but got up and went to Keith while he continued playing. The ride back to the shop was quiet; Keith passed out, and it felt like we had run out of words to say. When we arrived, Mr. Charles was washing the car and drying it.

"Y'all look like you've been to a funeral. How was Chuck E. Cheese?"

We both looked at each other with emotionless stares, then at Mr. Charles. "Ahhh huuuhhh, the cheese still stands alone, huh!"

We both walked away in opposite directions. Donte went back to work while I got Miss Chyna's keys and Keith and headed back home.

CHAPTER 13

The next week provided some ease. I was able to see Donte and not lose it, although we still didn't talk. One day, I was coming home from running an errand in Regina's car. When I pulled up, I saw P, Donte, and a few others sitting in front of P's building. As I got out of the car, I pulled out my phone, trying to look preoccupied, hoping no one saw me. However, I was immediately spotted by P.

"Yo, Sister Shar!" P yelled. I quickly looked up and waved, then increased my speed as I kept walking. "Aye man, come here!" he motioned for me to come over. I started to make up a lie but didn't. I grunted and took my time walking in his direction.

P, who was at the top of the steps, moved to the bottom. He placed himself across from Donte and Paul, who stood on either side of him. When I finally made it to him, I nodded to the group without looking at anyone but P, hoping this would be a quick interaction, but knowing P, it wouldn't be.

"What's up? Where you been hiding?" P reached out to hug me, and I hugged him back.

"I've been around; what's up with you?" I said, trying to hurry along the conversation.

"I've been coolin', ready for my baby to come home. You know Miss Chyna's gonna give her a welcome home party."

P was gleaming as he spoke. I smiled weakly and nodded. P looked at my reaction, shook his head, and kept talking.

"Look, I got Rayna something special for her welcome home gift. I want to know what you think."

Was he serious? Did he have to do this now? I wasn't looking at Donte, but being in his presence was overwhelming. "Look, I'm gonna go get it. Stay…"

"P, I gotta go handle something for Regina real quick. I can come back later if you're around."

P nodded, "Sure, hit me up; I'll be around." Glad he finally took the bait, I smiled and immediately left.

Leaving, I felt like I could catch my breath again. I didn't look back, but I felt like all eyes were on me. I hadn't noticed before, but I was sweating like I had the damn flu. As I turned to walk up the steps to the building, I saw Donte at least 50 feet behind me. He wasn't looking at me but at his phone. So, I rushed into the building and down the stairs to my apartment so I could get in before he made it inside. The more I rushed, the harder I began sweating, and I kept fumbling with the keys. Trying to steady my hands to unlock the door was becoming a task, but I did it. Once the front door opened, I immediately slammed my apartment door shut. I leaned against the door and took several sighs of relief.

"You did it, Shar!" I said out loud, proud of myself for avoiding Donte. As I stood up and was about to walk away from the door, I heard a knock. I looked through the peephole; it was him. "Oh fuck," I mumbled, then covered my mouth. Why was he here? He wouldn't just drop by without telling me; it wasn't his style. Donte knocked again, but I just leaned against the door and didn't answer. Why can't he just leave? My plan wasn't to avoid him forever, just until I was over whatever I felt.

He knocked two more times, then stopped. I thought the coast was clear until I heard my phone chime once and then again. "Fuck! Fuck! Fuck!" I mumbled, then reached for my phone, which happened to be in my pocket. I unlocked it and immediately turned the volume down. The messages were from Donte. I thought about not opening them, but I decided against it.

Him: *How long you gonna keep this bullshit up?*

Him: *I know you're on the other side of the door, Shar!*

When I heard him walk away, I felt foolish for continuing this thing between us. He was obviously over it; why couldn't I just let it go?

Still unsure about what to say to Donte, I kept my routine of avoiding him. Like clockwork, Miss Chyna would get home, and I'd be out the door before Donte came home. It was going so well until one day during naptime, both Keith and I were asleep when the door opened; it was Donte. He came home early from work. FUUUUDGGEEE. Okay, I can handle this, I said to myself. Donte walked in and looked like crap.

"Hey," he took a breath as he walked, "Sup."

I examined him further as he got closer to the sofa. "You look like shit."

He gave me the *really* face and said, "Thanks. I don't feel good, so Charles sent me home."

Negro, please, you look just fine, I thought to myself. But truth be told, he did look horrible.

"Sorry to hear that. Did you call ole girl so she can take care of you?" I said sarcastically.

"Damn, that shit really got under your skin," he said as he grunted to clear his throat. I was instantly pissed and reacted out of frustration.

"Nah, but clearly she's given you the fucking plague, so enjoy."

Donte was over the conversation. "Man, fuck you, Sharnel. My stomach's just a little messed up; can't keep nothing down." I immediately felt bad.

The whole reaction was totally uncalled for. It was well known that Donte had suffered from stomach issues since he was a kid. From time to time, he got really sick and was hospitalized a couple of times. However, I thought he had it under control since he hadn't been sick in a while. I felt remorseful at that moment, and it showed. I was about to apologize, but he left the room. Fuck Shar, too far!

Donte walked to his room and then went to the bathroom to shower. I knew Keith would be asleep for another 30 minutes, so I slipped out. I went to my apartment and grabbed some fresh ginger to make the ginger drink my granny taught me. I also grabbed some soup, crackers, and Pedialyte. I felt like such a sucker, but I couldn't help it. I had to make up for my actions somehow. I also knew he was really in pain if he came home; he rarely ever missed work. When I returned to Miss Chyna's apartment, I heated the soup and put the Pedialyte on ice. I placed everything on a tray and headed toward his room.

When I entered Donte's room with all the goodies, he was passed out. He looked peaceful as he lay under the blanket, almost snoring. I just watched him, wishing things were different between us. Why couldn't we figure this out? We might actually be good together if…this is crazy. I decided to take the tray back into the kitchen, but before I could walk away, he woke up.

Not lifting his head, he mumbled, "Can I help you?" I turned around with the tray in hand. He just stared at me.

"I thought you might need this; hopefully, you will begin to feel better." He didn't move, just looked pitiful. So, I set the tray on the desk and grabbed the ginger drink, then handed it to him. He just looked at it and then at me. "Look, it's the ginger drink," I hoped he remembered it from the laundry room. When he didn't respond, I kept talking. "Granny used to give it to Papa when his stomach bothered him. He had something like what you do." He looked skeptical but sat up in bed.

After he sniffed the cup, he took a sip. "Slow sips; it's strong, remember?"

He slowly sipped while staring at me in the process. "You ain't spit in it, did you?" he asked seriously. I wanted to react, but I'd done enough of that for today.

So, I smiled and sternly replied, "No, Donte, I might be an alleged whore, but I ain't an evil bitch."

He didn't say anything; he just continued to sip more and more. According to Granny, that meant it was working. "What else is on that tray?" he asked while he sipped.

"Soup, crackers, and Pedialyte," I said. "There's more ginger drink in the fridge; it should last you through the week, and you should be better tomorrow. If you need more, let me know."

He nodded. "I'll get the tray before I leave. Keith is about to get up soon."

Donte replied. "You don't have to."

I shrugged. "It's cool; just rest…hope you feel better soon."

I walked to the door, and as I was leaving, he mumbled, "You ain't a whore."

I wasn't going to react, but I couldn't help myself. "Guess 'evil bitch' is still an option," I chuckled as I closed the door lightly.

After Keith got up, I gave him a snack and occupied him with his favorite Thomas the Tank. I checked in on Donte once again before Miss Chyna came home. He was in a deep sleep. The tray now sat on the nightstand; the soup was gone, the crackers were open, and the ginger drink and Pedialyte were empty. I just stood there and looked at him. Fuckin' Donte, why do I feel this way about him? I couldn't comprehend my feelings or what that meant going forward. As I was about to leave, I picked up the tray but looked at the empty cup. "I wish I had something to fix us," I whispered. Just then, I set the tray down and got closer to him. I rubbed his back.

"I hope you feel better soon! Sorry I've been shutting you out…I'm done, I promise," I whispered. Then I leaned down and kissed his cheek. I wished I could watch him all night, but that wasn't an option. We were not even on speaking terms; we barely said anything to each other. So, I just left the room.

When Miss Chyna came home, I was washing dishes and was just about to sit Keith down for dinner.

She smiled, "Hey babies, how are y'all!"

Keith smiled, "Mom Mom, Donte's sick!" he told her as she exchanged hugs with us.

"I know, baby; he told me. I was going to come home, but he said Shar Shar was taking good care of him."

I could feel her smile, but I didn't look in her direction. I hoped he didn't tell her everything. She came into the kitchen and made eye contact with me.

"I see you taking care of my boys," then she walked toward the back to check on Donte. I packed up my things and decided to head home. When she came back to the living room, I told her about the Pedialyte and ginger drink in the fridge.

"You know, Shar, you did a great thing today. Thank you!"

I smiled at her and nodded. I hugged and kissed Keith and said goodbye since this was my last day babysitting. Before I exited the door, she said, "Just 'cause Rayna ain't here don't mean you can't come around…you never know; it may help." Miss Chyna winked, and I smiled again, then closed the door. When I finally got home, I was glad, but my mind was still on Donte. I hoped he was feeling better soon. I thought about checking on him, but I felt that was too much, so I stayed away, although it pained me to do so.

CHAPTER 14

Miss Kena and I sat in silence as she braided my hair. "Girl, you good?" she asked.

"Yeah, I'm cool, why?" I asked.

"You feel like you got a weight on your heart and mind today."

Dang, was it that obvious? It had been a few days since I had seen Donte, and it was starting to eat at me again. I meant what I said; I was done ignoring him. I didn't mean for my feelings to be a badge, but I was wearing them loud and proud apparently.

"You got a love jones maybe?" she asked. We both laughed, and Miss Kena offered some advice. "You know where I'm from, love is a beautiful, scared thing shared between two people. It's not set with all the boundaries and daggers you young people put on everything. If you love a person, you love them. If you want to be with them, you be with them. If it's not meant to be, love them from afar, free from the pain. You will tear your heart and self in two trying to avoid love. And know what happens then? You develop all these illnesses and ailments all because you didn't let love flow free. Love is a beautiful thing from God; why should we not enjoy a gift from His majesty, hmm?"

Miss Kena's words were like kryptonite to my heart and soul. I was feeling love. However, I wasn't just in love; I was in love with Donte. But I was too afraid to find out if he truly loved me after last time. I wasn't gonna ask, nor was I going to bring it up ever. He shitted on me once, and that was enough.

"Sharnel, do yourself a favor…don't be afraid to try." I looked at Miss Kena, surprised; it was like she was reading my thoughts. "What's for you will never fail you because you can't lose what has always belonged to you." I smiled and nodded again as Miss Kena hugged my neck.

After paying Miss Kena for my hair, I decided to get away from the apartment and go out for some dinner. Regina wasn't home (surprise, surprise), and I was over carryout and takeout food. I would have to Uber because she took her car, but I was perfectly fine with that for once. I decided to take a trip to Annapolis for dinner at one of my favorite spots. So, I put on a white summer casual slip dress with spaghetti straps and platform wedges. I grabbed my keys, AirPods, a multicolored wrap for my shoulders, and my purse, then headed out the door. When I opened the door, he was about to knock.

"Sup?" He looked like himself again, and I was glad.

Donte stood there in a white T-shirt, black basketball shorts, and black slides with white socks.

"How you feeling?" I asked, slightly smiling.

He took a step back and nodded. "I'm well, and you?"

He glanced over my outfit and raised his eyebrow. Feeling nervous, I moved my braids back over my shoulder so I had a reason to look away before looking at him again.

"Am I interrupting something?" He looked a bit disappointed, but I was glad to see that. I thought about telling him a lie, but I was over playing games.

"Nope. I was just taking myself to dinner in an Uber. I'm over carryout and the local food."

He stood there emotionless as usual, which I expected. I could tell I looked good because he kept looking me up and down.

"Oh, okay, sounds cool, but why an Uber?" he asked as if that was weird.

"No car tonight, so it's just me and some rando in a car," I said, feeling lame.

He just nodded. "Well, y'all have fun, I guess," he replied.

As he turned to walk away, I acted quickly. Time to bite the bullet and rip the band-aid off. "Would you like to join me for dinner?"

He turned around and frowned a bit, as if he was shocked but intrigued. "Nah, I can't; just helped Mom with the rent, so I'm kinda slow right now."

I paused and nodded. "I get it."

We were both quiet, and then he spoke. "Well, I'mma let you get on your way; just wanted to say thank you for the other day. That stuff you gave me helped like shit; good looking out," he still sounded a bit disappointed.

"Sure, no problem. Glad you're feeling better." He was about to walk away again. Why did it have to end like this? I'd been waiting for this moment; this can't be it.

I started to think about Miss Kena's words and felt sick, so I rushed the words out before I actually hurled. "Hey, look, I know you don't got it right now, but how about we split a DiGiorno pizza with stuffed crust and just watch TV?" When I finished, I was catching my breath, trying to compose myself again. He didn't turn around, but he did stop. "Then maybe we can go out another day…as friends or something," I added.

Donte turned around, confused. "Did you just ask me on a date, Shar?"

I was officially humiliated, and it showed. I did, but he didn't have to point it out. I mumbled, "Never can make anything easy, huh?" I was about to get mad, but I swallowed it. This wasn't that type of moment anyway.

"Look, you in or nah?" I mumbled, trying to hide my shame.

He smirked. "Okay, cool, but can we do it here? I'm not about to watch Keith's kid-friendly movie collection; I'm tired of that shit."

I laughed and nodded in agreement. I had enough of Thomas the Tank and his friends while babysitting.

I opened the door wider for him to enter the apartment, and he came in. Donte went and sat on the sofa while I locked the door. As I walked down the platform and the two stairs into the living room, I was glad I finally spoke up and that we were finally hanging out. I stopped behind the sofa opposite him, which led to the hall.

"Well, let me go get changed; I'll be right back." He looked me over again and nodded, then looked back at the TV.

"Can you take the pizza out and preheat the oven, please?"

He looked at me again. "I got you," then he headed to the kitchen, and I went to my bedroom. Of all nights, I can't believe tonight we were finally in the same room and had not argued—yet. It was still early, but I was excited. Maybe this time would be different.

CHAPTER 15

As I prepared for dinner and a movie with Donte, I was nervous. I couldn't believe we were finally getting some time alone. It seemed like every time we got a few moments together, they were interrupted, or it ended in an eruption. I decided to ditch my dress and go with a cute green, extra-soft casual jogger set, which consisted of a short top and leggings to match. Something that hugged just right but was comfortable in case I started sweating, which seemed to happen around Donte. I took my braids and put them in a secure bun. After making sure my perfume was still good and my lips were shining, I headed back into the living room.

When I entered the living room, we made eye contact as Donte was flipping through the movies to find something to watch.

"Can I get you anything?" I asked.

Without even looking my way, he replied, "Yeah, whatever you have is cool."

Really, sir? I spruced up for you, and you ain't even give me a good look. This is BS. I just rolled my eyes and made my way to the kitchen just as the preheat was done on the oven. After putting in the pizza, I decided to make a little beverage I enjoyed with fresh mango, orange, and pineapple juice and ginger, of course. I hoped the pineapple was sweet enough.

As I was blending everything together, Donte entered the kitchen with a frown on his face. "Man, I didn't think you were going through metamorphosis for something to drink. I was thinking water or ginger ale," he snapped as he stood in the doorway. "It better not be any alcohol in that; you know I don't drink." I just stared at him.

"Why must you be so damn extra?" I said. "I know you don't drink; neither do I!" I shot back dryly. "You said whatever I was having, so this is what we're having," I added with a lot of sass. Then I relaxed my tone before making my request. "So, taste it and let me know if it needs anything, please."

He came closer, and I raised the spoon to his lips. He stared at me as he took a sip. Which was awkward. As he tasted the drink and nodded in approval.

"Yeah, it's cool," he replied in his emotionless demeanor.

"Damn, can you add any type of enthusiasm to your responses?"

He moved close enough to enter my personal space, putting us chest to chest, and stated in a high-pitched voice, "What do you want? OMG, that was the best drink I ever had in my life, babe. You're the best, like DJ Khaled."

Looking up at him, I moved even closer and said, "YES! Please just say that instead of the usual, just once, please."

He lowered his head closer to me, enough for us to inhale each other's breath. "Nah, I'm good."

Then he got a glass from the cabinet in front of him and filled his cup. He looked at me as he took his first sip and walked out of the kitchen, not before stopping to raise his glass as he proceeded to the sofa. This dude, ugh! But wait, did he call me babe? I immediately began to mull over the term. He knows he loves me, so he needs to stop playing. I continued cleaning the kitchen until the pizza was ready, then joined Donte on the sofa with our food.

I handed him the plate and waited for him to pray. He prayed, and we began eating.

"So, what movie did you decide on?" I asked.

"I don't know, man; too many. You choose… don't pick any girlie shit," he replied as he took another bite. Why was I not surprised? Typical Donte! "Ugh, you had one job you and now you're gonna tell me how to do it."

I rolled my eyes, and he handed me the remote. I snatched it while he kept eating unbothered. I really didn't care about the movie; I wished we could talk about anything but not argue, but we never seemed to do that. That bothered me the more I thought about it; there was a divide we couldn't get past. Hell, I would even settle for sitting in silence and vibing out to music before watching a movie. That, too, could lead to an argument about what to listen to. This was a start, so I'd take it.

For the next few minutes, he vetoed every single option I suggested. "I don't like that… that shit's boring… that's some girlie shit… nope… oh hell nah… seriously, Shar!" I was over this already, but then we finally settled on a classic movie, *Scarface*. How romantic—machine guns and yayo! As soon as I started the movie, we instantly began arguing about who was wrong, Tony or Manny, in reference to Manny dating Tony's sister and whether Manny deserved to die. Of course, when I said Tony was wrong and Manny didn't deserve to die, I was wrong on both fronts.

"Tony crossed the same line with Frank," I argued.

"Nah, but Manny was his right-hand man; that was fucked up" Donte argued. So, I decided to pose a real-life scenario.

"So, is P wrong for dating Rayna? He's your right-hand man, right?" I asked, still eating my pizza. He wasn't ready for that one and thought about it.

"Nah, that's different. P stepped to me first, and I gave him my blessing. Tony told that nigga to stay away from her, and he did it anyway; that's a violation," he replied.

I just nodded because he had a point. I thought it was sweet that P would do that. I was happy for Rayna; they deserved each other.

I posed another question that I had asked before but never got a clear answer to. "Since you look at me as a sister or whatever, would you approve of me dating someone you know?"

He raised his eyebrow and looked at me from the corner of his eye. So, I thought quickly, "Like the dude the other day at your job who asked who I was."

He gave me the *really* face and looked back at the movie. "First of all, that ain't my friend! I just work with him, and he's trash… but if that's what you want! Thought you would have learned your lesson from the last time!" he said with a nonchalant tone. I was about to reply, but he continued, "Second, I never said I saw you as a sister." I rolled my eyes.

He had a point, and the more I considered the question, I realized I could have worded it better or left it alone completely. However, we were discussing it now, and I wanted to know his true feelings. I nodded and waited for him to continue. "Plus," he looked at me from the corner of his eye, "I kissed you, Shar; I don't kiss my sister or just anyone like that!"

Being funny, I said, "Which time?" He slightly laughed, shaking his head, then looked back at the movie. I still needed to respond to his remark, so I took the opportunity.

"No! That's not who or what I want!" I said with certainty but had a follow-up question. "So, what do you…"

"Before you say anything else, I don't know… I haven't processed this yet," he said, motioning between us.

I nodded. "Enough said," I said gently. However, I had another question, so I asked it. "But you kissing me, that meant something, right?" I asked, waiting for a response.

Donte looked back at me flatly and said, "Did you kissing me the other day mean something?" He was awake the other day and likely heard what I said. Knowing he heard me made me nervous, but I just leaned into it.

"Yeah, it did."

Donte nodded. "Then you got your answer."

He went to say something else, and I held up my hand. "What you said was enough for me; no further explanation needed. Take your time; I'm not rushing you."

I smiled softly, and he nodded. Giving him space would also give me some while testing my patience. The rest would be what it would be; I was just glad we finally agreed on something without cursing each other out. Maybe we could make it one night without having a serious argument.

Once we finished eating, I collected the plates and cups and put them in the kitchen. When I returned to the sofa, he was still watching the movie. We sat on opposite ends of the sofa. I sat down, grabbed the blanket that lay along the sofa, and placed it over my legs, which were on the first two cushions. Donte never moved; however, after a few moments, he made his way closer to my side of the sofa. He stood up, moved the blanket, lifted my legs, and sat on the second cushion. Then he placed my legs across his lap.

When he put his arm along the sofa, I scooted closer, leaning on his shoulder, and he cradled his arm around me, placing his hand on my shoulder. That's how we stayed the rest of the night. He never said a word, and neither did I; it was perfect. This was how it was supposed to be. By the time Tony was telling people "to say hello to his little friend," we were knocked out. We both were exhausted, thinking about the words unspoken and the feelings we had exhausted. I was relaxed until I woke up to an uneasy feeling. Donte wasn't gone, but we had company.

When I opened my eyes, Tony was blasting everyone with his gun. I was startled by the presence of Uncle of the Week, Roy, who sat on the arm of the sofa opposite Donte and me. I hated this dude; he didn't say much, just kept tossing his money around, and Regina ate that shit up. I, on the other hand, hated it because when he did speak, he was rude and disrespectful. He acted like he was smarter than everyone else and that only his perspective mattered. I watched Regina shrink around him, and that pissed me off even more. He sat there now, smoking a cigar with a look on his face like he owned the place. He kept puffing and just nodding his head without saying a word. I nudged Donte, who didn't even flinch; he just opened his eyes calmly and met Roy's stare with his emotionless glare and never said a word.

I broke the silence. "Can I help you? Regina ain't here," I said with an attitude.

"Yeah, I know… she's in AC with the ladies this weekend," he replied, still looking at Donte, who still didn't move.

"So… why are you here? Don't you have a home or somewhere else to go?" I asked.

He laughed and then turned his eyes to me mid-puff. "Yeah, and I am home. Your mama said I could stay here a while, so I invited some of my buddies to play cards tonight! So, if y'all can take this shit somewhere else, I'd appreciate it."

He got up and began turning on all the lights in the house. Boy, I wish I had a gun like Tony right now. I got up and folded the blanket, but Donte didn't move; he just sat up straighter but never took his eyes off Roy. What the hell am I gonna do now? I couldn't stay… Before I could finish my thought, Donte, still following Roy with his eyes, said, "Go get your stuff; you're not staying here."

I looked at him, and for a moment, he glanced at me and motioned with his eyes for me to go. Too afraid to leave him out there with Roy, I grabbed his hand and motioned for him to come with me. Reluctant at first, he didn't move, but after a few gentle pulls, he finally got up.

When we got to my room, he stood in the doorway facing the living room. Roy had turned on music and began making his way down the hall to Regina's room. He and Donte exchanged glares, and then he went into her room and slammed the door. I continued packing my things. "So, this is your little room, huh?" Donte finally broke the silence. "Like pink much?"

I just rolled my eyes. I knew he was trying to lighten the shitshow we were in; I appreciated it. Pink was my favorite color. Maybe it was a little much, but at least it was classy. Besides, what did he know? His damn room was pretty much black. "It's my favorite color," I replied.

"I know," he followed.

"What else do you know, Inspector Gadget?" I replied since he was such a smartass.

Before he could answer, Roy chimed in, "I know y'all better hurry up before the fellas get here." Roy, who had now changed, continued smoking his cigar and headed to the living room.

Donte grabbed my bag, and we headed back into the living room toward the front door. I made sure to lock the doors of the spare room before I left. I had no idea what type of friends Roy had, so I had to be cautious.

I made a beeline to the front door; Donte was behind me but a few paces back. When I opened the door, Roy's card buddies had just arrived with snacks and beer in hand.

"Hey, sexy, where you going?" one guy replied.

"Yeah, we need some entertainment for when we're done! I got $500 if you let me have my way," another guy replied.

Usually, I would have said something smart or immediately replied, but I froze. The thought of their advances becoming a reality sent fear throughout my body. I wanted to move and leave, but I couldn't. I just stood there and didn't say a word. However, when one guy went to touch my hair, I finally snapped, about to address him for attempting to disrespect me.

But Donte came from the other side of the door and stopped him mid-air. The guy knew he had obviously made a mistake. "My bad, playa; we ain't mean no harm… just having a little fun."

Donte didn't say a word, but based on his demeanor, he didn't need to. That *get the hell outta my way or it's about to be a problem* vibe was there. The fellas parted ways, and we walked past them.

I was about to say a few choice words, but Donte shook his head no and ushered me up the stairs. As I walked up the steps, I could feel Donte on my heels as if he were my shadow. I couldn't believe Regina would allow him access to the house with me there, especially without telling me. Why didn't she think? Better yet, why didn't she care? What if something happened to me? As the thoughts flooded my mind, I got angry and felt like I was reaching my breaking point or something. When we finally reached his apartment, he opened the door, and Miss Chyna was sitting on the sofa talking on the phone.

She glanced in our direction and knew something was wrong. "Hey, I'ma call you back," she said to whoever was on the phone.

"What's wrong with y'all? Shar, baby, what's wrong?" she asked after looking into our faces. I could barely explain everything to her as I felt the rage take over my body. Donte just went into the kitchen and stayed there.

When I finished, Miss Chyna nodded and gave me a big hug. "You did the right thing, baby; you can stay here as long as you need to. Rayna decided to stay with her dad longer, so her room is your room even when she comes back. I'll go make sure it's ready, and Keith will be happy to see you as well." Then she hugged me so tight as if to solidify her words. It was just what I needed.

I grabbed my bags and went to Rayna's room to put them down. Then I made my way back to the living room.

"Miss Chyna, I need to go get some air… I'm not going far." She just nodded, and I was out the door. The sense of rage now felt almost like a panic attack. Donte was still in the kitchen when I rushed out. I wanted to go back home and make noise, but I decided against it. I wanted to go outside, but I didn't want to risk running into Roy or his people. I felt trapped, so I went to my spot in the laundry room.

When I finally made it there, I broke down crying. I couldn't stop the tears or the emotions pouring out of me. I put my forehead against the wall and screamed, letting it all out. I grabbed my phone and called Regina; she deserved to feel some of this as it poured out of me. However, she didn't answer, and her phone went straight to voicemail. When her voicemail message finished, I was ready to leave a message, but the box was full. I ended the call, even more pissed off.

I needed to get whatever I felt out, and before I knew it, I was talking out loud. "How could she be so stupid! Let that bum-ass dude stay in the house with me alone! What if something happened to me? What if they would have…" The thought of rape made me want to throw up. I had never actually experienced sex, but I'd been violated on several occasions. In those situations, I froze just like I did in the apartment, and that made me mad. It was as if I felt I deserved it since I didn't fight back.

Thinking about my reaction in those situations, including this one, made me angrier. I punched the concrete wall a few times. I didn't feel any pain, but I knew it would hurt later. As my body shook, my vision was filled with tears. I couldn't breathe because the emotions had taken over me. "I can't understand why she can't just be a real mother who gives a damn about me." I spoke as if I was waiting for the universe to respond, but there was no one there but me—or so I thought. I didn't hear him come in, but I felt him in that moment. Usually, I would try to straighten up, but I didn't have the strength. I felt weak, sick, just completely empty inside. My hands were throbbing, but I didn't care; what's more pain when you're already broken?

I barely had the strength to turn away from the wall. Donte stood behind me and put his hands on my shoulders. I was tired, but I didn't have the strength to sit down. He eventually sat on the bench attached to the nearby folding table and slowly pulled me back with his hands by my hips. He turned me around slowly and sat me down on his lap, and I just melted into him. This made me cry even harder; he was drenched in my tears and covered in all the emotions I had to let go of. He didn't say a word but held me tighter in the hardest moments of my life. He gently caressed my back as I calmed down. When I finally came to, it felt like hours later. There was nothing else to feel, say, or think… I was just broken to the point where I couldn't even move.

If you've ever felt empty, it's like you deserted your body and can't even conceive when you will ever feel full again. That's how I felt—so lost in my thoughts and feelings that reality did not exist. I sat for so long in my thoughts that I forgot Donte was still holding me. He never said a word, but I could feel him breathing, and eventually, our breaths became in sync. I couldn't look at him; what was there even to say? I slowly pulled away from him so I could wipe my face and blow my nose. He sat patiently while I worked up the courage to look in his direction. The feeling I usually had when I met his gaze was gone. I was a blank canvas, and I didn't care if he saw it. When I turned around, he searched my eyes for any emotion and found none.

He motioned for me to come back and sit next to him. I sat on the bench and put my head down on my folded arms while looking at him. We didn't say anything; we just looked at each other. Eventually, he pulled my arm, and I lifted my head as he put my arm around him. We hugged as he rested his chin on my head. When I sat up, he kissed my forehead and stood up. He nodded, and I did the same, then he ushered me from the laundry room to the apartment. When we arrived, it was dark and felt empty. He guided me to the kitchen to get an ice pack for my bruised knuckles. He placed the ice over them and I didn't even flinch. I looked up at him, and he stared at me.

"What do you think of me now?" I whispered. "Are you still intrigued by these pieces?" I didn't move, and neither did he.

"Nothing has changed, Sharnel," he said while looking into my eyes. I heard him, but part of me couldn't receive it, so I held on to my doubt and looked away from him. We were both quiet, then he finally broke the silence.

"C'mon, let's sit on the sofa." I didn't respond, just followed him to the sofa. Donte grabbed the remote and turned on the TV; he didn't even turn it up very loud, but I didn't care… I just wanted to be in deafening silence. He grabbed the pillow and the blanket, laid the pillow across his legs, and I immediately fell into place. He laid the blanket over me, and that was that. With his hand on my back, I eventually fell asleep.

When I woke up, I was almost unsure of where I was. I was scared for a second until I saw Rayna's picture of her and P on the nightstand. They looked so happy. As I began to wonder about their relationship, I contemplated whether I would ever find that happiness... hell, would I ever find security? It was too much to process, so I rolled over to face the wall and fell asleep. When I woke up again, it was dark. I lay there and wondered what was next. What if Regina never came back? Would I ever be able to go home? If she did, would she believe what I told her? What if Donte hadn't been there? I started to feel sick all over again. I cried myself to sleep again; the what-ifs became too much. I thought I heard someone come in later that night, but I was too numb to see who it was. I figured it was Miss Chyna just checking in.

After coming out of a 48-hour trance, I finally sat up in bed. When I found the strength to actually get up, I heard Keith whisper, "Is she coming out today?" That made my heart flutter a bit. I couldn't hear the response, only the footsteps down the hall. In between my sleeping spells, I purposely waited until everyone was gone or sleep before I made any moves. I avoided everyone, only going to the bathroom when no one was around. At night, Donte's door was cracked, and the light was off when I walked past. He didn't come out, and I didn't go in. He never slept with his door open, so that made me feel a little special.

When I finally got up for good, everyone in the house was gone. I went to the bathroom and showered for what seemed like an hour, got dressed, and made the bed. When I made it to the living room, it was empty, but I could still see Donte and me on the sofa from days before. I imagined him carrying me to Rayna's room, putting me in bed, and covering me. Then kissing my cheek, just like he had at P's house the night before graduation. That thought made me smile. If I was sure of anything, I was sure he cared. I surveyed the empty room and noticed a note on the table in the dining room from Miss Chyna.

Hey Baby Girl, there's lunch in the fridge. Eat as much as you want and just relax. We will be waiting when you're ready to come out. Call me if you need anything; love you. P.S. – Rayna has been calling every day to check on you; she will be home soon.

I love that lady. I made my way to the kitchen and found a sandwich waiting for me. I grabbed half the sandwich and some water. I didn't know if I would eat it, but I should try. As I was about to exit the kitchen, I heard keys in the front door. Maybe Miss Chyna came home for lunch? It didn't bother me; if anything, I'd welcome the company. I sat down at the table and waited for the door to open; it was Donte.

When he saw me at the table, he didn't say a word. I nodded, and he returned it and closed the door. He walked from the door down the platform and two steps to the dining room. He took a seat in the chair next to mine, so we were face to face.

Looking at my untouched food, he said, "Not hungry yet?"

I replied, "I just sat down; the other half is in the fridge if you want it."

Without taking his eyes off me, he nodded. Why does he keep staring? What is it that he wants to say? However, I was the one who needed to speak first so I spoke nonchalantly. In my mind, if I spoke as if nothing happened maybe I could resolve what was plaguing me faster.

Clearing my throat, I spoke, "thank you for the other night, I appreciate it."

Nodding his head and looking away as if to consider my words and reaction, he said, "You good, glad I was there."

My mind flooded with what-ifs, and I began to feel sick again. I pushed the sandwich away, unable to eat it. "If you hadn't…" I started, but my voice cracked, and he cut me off.

"I'm glad I was," and he touched my hand. But the touch was too much, and I eased away. Donte didn't look insulted; if anything, he looked like he understood.

I cleared my throat and tried to regain my composure before continuing, "I'll be outta y'all's hair today. Regina should be back, and I guess everything will be back to normal." I stated the words as if I truly believed them, but the thought of going home made me depressed. I wished I could be anywhere but there, especially with her.

Donte didn't say a word, but his face displayed uncertainty about my thought process. "Maybe I'll take her up on that offer to go to Atlanta; she claims I know someone there or some shit. Maybe I'll go… only never come back. Not like she or anyone else would give a fuck!"

As the words left my lips, Donte's reaction looked like I had hit him with a mac truck or something. "Fuck you mean, you going back?"

He couldn't comprehend the words I was saying. "Atlanta, and not coming back?!?!? That's some funny shit, ma G." He was disappointed by my statements. He got close to my face so I could see his reaction clearly.

"Sharnel, you just gonna run away like some little ass kid because of that bitch-ass nigga? We talked about this, man. You already know Regina ain't shit! But you running anyway? REALLY, SHARNEL!" Donte yelled.

I didn't even react; I just sat there, broken, unable to respond as he continued. "Fuck outta here! Who the fuck you got to protect you in Atlanta? Explain that shit to me! Your ass don't like too many people, so who you gonna run to, huh? You want security, but your ass always fucking running as soon as shit gets rough." He stood up and walked to the other side of the room. I just sat there with a blank expression. What he said made sense, but I still didn't understand his reaction. I was too numb to comprehend any of this.

I mustered up the only words I could find. "Donte, what do you want me to do, huh? Stay here forever? I can't keep crowding y'all like this." It was an ideal situation in some ways, but unrealistic in others. I was calm at first, but as the words came out, tears formed in my eyes. Then all the pain rushed back to me, and I started to lash out. I stood up as I continued. "She already made it clear this dude and all others are more important than me! I'm sorry if I can't just suck that shit up; it hurts ALL THE FUCKING TIME! So yes, as much as I don't want to… if I can get away from it and her, why the fuck not!" I stopped to catch my breath and tried to wipe my face as tears trickled down, but it was pointless. "If you hadn't been there, who knows what would have happened to me?"

Now I was crying for real, but I didn't care. I stepped closer to him as I cried hysterically. "I don't have a job, no damn future at this point, just a fucking hopeless crying ass female." The words were harsh, but it's how I felt, so I leaned into them. "Nobody wants to deal with that especially one begging someone to love them, right?" That last piece was a dagger to his heart. I felt it as I said it, and his face showed it. "Don't nobody want to deal with that shit, nor should they have to! Fuck outta here!" I yelled, crossing the line of no return. It was as if I had just spit on everything we had gone through in the past 48 hours, then added lighter fluid to it and watched it burn.

Donte backed away from me and gave me an astonished look that reflected his next words: "FUCK IT and FUCK YOU." I was completely done—just push me over into the grave and cover me. In my mind, he confirmed that I was not worth it. I stood dazed, nodding my head.

He walked back out the door, slamming it so hard that the windows rattled. I packed my stuff and headed back to the third floor. Might as well enjoy the hell that is my life; whatever happens, happens. I walked back into the cold, dark apartment and looked around. It was apparent Regina had returned, but Uncle of the Week had made his exit. I made the trek to my room and closed the door. I just sat in the room, which felt dark and lonely. I texted Miss Chyna, thanked her, and let her know I had left. She commented that she understood, but her door was always open. I knew hers was, but Donte's was shut, and I think I bolted it shut this time. Fuck Sharnel, you really did it this time.

CHAPTER 16

The next day after returning to the apartment, I finally came out of my room. As I made my way to the bathroom, there was movement in Regina's room. "Sharnel, when you finish, come on in here!" After Regina didn't answer my call the last time, I had no interest in being in her presence, but it was time to have it out. After taking my time in the bathroom, I entered Regina's room, which was filled with boxes and packing material. Seeing everything, I immediately became pissed. I knew she didn't think I was moving with her and Uncle of the Week after everything that happened.

I looked fiercely at her, waiting for an explanation. "I'm moving out, so what are you going to do?" she asked as if it were nothing.

"What do you mean you're moving out?" This was the last thing I needed to hear right now; I still had nothing planned and no job. Regina knew this, but again she didn't include me in her plans. This is why I couldn't be bothered with her.

"Well, you're going to be of age, and I've done my job, so I'm moving with Brad," she said proudly. Who the fuck was Brad? Not that it mattered. In my eyes, he was already just as horrible as the other Uncles, especially for leaving me ass out. I just stared at her. It was now pointless to even tell her about my interaction with Roy; she had moved on and was apparently moving out.

I just stood there in disbelief and finally spoke, "Where are you moving to? When were you going to tell me?" I said, exhausted from the conversation and yet another layer of bullshit added to my life.

Regina acted as if my questions were intrusive and snapped back, "Look, I'm telling you now. We are looking for a house about an hour from here, and besides, it's time you live on your own." I pondered her statement with a look of confusion and just balled my aggression inside without saying a word. "I mean, you stay at Chyna's so much, maybe you should live there. Maybe you and Donte can finally be a thing!"

Was she serious? Is that the only option she saw for me—banking on a man like she did? Not wanting to entertain Regina anymore, I wanted to leave, but she continued talking, so I stayed. "Maybe they will let you rent the apartment, huh?" she replied as if that were a realistic possibility.

"What am I going to pay them with? Hopes and dreams?" Regina just shrugged. "Look, I paid for this month and the rest of the summer through September. That's plenty of time for you to figure your shit out." I didn't even reply because it didn't matter. It was time to spring into action; I had to make a plan, and soon. This conversation was pointless, and I was over Regina and her foolishness. I went to my room to pick up my keys and hurried out the door. As I walked toward the front door, she yelled, "You could say thank you, Sharnel, ungrateful ass!"

After slamming the apartment door, I locked it and took a breath. "God! What is my life? She gets on my damn nerves!" I said aloud as I stomped up the stairs, huffing and puffing, mumbling a few other choice words to myself. "Calling me ungrateful… is she out of her damn mind!" I was so lost in my thoughts that I didn't see Keith, Miss Chyna, and Donte approaching the front door of the building at the same time I did.

"Shar Shaaaarrrrrr!" Keith yelled and hugged my legs. Urgh, this kid is too cute. The hug felt like the greatest joyful pain. I immediately tried to change my expression to greet my favorite little guy with a hug and kiss. He could kick me in the face, and I'd still love him. Despite my obvious exhaustion, I pulled it together.

"Hey, Keithy Face! Hey, Miss Chyna! How y'all doing?" I purposely didn't address Donte; he said fuck it and fuck me, so that was that.

Miss Chyna shook her head as I purposely shaded Donte, who brushed past them out the door without acknowledging me either.

"You didn't say hi to Donte, Shar Shar," Keith said unsurely. I smiled; this kid is too damn smart. So, I came up with a quick reply.

"I wanted to say hi to you so bad I forgot my Keithy Face!" I picked him up and hugged him tightly while he screamed. Miss Chyna's reaction immediately called bullshit.

"Y'all need to grow up, Miss Chyna," she said, shaking her head. Here we go, Miss Chyna was going to let me have it. It didn't matter; I was numb enough. What was one more tongue-lashing? We proceeded out the door.

"Keith, go find Donte; let me and Shar talk a minute." We could see he was at the car warming it up for them to leave.

Once Keith ran off at full speed, she continued, "I know y'all are mad at each other for what only God knows now! But this gotta stop; I can't deal with either one of you. He's walking around pissed and mumbling."

I instantly smiled at him being miserable too, but she corrected me immediately.

"Don't smile; you're just as wrong as he is and acting the same way. I'm sick of you both!" I stopped smiling, and she continued while stopping to face me.

"Look, baby, I know you got a bad deal and it's tough. Lord knows I have been there, but you gotta let someone in, honey. You can't stay to yourself to 'protect yourself.' You deserve love… furthermore, love ain't supposed to hurt." She took my face into her hands, and the damn tears fell again as she continued, "What I'm about to say is not to sway you in any way… it's just my observation, okay?"

I nodded and waited for her to continue.

After taking a breath, Miss Chyna spoke from her heart. "You deserve love, and my son loves you… he always has. He's just as locked up inside as you are, but when you two get together (even if y'all are bickering), I've never seen you both so free. But neither one of you can pour into that love until you fix yourselves as individuals." She began to wipe my tears and continued, "Now, I'm not saying don't engage until you're fixed; I believe y'all being at least cordial will help repair the brokenness a little faster. Y'all just need to stop shutting each other out! Now I'm not telling you anything I haven't already preached to him." She took her hands down from my face and grabbed my hands in hers, then said, "Just remember, nothing will change if you leave now… it will only put a growing ocean between you two."

Once she finished, Keith and Donte were walking back toward us. Fuck, he's going to see me crying again. Urgh, get it together, damn it. Miss Chyna released my hands just as Keith ran up to embrace her.

"Time to go, Mom Mom!"

Donte approached us and didn't say a word; we both stared at each other. I knew he saw my eyes were wet from the tears, but he didn't even seem fazed, which hurt, but I got it.

"Well, we gotta go, but our girl will be home tomorrow. So, be ready for family dinner at 7 p.m.; I don't care what your excuse is," she said, then pointed and looked at both of us. "You better be there."

Never leaving our gaze, we both nodded, and they went on their way while I went mine. So, he's miserable too, huh? Good for him, evil ass. I knew our argument was completely my fault, but it's true; misery loves company, so mentally, I was glad he was sitting on the mental sofa too!

Later that day, I went back to Miss Kena's to get my hair done. The braids felt like they held my trauma, and I needed a fresh hairstyle. I decided to go with a summertime ponytail. It was straight; my hair was slicked back with a slight bang swooped off to the side. It would hold me about two weeks while I decided on my next move. Lucky for me, she was too busy tending to her kids to talk today… I wasn't mad at it. Less talking meant I could be in and out while not tapping into what was plaguing me.

"Trying something new today, huh?" Ms. Kena replied once she was done.

"Yes, ma'am, trying to change my karma a bit."

Ms. Kena laughed, "You don't change karma; you just manifest change to attract new energies, ma dear."

Now that was something I could get with; the energies lately were completely fucked! So, I welcomed anything that reflected change, which now started with this new style.

I tried to pay Miss Kena, and she refused, saying, "No, ma dear, I hear your mama is moving, so I want you to use the money to stay here… we're gonna be lonely without you. Let us know what we can do."

Damn, nothing was sacred in this neighborhood. Everyone knew your business before you did. I couldn't do anything but smile and shake my head. She kissed my forehead, and I could feel the emotions build up again. Damn, I gotta stop being so emotional; this shit is getting old. I thanked Miss Kena and told her I would keep her updated.

It was after 10:30 p.m. when I left Miss Kena's apartment. As I left her apartment, I ran into Mr. James, who was letting in baby mama number 3 (or 4). He smiled as he held his apartment door open.

"Ohhhhh, who you trying to look cute for? You're gonna make my man Donte beat somebody up." Mr. James winked; his comment caused me to laugh out loud, and I rolled my eyes. As I made my way down the next flight of stairs, I wasn't ready to head home, so I decided to sit out front of the building. However, there was a crowd outside, so I almost decided against it but went outside when I saw P. Him, Paul, and a few other dudes were just sitting and talking mess.

"Okay, new duo, I see you!" yelled Paul. "Looks good."

I appreciated the compliment, but Paul was being messy. Plus, Tonya would flip her lid if she heard him talking to any girl.

"Thanks, Paul," I said, keeping it short and sweet while walking to the third step and stopping to lean against the wall by the handrail.

I was about to speak to the remaining fellas with the same sincerity, but then I saw Trav, who just walked up. His face pissed me off.

"Hey y'all," I spoke dryly. "What's up?" kicking myself for coming outside.

"Sup, Sista Shar!" P said, nodding my way. I returned the nod.

"Ain't y'all on the wrong stoop?" I asked since P lived in the next building.

"What, you neighborhood watch or something?" Trav asked, annoyed.

"Yeah, I am, and we don't allow riffraff around these parts," I said with an instant attitude.

"Be cool, Sista Shar; we just came to see a man about a horse and got caught up in a conversation," said P, which meant he came to get some weed from Mr. James, who secretly grew his own strain. P continued, "But I will be here more often since my baby is coming home tomorrow. I can't wait to see her… you coming to dinner tomorrow?"

I had completely forgotten about that. "Yeah, I'll be around there," I rolled my eyes at the thought of sitting like a happy family.

"Cool, I'm sure your husband will be there," P joked, then went inside to meet up with Mr. James. I'm sure he was trying to make me smile or give some other positive reaction.

However, before I could respond or react displaying my annoyance, Trav jumped in. "Oh, that dude Donte is the one getting in the 'virgin ass'; no wonder she's out here acting brand new," Trav said very salty.

Oh no he didn't. "The fuck you just say to me? Don't worry about what's going on here," I snapped back.

Trav smiled and stepped closer to the bottom step, putting his attention on me. "Yoooo, so that's the dude who almost saved you from almost getting…" I flew off the step and hit Trav right in his mouth. His lip was bleeding, but he just smiled while wiping his lip.

"You should watch who you step to, Sharnel; you never know who they're connected to," Trav said, spitting blood on the ground, still smiling.

I didn't know how he knew about the other night, but it didn't matter. His words sent me into a fury, and I let him have it not only for that time but for all the times I didn't react. I swung on Trav and kept swinging, cursing him out in the process.

"The fuck you say!" I purposely scratched him, which made him angry. Based on his body language, I knew he was going to retaliate. I was ready; there wasn't anything he could do to me at that point. However, when I went to match Trav's energy, P held me back.

"Yoo, Shar, what the fuck, man! Calm the fuck down!" P yelled, tightening his grip, but I was still going. I knew better than to put my hands on any man, especially after everything that happened with Eric. However, Trav wasn't a man; he was a coward. He was intentional about his bullshit and wanted me to react, so I gave him what he asked for. It was stupid, but I owned it and whatever happened next.

As P held me back, Paul leaned over to him and whispered something. "Da fuck!" P yelled as I kept charging at Trav. If he knew what Trav's statement meant, then Donte had told him about our interaction with Royal and his friends. P purposely loosened his grip for a few seconds, which allowed me to get more jabs in, which Trav successfully blocked.

"Say it again, go ahead and say it, say it again…you bitch-ass nigga! I will make you pay, you college boy gangsta; don't you ever disrespect me like that," I screamed.

The moment was short-lived, and P tightened his grip even more than before. Through tight lips, he whispered in my ear, "Shar, relax, man…relax!" I felt him loosening and tightening his grip as if to get my attention, but I didn't respond; better yet, I couldn't. I was on fire and wanted to hit Trav again. Trav's face was now red, and he finally charged at me, but Paul eventually stepped in and held him back.

"Fuck you, bitch! Thought you'd learn from Eric hitting your ass! But nah, that nigga dickin' you down got you feeling bold, huh!" I pushed harder, charging at Trav not only for his insinuation but now for lying on me.

Trav was about to say something else but was interrupted. "Something you want to say to me, Trav?" Donte stood emotionless beside Trav, waiting for his response. Trav turned to the side and stood eye to eye with Donte, whose demeanor was calm, which wasn't a good thing. I didn't even see him walk up or know where he came from. But his presence caused P to loosen his grip completely but not let me go.

"Nah, shorty obviously can't take a joke," Trav replied, looking at me then back at Donte.

"Nah, my dude, you was wrong…you provoked her with some bullshit," P replied seriously.

Donte looked at me for confirmation, but I didn't make eye contact with him. I kept my eyes on Trav.

Donte nodded, "Let her go, P; she good now," he said, now looking at Trav. P slowly backed off but stayed close enough to react if needed.

"Since it was a joke, how about you repeat it to me?" Donte stood calmly and waited for Trav to respond. Trav was silent and mentally weighed his options. When there was no response, Donte nodded and continued. "Now, Trav, do me a solid and apologize to her," he said in a calm voice, motioning towards me with his head.

Trav looked at me and then back at Donte. Feeling bold, he sarcastically laughed, "I ain't responsible for her feelings; ain't that your job!" I was hot all over again. Before I could move, Donte put his arm out in my direction for me to stop. Why the hell was he holding me back? Da fuck!

Donte cleared his throat and stepped closer to Trav. His relaxed demeanor disappeared, and he spoke grimacingly while putting his hands in Trav's face. "I'ma ask you again…" He didn't need to say anything else, as his words were enough for Trav to rethink his decision. Looking at me, Trav met my gaze.

"I apologize."

Everyone knew Trav was all talk; he'd never been in a fight with a dude ever. However, it was rumored he smacked around his ladies with no problem. In my mind, this was yet another reason to stand toe-to-toe with him and smack his ass around. He then turned to Donte, "My apologies, brah; that wasn't called for." Donte just nodded, and Trav walked away as if nothing ever happened.

Donte wasn't one to hold grudges, but he would remember Trav's actions and deal with him accordingly going forward. I was stunned; I couldn't believe what I just saw. Now I was pissed at Donte, who was now talking to P while the other guys began talking amongst themselves as if nothing ever happened.

I turned to Donte pushing his arm to get his attention. "Fuck that apology; I wanted his head and now!" Donte's face warned me to relax, but I didn't care, so I continued my tirade. "That's it! His bitch-ass gets to walk off; I should have hit him again!" I yelled, pointing at Trav. Donte hadn't realized I was the one who hit Trav, although he wasn't surprised. He shook his head in frustration when he saw my knuckles, which were bleeding. He grabbed me by the arm and led me into the building while all the dudes watched us walk inside.

Unfazed by their stares, I kept fussing and yelling once we were inside the building. I didn't care if all eyes were on us. Still holding on to me, Donte was about to walk upstairs, but I snatched away from him in frustration.

"Do you know what he said to me? Huh?"

Donte just stood there, looking like he didn't care.

"I can't believe that's all he got; salty-ass dude for nothing...I can't believe you..."

Donte flared his nostrils. He obviously had enough and did something I'd never seen him do. He scooped me up and threw me over his shoulder and headed upstairs. I looked outside, and P just shook his head before he and the others walked away. Was he serious? This was complete bullshit! I hoped he didn't think this would shut me up because it wouldn't! Donte was uninterested in anything I said, but I kept ranting as my ponytail flapped upside down.

"Put me down! I can walk on my own! You gonna mess up my hair!" I yelled. He just kept grumbling about something as I continued. Once we got into Miss Chyna's apartment, he didn't put me down.

He kept me on his shoulder, went to the kitchen to get the same ice pack as before from the freezer, and then walked down the hall to his room. It was then that I lowered my voice to a hiss.

"We're inside; you can put me the fuck down now!"

He still was not listening and opened the door to his room. He slid me down from his shoulder and sat me on the bed as I kept fussing. "You gonna continue to ignore me, or answer my questions or nah, Donte?"

He went back to the bedroom door, slammed it shut, and locked it. It was then that I stopped talking.

He watched me and very sternly said, "Are you finished?" He was obviously annoyed and tired of my shenanigans.

"Whatever, Donte; I'm tired of fussing anyway," I said, then just laid back on the bed.

He approached the bed with the ice pack, took my hand, and placed it on my stomach, then put the ice pack on it. I winced at the feeling of the ice on my bruised knuckles. Then he hovered over me on the bed.

"This shit is getting old. You need to relax with that angry shit. Control your emotions; you're too old for this shit."

Now I was pissed all over again. I had every right to defend myself. Trav was in the wrong, and he should know that. I was about to get up so I could give him another piece of my mind. However, Donte already peeped game and held me back with one hand.

"Sharnel, relax, man! Stop fighting me on everything! You can't always get your way! Just relax before you make things worse, damn."

"Urgh, fine, I'll lay here, but I ain't gonna like it," I mumbled, then folded my arms in protest.

He stood up and sat on the edge of the bed, holding his head as if it hurt. It was almost midnight, and we both were obviously tired. I knew going home wasn't an option, so I got comfortable.

"Guess I'm spending the night! Can I at least get a scarf for my hair, please?" I said, annoyed.

Donte looked back at me and grunted. He went to his closet, got a shirt and shorts, tossed them at me, then left the room, and I changed. When he came back, he had a scarf from Rayna's room. I tied my hair, laid down on the pillow near the wall, and he cut off the light. I could see him walk toward the bed since the moon was shining through the slightly opened blinds. I watched him take off his shirt and put on his lounge pants. Neither one of us smiled; we just looked intently at each other. I didn't take my eyes off him, and he didn't look away either. He opened the blinds a little more, and I could see him even more. Then he laid in the bed next to me and stared at the ceiling, and I did the same.

We were quiet and took in the light while processing what happened. I loved moonlit nights, so this was perfect in my mind.

I didn't even care if we spoke. I was glad to not be alone tonight; I could use the company, even if it was silent.

Without even looking at me, he spoke. "Why you let him get to you like that?"

While staring at the ceiling, I replied, "He was speaking on something he had no idea about, making a joke that I should have…" I stopped and then continued, "Who and what we do ain't got nothing to do with him. He's just mad 'cause I don't want his dusty ass," I replied.

"You know he was trying to get a rise out of you, so what was the point? Do you really think your reaction was defending us?" Donte asked skeptically.

"Us?" I boldly asked. He didn't reply, so I continued. "Whether there is an us or not, I don't allow no one to disrespect what's mine."

Donte grunted; I was missing his point, and I knew it but kept going. "I don't care if all we do is fight and hurt each other; it's none of his damn business!" Then I finished with, "Even if that's not how it's supposed to be!"

He seemed a bit surprised by my response as his face softened, and he turned his head toward me. "What's yours?" I didn't know what to say, so I didn't reply.

"I don't know, man," he said before looking at the ceiling again.

I wanted to protect his space and time, but I had to get something off my chest. So, I turned toward him and gently turned his face toward me.

"I hear what you're saying, Donte; I do…but I also feel what you're not saying. 'I don't know' is not enough; it's obviously more than that because we keep finding ourselves here." I touched his arm, rubbing my hand up and down it. I thought I was done, but I was about to say something that made my throat want to close. But I couldn't help it. "I love you, Donte. I can't apologize for how I feel or wanting to protect you, even if I did/do overreact a bit."

He just looked over at me and didn't immediately react. I removed my hand from his arm, then looked at the ceiling while I began to panic mentally. What the hell did I just say? OMG, Shar Shar Shar, what the hell, woman…his ass didn't even respond. Fuck, fuck, fuck, fuck! I immediately wanted to get up and throw up at the thought of my confession. Then he grabbed my hand and pulled me closer to his body so that he could hold me. He made sure there was no space between us; that's what we needed at this moment—no more space. It was then that I felt better.

As he held me, I could have melted right there. Maybe passed out. He didn't need to say anything; this was everything. I could have lived in this moment forever. I slid a little higher so I could be eye to eye with him.

"I love you, Donte." I couldn't help myself, so I lifted up to kiss his cheek slowly. When he didn't resist, I kissed him again, closer to his mouth. When he still didn't resist, I kissed him once again, but with more passion on his lips. I grinded my body against his. Kissing him was becoming the best experience I'd ever felt. My lips on his skin and his body touching me completely relaxed me. All the aggression, tension, and anguish we both felt disappeared. As I planted another small kiss, I could feel his grip get tighter on my waist, and I could feel him further melting into my skin. He didn't push me away at any point but drew me closer as if we were one skin. I couldn't breathe; it was so intoxicating. I didn't want it to end. Having him at this moment made everything that happened worth it.

We kissed for what seemed like hours. I was ready to take it all the way. However, when I tried to pull him on top of me, he resisted... I knew I had found my boundary. The moonlight allowed me to see his face more clearly; he looked almost high. I kissed his lips once more, then slowly made my way to his neck, kissing every inch of it. I could feel him grip my ass. As much as I wanted to seize the moment—and I knew he did too, as I could feel Donte's arousal—sex was completely off-limits, so I didn't push it.

In the midst of our touching and kissing, he whispered something in my ear. I couldn't make it out at first, but when he said it again, I instantly caught it: "…I love you too, Shar." He finally said it, and I knew he meant it… YESS! I was freaking out in my mind. I tried to pull him closer, if even possible. He laughed and backed away, which indicated he wasn't having it.

We settled back into our respective positions and lay side by side while we looked at the ceiling. Neither of us said a word, but when he looked over and smiled at me, that sealed the deal for me.

"You finally got your answer. You satisfied?" he said sarcastically.

I nodded yes.

"But you already knew the answer; you've always known," he said, then rolled over and kissed my cheek. I was in love for real. Donte A. Wright was the man for me. I couldn't stop smiling and replaying what had just happened in my mind! Donte just shook his head as he watched me.

He looked back at the ceiling, then spoke again, "So, you still running away?"

I shook my head no. "Well, not permanently. I mean, I am going to the beach for a while… but I will be back, I promise."

He just nodded. "And I'll calm down, I promise." I rolled over on my side to face the wall, then slid closer to him. He rolled over and held me, placing his mouth close to my neck while he held me from behind.

"Shar, I still need to process this," he said, squeezing my waist a bit. "But I do love you, and I want you."

I nodded and turned around one last time. "Maybe we can talk about it when I get back." He didn't respond, just looked at me.

"But I want you to know, I don't want anyone else, Donte… it's always been you." He kissed me again slowly, and I rolled back over. We eventually fell asleep holding each other, spooning as some people call it. Having him hold me was the safest I'd ever felt in my whole life. I woke up a few times that night to make sure I wasn't dreaming. It was real; I could feel him breathing and holding me. I kept mentally pinching myself to ensure this was real. I couldn't stop smiling and inching closer to him, as if that were possible.

I thought Donte was asleep until I heard him mumble, "Take your ass to sleep, Sharnel!" Then he kissed my neck and went back to breathing deeply. It was perfect! No matter what happened, I knew he'd always be there for me. I wanted to move forward and just figure it all out together, but I understood waiting and would do so… hell, I'd waited for him this long.

I thought back to a conversation with Tonya, not too long after we made up.

We were sitting on the front steps of the building like usual, just her and me. She apologized for her comment regarding Donte. I explained I was sorry for hurting her feelings, but I couldn't apologize for my reaction. Tonya said she understood why I had love for the Wrights, but she specifically asked me why I liked Donte. I took a moment to think about it. The truth was, Donte and I shared a lot of intimate moments. I was open with him in ways I wasn't with her and Rayna. I didn't want to explain all of our interactions, so I told her, I liked him because he understood, protected, and never judged me. Which was true, but there was more to it… a lot more. Miss Chyna was right; he opened up to me in many ways, and I did the same. He wasn't always as forward as I was, but he did show it with his words and actions, both seen and unseen, which I didn't always acknowledge, especially when he pissed me off. Besides the family, P, and Mr. Charles, Donte didn't put himself out there for anyone. Even Trina with he was a shell of himself, she would have realized if she truly knew him. I ended my statement to Tonya by saying, "We just have something deeper than words… he's seen and been through a lot with me." Tonya smiled, "I can see why you're so protective of him… I hope it works out for you, Shar. I'm happy for you… I hope to find that one day." I smiled, then nudged her shoulder. "You deserve it and you're worth it… just remember, don't search for it; that shit will find you."

I smiled at the thought, then took my hand, put it on his, and finally closed my eyes. When I awoke, he was still holding me as if he had never moved. The sun peeked in through the blinds; it was beautiful. I just enjoyed the peace for a while. I knew we had to get up soon because Rayna would be arriving, but I was in no rush… this was where I belonged. I was about to close my eyes again; however, I instantly panicked when I thought about Miss Chyna. OMG, what if she saw me leaving? The thought snapped me out of my little oasis, and I freaked out. I started to ease away from Donte, but when I rolled over, he was awake. He didn't say anything, nor did I, despite the horrified look on my face.

"How you feel, Rocky?" he asked with a straight face.

"My hand hurts like hell, but I'm good," I replied and smiled at the sight of his face.

Then there was a knock on the door. I jumped and moved to get up, but he stopped me. He mouthed, *relax* I laid down and covered my face with my hands.

"Donte, we gonna be late if you don't get up so we can get Rayna," Miss Chyna yelled.

"I'm up!" he replied, then moved my hands and shook his head almost laughing.

He was about to embrace me with a kiss when Miss Chyna spoke again, "Oh Donte, ask Sharnel if she can watch Keith while we go to the airport. I know she's in there!" Miss Chyna laughed as she walked away.

I was horrified again; Donte just shook his head. "Dang, your mama knows everything," I replied.

"Yeah, I'm sure the neighborhood watch told her about your main event last night," Donte replied.

Of course, they did, why not! I thought about everything that had happened. I didn't regret my interaction with Trav, but I regretted that Donte got involved. I absolutely hated that.

Donte kissed my cheek, got up, and went to his closet to pick out clothes. I lay in his bed, just looking at the ceiling. "Donte, I'm sorry about last…"

He said, "Let me stop you there," then faced me. I finally sat up in bed and leaned against the headboard so I could see him. "I know you can handle yourself. You had already hit Trav and were going for more before I got there." He stopped, then came closer. "If we gonna do this," he said, motioning between me and him, "you gotta let me protect you. But that temper can't be the reason why. Fix that shit!"

I knew he was serious, so I nodded okay then he walked back to his closet.

"Shar, I gave you that necklace not only because of Granny, but because it symbolizes maturity and change. A reminder to for you to calm the fuck down, stop fighting the same bullshit you've moved passed. Didn't think I needed to write that shit down, but maybe I should have, huh?"

I immediately frowned and rolled my eyes. I knew what the damn dragonfly represented I'd done my research—such an asshole. Donte laughed at my reaction to his bullshit response but then got closer to me and whispered, "It's also a reminder that I'm always here to protect you, got it?"

I softened my face, nodded okay and he kissed me before he went back to his closet. "How long you going to the beach for?"

I finally sat up on the edge of the bed to stretch. "I'll be gone about a week."

"Who else is going with you?" I took a breath because I knew this was not going to end well. "No one… going by myself!"

He shot me a look as if I had said something wrong. "What, Donte? I'll be fine alone."

He shook his head, then turned back toward his closet. "You know I don't like that shit, Sharnel!"

I knew it, but it was what it was. "Well, I already planned it, and it's paid for… I'm not backing out. I deserve this…"

"I know, and I'm not saying you shouldn't go. I'm just saying you shouldn't go alone." I folded my arms and rolled my eyes. "Matter of fact, how you getting there?" he asked as he decided on a shirt.

"I'm driving, Donte… Regina is giving me her car for the week."

He shook his head again. "So, you're driving three-plus hours to spend the week by yourself?"

I slid off the edge of the bed and stood behind him, leaning my head against his back. Then I put my arms around him and laced my hands across his stomach. I whispered, "Yes, and I'll be fine." I was expecting him to protest again, but he didn't.

He just continued what he was doing, then switched subjects. "Don't think I didn't notice you trying to get some last night," he said, looking from the corner of his eye.

I just laughed, still holding on to him. "You ain't ready for that yet!" I laughed again and was about to call his bluff.

"We'll get to that when the time is right, cool?" He waited for me to say something.

"Okay, Donte! Let me head out and get cleaned up before y'all leave. I'll see you later." I gathered my clothes, then headed to the door. He grabbed me close for one last kiss before I left, not before whispering, "Don't let last night go to your big head," then he squeezed my butt. He opened the door and rushed to the shower, and I headed home. This dude.

CHAPTER 17

Miss Chyna and Donte were off to pick up Rayna while Keith and I went to Miss Kena's house to prepare decorations. Miss Kena and I blew up balloons and tied them to weights while the kids played in her room. "Ma Lord, did Chyna think Rayna gone to war? Why so much stuff, eh?"

I just smiled and shook my head. "Nothing is small with this family." We continued to blow up balloons. In true kid fashion, they got bored playing inside and decided to go out front. Since Mr. James was out front with his kids, Miss Kena let them go outside. As I was putting helium into a balloon, Miss Kena looked over at me.

"Sharnel, can I ask you a question?" I nodded my head and kept blowing up the balloon. "I know you're a virgin, but have you ever been… touched?" I could tell from her tone she wasn't sure how to broach the subject, but she seemed concerned.

I didn't say anything, but from the look on my face, she knew I had. "Was it more than once?" I just looked at her, nodded yes, and kept blowing up the balloon. I stood there and thought about some of the times I had those near-sexual experiences. I was young, naïve in a lot of ways. I thought back to an article I read about the symptoms of overly sexualized teens. I always wondered if I was one of those people. At an early age, I knew what sex was; it was all around me, and I'd even heard it while I was in the same room. As uncomfortable as it made me, I was drawn to it. I was curious; I felt like a fiend for a drug I'd never tried. I'd only kissed boys, but I knew what it felt like to be groped, to feel a rush of hormones all over my body. I'd even let a penis touch my lip one time. I was humiliated when he went back and told everyone what I'd done. I swore I'd never let anyone do that to me again. It started a new mindset for me: never let anyone punk you. So, I decided to take control of myself and never give myself to anyone else until I was ready.

Although none of the uncles of the week ever touched me, I had some who looked at me a little too hard or hugged a little too long. I was so lost in my thoughts that I put too much air into the balloon; it popped, scaring me and Miss Kena. The sound startled me so much that I was paralyzed. My hand was shaking so much that Miss Kena had to come over and relieve me from the balloons. She took over blowing them up, and I put the weights on instead.

"Miss Kena, can I ask you a question?" I said after a few minutes. She stopped what she was doing and nodded. I cleared my throat.

"How did you know?"

She stared at me. "I know that howl anywhere." I knew then she heard me in the laundry room. I also realized she too had experienced something similar. "Only, I didn't have someone to hold me and protect me until years later," I knew she also saw Donte that night as well. I felt relieved that she understood, but sad that the two of us had a trauma bond.

"One more question, did you ever feel dirty or uncomfortable with the thought of sex after it happened? Like, did you blame yourself?" I asked, trying to understand what I was feeling.

She grabbed my hand and looked into my eyes. "Sharnel, baby, I felt it a lot. The shame I felt was overwhelming. I felt like that was everything people saw when they looked or talked about me. Like I was nothing but a girl who had been marked, kinda like a scarlet letter." She got quiet but then continued, "Then I found love; I found a great love… I found the love within. I found me. I rid myself of the shame and judgment. It was then that I allowed myself to truly fall in love. It was beautiful; it still is, and I hold it with me every day." She shook her head as if to bring herself back. "Now you have already found you… just need to open your eyes. Don't be afraid of being you… the healed version of yourself. God has blessed you; allow it to consume you, and for God's sake, open your eyes… what you need is already here." We both shared a smile. Miss Kena had done it again; I was reset. When we finished, the balloons and weights were perfect and ready for whatever Miss Chyna had planned next.

Since Miss Chyna went all out to welcome her baby back home. Rayna's welcome home ended up moving to the courtyard of the building because so many people wanted to have dinner. Mr.

Tony, Rayna's father, decided to escort her home, so of course, he was in charge of the grill. I remember him visiting when we were kids; he was so cool. Everyone loved him, and he treated everyone's kids like they were his own. He was one of the few men Donte's mean ass got along with, surprisingly. So, I was excited when Donte texted me and told me I couldn't wait to see him. When they got back, in true Rayna fashion, she ran off to see P, so I knew I would see her later.

When Miss Chyna walked into the apartment, Keith and I were watching TV. She asked me if I could get him ready and then help her with side dishes for dinner while Donte and Mr. Tony were outside putting together the grill they'd just brought. After I got Keith ready and laid him down for a nap, I met her in the kitchen to help.

"Hey baby, thank you for helping out…that daughter of mine is probably somewhere making me a young grandmother, unless I already am?" Miss Chyna stared at me, waiting for confirmation. I was shocked until she laughed, then I loosened up. "You know I'm messing with you; I know you're still a virgin," she said as she bumped me with her elbow.

In the back of my mind, I knew Miss Chyna wouldn't trip about me staying in Donte's room. Despite my advances last night, there was no way I'd ever have sex with him in her house. I had way too much respect for her, and it would just be weird as hell.

"But know, I do want grandbabies at some point— not too soon, but one day, please."

I just shook my head, and we finished preparing the sides. I loved Miss Chyna; she made situations like these easy and never uncomfortable.

After we finished cooking, I decided to go home to find something to wear. "Aight, Miss Chyna, I'm going home to get ready." She gave me the eye, then nodded.

"Okay, baby, well call or text me when you get there, and call if you need anything, got it?"

I smiled confidently and hugged her. "Yes ma'am, I definitely will." I walked towards the front door, and Miss Chyna walked towards her room to do the same while Keith took his nap.

After locking the door, I headed downstairs and ran into Mr. Tony and Donte. Seeing Donte caused me to smile immediately; however, I was also happy to see Mr. Tony.

"Hey Mr. Tony, I'm so happy to see you." Mr. Tony was always jovial and had jokes, so I wasn't surprised by his first comment and actions.

"Hey Tyson, how's my favorite girl?" he asked, acting like he was shadow boxing. Lord, who didn't know about last night? I wondered if he knew everything. The thought of my night with Donte made my stomach flutter while I smiled even harder. I gave Mr. Tony a big hug while glaring at Donte, who shook his head.

"How you been? Looking good as always!" Glancing over at Mr. Tony, he looked amazing. He didn't look a day over 45, if that. He always kept himself in shape and wore the latest gear, which also helped his young image. He was the true definition of a hustle man—smart and always on the move. I think that's one of the reasons Rayna was drawn to P; he reminded her of her father.

"Yeah baby, you know the women in my life keep me young," he said while dusting off his shoulders and tapping Donte, who just shook his head.

"Where you off to?" he asked in a concerned voice. Donte turned towards me and waited for me to answer.

"I'm just going to my apartment to get ready." When both Wright men gave me the *oh really* face, I couldn't help but smirk. So, I went into damage control mode while trying not to laugh at their expressions. "I promise it will be less than an hour," I said, answering Mr. Tony but trying to assure Donte I was good. He didn't like my answer, but he didn't budge. "I told Miss Chyna I would text/call her once I made it in and if I needed anything." Still nothing; he was not happy.

Seeing Donte's face, Mr. Tony said, "Let us escort you home then, just to make sure everything is cool." I nodded, and both men moved aside as we all headed downstairs.

"I hear you're going to the beach," Mr. Tony said. I kept walking.

"Yes sir, going in a few days for a week," I said proudly.

"Well, that's good baby girl; you enjoy yourself, but as a father and seeing you as one of my own…I wish you would…"

Before he could finish, we arrived at the apartment door. "I'll be fine, Mr. Tony; I promise I'll be extra careful," I replied, looking at him and Donte. Mr. Tony put his hands up and smiled. I opened the door, and the apartment was dark and cold as usual. I turned on the light, and they both stepped in. Mr. Tony looked around.

"Aight, everything seems cool. You sure you don't want us to stay?" he asked, concerned.

When I shook my head no and smiled, he said, "Okay, it's good to see you, baby; we're gonna see you soon, right?"

I answered, "Yes sir, just going to change, and I'll be right out."

Donte grunted, knowing the words "right out" were the opposite of what I meant. He always complained that I took too long to do anything. But in this case, I would try to shave a few minutes off my normal time. He needed to relax!

Mr. Tony nodded. "Good, good. I want to catch up with you…see what's going on with my other baby girl! So, be prepared to share a drink with your ole' man, deal?" I smiled and hugged him.

As both men walked past me out the door, I purposely rubbed Donte's hand, and he rubbed mine back. Halfway up the stairs, Donte turned around and mouthed *hurry up!*

I winked and replied, *OK relax* as I blew him a kiss. As usual, I didn't close my apartment door until I heard them open/enter Miss Chyna's apartment. So, I caught a glimpse of a conversation between Mr. Tony and Donte.

"Baby girl, done grown up…you ain't wifed her yet?" Mr. Tony said.

"C'mon on, Tony man, not you too," Donte replied.

"Just saying, you tripping; that's a fine woman and won't be single for long!"

Not hearing Donte reply, I knew he shook his head; however, I was not ready for the next comment. "Shit, did you at least hit it or peek at it?"

I held my laughter in because I knew Donte was embarrassed. After hearing Donte grunt, I closed the door so I could laugh freely. Poor Donte. I could only imagine what his face looked like. However, Mr. Tony had a point; he had better move fast or he'd miss me…or have to scare someone else away with his angry-ass expression. I smiled at the thought of us being together and rushed off to the shower.

It took me a little while longer than expected to get dressed. After showering and changing multiple times, I couldn't decide what to wear. I was trying to hurry up, but Donte kept texting me.

Him: *You know I don't like this…hurry up, Sharnel. In and out…don't be dragging ass like usual.*

Donte's use of my first name let me know he was irritated, but what was new? I tried to assure him I was good, but he did not care.

Big Head: *I'm moving as fast as I can…would be sooner if you would relax, Sir!*

After another 20 minutes, he texted me again.

Him: *Be outside in 5 minutes or I'm coming in.*

Big Head: *I'm almost dressed, so relax!*

So, I tried on a few more outfits before I decided on a black plunged halter sleeveless pleated long romper knit jogger maxi jumpsuit with pockets and flat sandals. My ponytail was still intact, so my hair just needed a little pruning. I tried to hurry and put on my studs and bracelets quickly as my phone kept going off. "Urgh, I'm coming," I yelled as if someone could hear me.

I turned off the lights and made my way to the door. A bothered Donte was already outside. "I was on my way out the door, I swear," I tried to say quickly.

He just looked me up and down and visually called bullshit on my words. He waited for me to lock the door and motioned for me to go up the stairs outside.

"Urgh, always mad," I said as I walked to the stairs. But I knew I looked good because I could feel him watching me walk.

"Can you not shake your ass as you walk, man?" Donte said flatly.

When we got to the front door, I turned around and smirked at him. "You could have covered them up a little more too." Donte pointed at my plunged top, referring to my breasts, which made me smile even more.

Of course, his face was emotionless as usual. "Make sure this outfit stays home," he said as he held the building door open.

"You ain't my man," I said sarcastically, then laughed. Donte gave me the *really* face and motioned for me to walk through the door.

"Oh yeah…keep that same energy when you come back from the beach," he mumbled as he slightly rubbed his hand across my butt as I passed. I smiled, looked behind me, and winked, then we made our way toward the festivities.

CHAPTER 18

Everything was in full swing once we arrived. Rayna happened to have arrived with P as Donte and I walked up. "SHAAARRRRR OMG, there's my bestie!" Rayna ditched P and ran straight to me, embracing me with a true sisterly hug. She looked amazing; the Miami heat had done her well. Her skin glowed, and she looked refreshed.

"OMG let me look at you; the south done did ya right, girl!" I whispered, impressed by her figure.

"Girl, you have no idea," she whispered back. Rayna turned so I could admire her voluptuous figure. You could tell she gained weight in all the right places because she was killing it in her white capri pants with a blue tube top. Her braids were retouched and flowed down her back, stopping right above her ass. I also wondered about the glow she possessed.

"Where is Tonya?" Rayna asked as we walked further into the gathering, arm in arm.

"Well, her mom convinced her to stay a bit longer with her family, so she'll be home next week."

Rayna nodded, then turned to me, stopping our progress. "Okay, so what's this about you going to the beach alone? Not gonna happen, Shar!"

I looked for Donte a few paces away from us and rolled my eyes. "Why is this everyone's topic of discussion? I'll be fine!" I said, slightly annoyed.

"Because it ain't a good idea!" Donte mumbled as he passed by. I rolled my eyes again—damn, who else did he tell, crybaby ass!

"He got a point, Shar! I know you need a break, but…come on!"

Grabbing Rayna's arm again, we continued walking. I was over the beach advisory committee and hoped she would change the subject. I was so excited for Rayna to be back. It was weird not having her around for so long. I didn't call or text much while she was gone because I wanted to give her space as well as myself. I couldn't wait to catch her up, but I'm sure there wasn't much she didn't already know thanks to Donte and P.

Feeling hungry, I guided Rayna towards the tables where everyone would sit. Miss Chyna didn't believe in sitting spaced out, so she lined up the picnic tables so we could all sit together. We all grabbed hands so Mr. Tony could pray, then went to the food table to make our plates.

"Sooooo, I heard you were out here protecting your boo last night, what's up Sharnte?" Rayna said, laughing at her mock-up of mine and Donte's names.

"OMG, the night that will never end," I said, slightly smiling while looking over at Donte, who was chatting with P. "And shut up; it wasn't even like all that." I tried to switch the subject, but Rayna would not let up.

"Ummm hmm, seems like a lot has happened since I left," Rayna said, peeping my smile. "We definitely need to catch up sooner than later."

At the food table, we picked up plates and utensils as Rayna smiled. "Make sure you grab two plates, Shar!"

I laughed and pushed her jokingly. "Umm, you're the one who really needs two plates! P don't play them games!"

Rayna rolled her eyes and smiled. "Yeah, I do need to feed my baby, again! Been too long!" She said, shaking her ass a little while smiling as we looked over at P and Donte, who sat at the table. We both made two plates. I put foil on Donte's plate, knowing he may or may not eat it, then we headed to the table. When we sat down, Donte and P were no longer there; however, they were making their way back towards us.

"Ohhh Donte, come sit across from your boo!" Rayna yelled.

I was so embarrassed. I never said we were together, but Rayna didn't care. "Note to self: kill Rayna later."

Rayna obviously had a few sips before the party, so she was on ten, and it was still early.

"Alright, Rayna, back off a bit," Miss Chyna suggested calmly. Rayna rolled her eyes but obliged her mother's request.

P sat in front of Rayna, smiling as she smiled back. Great, now I get to look at them making love faces all night. Urgh. Donte sat across from me, but his energy was directed at his sister, whose comments were too much for him. Rayna handed P his plate.

"Here you go, Boo," P winked at Rayna, and she stuck her tongue out seductively. I shook my head and tried to wipe the image from my mind. Then I started eating from my plate while the wrapped plate sat on my side of the table. We all began eating while Donte looked at me as if to ask where his plate was.

"Is there a problem, sir?" I said flatly as I picked up my fork to eat again. He nodded and smiled. I took my second bite and then handed him the covered plate.

"I thought so!" he said as he inspected the plate. I smiled as he gave his usual head nod and began to eat.

"You know better than to do your boo like that, Shar!" Rayna said, laughing. Donte, P, and I just shook our heads.

As we continued to eat, I looked around for my water, which I had forgotten to grab.

"What did you forget, Shar?" Rayna asked.

"My water!" I said as I was about to get up, but Donte placed two cold bottles he had on the seat next to him on the table. He opened one bottle and then placed it closer to me.

"Thank you," I said.

"Damn…got niggas opening bottles and shit!" Rayna laughed.

I nudged her, but I could tell Donte was over her commentary. However, Rayna didn't care; she turned her attention back to P. Which was cool—maybe she would move on from Donte and me. They continued getting on my nerves with all their cute faces and lovey-dovey actions. You could tell Rayna definitely missed him and was not shy about it. However, that was an intermission as she switched her attention back to Donte and me.

"Soooo, lovebirds, what y'all been doing this summer?" Rayna whispered between bites, looking at Donte and me. P kept his mouth closed and looked down while shaking his head.

"Relax, babe," he tried to urge her.

As I continued eating, I thought about all our interactions before and during the summer—some that Rayna knew about and others she didn't. If she only knew! So much had happened—ups, downs, and what the entire hell—but here we were. I smiled at the thought.

"Wait, y'all had sex?" Rayna said a little too loudly, causing everyone to look in our direction.

Donte dropped his fork. "You got one more time."

I just lowered my head, and Rayna waved him off as if he didn't matter.

She leaned over to me and mumbled, "Well, did y'all?"

I just looked at her and shook my head no. I wanted to look at Donte, but I was too embarrassed. Plus, I knew he was beyond pissed at Rayna, who was again unbothered by her actions, so I kept my head down and waited for yet another moment to pass.

We were quiet for a few moments. Then P leaned over to whisper to Donte, who was focused on his plate. He looked up with an emotionless expression, then looked my way. When I searched his face but didn't get a reaction, I turned to see what was behind me. It was Trav making his way toward the table. I felt anger rush over me and turned back toward Donte. I was about to move when suddenly I felt Donte MMA his legs around mine under the table. I couldn't flinch or move; I was trapped. Obviously pissed, I glared at Donte, but then I thought about what we discussed this morning and the "promise" I made him, and I decided to calm down.

When Trav approached the table, you could hear a pin drop. I had to give it to Trav; he was bold for coming over and even bolder for what was about to happen next.

"Hey, Miss Chyna, Mr. Tony… everybody," he said in the sincerest voice. Mr. Tony nodded as he sipped his beer, looking at Trav, while Miss Chyna spoke up.

"Hey, Baby, come sit down, grab a plate… join us; you're welcome at this table," she looked at me and Donte.

I nodded in agreement that I would chill. I would never disrespect Miss Chyna; plus, I knew we were all going to chill in front of her. Trav intentionally smiled at me, then went to make his plate. Dumbass! He thought this was getting one over on me; however, these were my people. If he was invited to the table, it was a litmus test—he would surely fail, believing he was in "no danger." If he acted out, I would be the least of his worries. Eat up, mothafucker; hope it gets stuck on the way down. I continued eating and smiled at the thought.

When Trav got his plate, he sat down at the next table on Donte's side. He was too close for comfort, but I still couldn't move because Donte still had my legs in a lock. Trav kept trying to get a rise out of me by looking in my direction, but I didn't take the bait. When he wasn't successful, he directed his attention to Rayna.

"What's up, Rayna? Welcome back." Rayna smiled weakly, and before she replied cynically,

"Hey, Trav, thank you! How you been?"

Trav smiled through his busted lip and looked at me when he responded, "Good, I can't complain."

This sorry bastard—urgh, he was lucky I promised Miss Chyna and Donte. I rolled my eyes, still focusing on my plate. We were all quiet, then Rayna dropped her fork and folded her arms.

Seeing her mood shift, P whispered, "Babe, not now…" She smiled at P as if she was going to indulge his request. However, Rayna didn't play about anyone who disrespected me.

She turned towards Trav and stood up, yelling, "Oh yeah, your busted lip says something different! Matter of fact, I heard you got—"

Miss Chyna smacked the table, yelling, "Enough!?!" She locked eyes with Rayna, who was about to say something else but decided against it.

Rayna laughed, then glared at Trav, who acted shocked and oblivious to what her next words would be. P immediately got up, took Rayna by the arm, and escorted her from the table upstairs. He whispered to her as they walked, and she fussed along the way.

"Nah, P, how his bitch ass nigga gonna come—" Rayna yelled until the front door of the building closed.

I watched her continue to yell all the way upstairs. I just looked at Donte and thought it seemed all too familiar, minus the throwing her over his shoulder. I just shook my head and smiled, then continued eating.

Trav continued eating as if nothing was wrong. He never said another word but ate until his evil heart was content. After we finished eating, he thanked Miss Chyna and Mr. Tony, then left. When he was far enough away, Donte finally let go of my legs under the table. I was about to get up to throw my plate away; however, he took the plate.

"Nah, I got it. Relax!" he said intently. I wasn't going to run after Trav, but he didn't care. I just sat back down. Moments later, Rayna came back downstairs, a little more sober than she was before. After we finished eating, Miss Chyna turned on the music. Some people talked, played cards, and just enjoyed the vibe.

I decided to help Miss Chyna with cleaning up. Rayna mingled, and Donte was playing cards with P and other people from the neighborhood. As I was coming back from taking the food upstairs, I heard a voice. "Aye, let's talk for a minute." It was Trav. He was tucked in the space under the stairs near my apartment. I took a deep breath and turned around to appease his request.

"Speak your peace, Trav."

He took a breath and let it out in almost a whisper. "I don't appreciate you embarrassing me like that yesterday. I ain't do shit to you. You came for my head for no reason."

My patience was running thin, but I let him continue.

"Shit, you owe me an apology in front of everyone for your behavior."

Was he serious? Like hell I would even entertain that request.

"Look, I told Miss Chyna I would be cool, so I'm going to do just that. I can't, however, do what you're asking," I calmly replied and turned to walk out.

"That's okay; your boy can't protect you forever. I'ma get what I want, and then some!" he said as I heard him licking his lips. I was about to walk out when he laughed and said, "Next time I'll get my uncle and his friends to bust that little virgin puss wide open."

His words stopped me in my tracks. He was related to Roy! How in the hell? Now it made sense how he knew what happened. Now I really wanted to put him in the ground, but I caught myself. I promised Donte, and that was his only saving grace. I went out the front door, and he mumbled, "See you soon, Sharnel. Ole boy can't protect you forever!"

Unsure what his words meant but knowing Trav, I would see him again. I tried to act normal, but I couldn't. I needed a moment to process what happened. Luckily, everyone was distracted, so I slowly walked toward the parking lot. As I walked, I felt okay, but as I got closer to the parking lot and out of sight, I sped up. I started to feel like my breath had left my body. Feeling lightheaded, when I reached the street pavement, I threw up everything I had eaten. I was glad no one saw me hunched over between the cars. I continued throwing up and felt like I couldn't stop. When I finished, I heard a noise and immediately jumped but relaxed when I saw it was Mr. Tony, smoking a cigarette. He extended his hand, helping me away from the puke, then handed me water and a napkin from his pocket.

"Baby girl, what was that all about?" I didn't say anything, thinking he was referring to the puke. However, he wasn't.

"I saw Trav go in the building, but he didn't come out." I now caught his drift; I thought about saying nothing, but I knew that wasn't going to fly. As I was about to respond, I saw Trav walking down the opposite sidewalk a yard away from us. He moved swiftly while talking on the phone, and I followed his every move. He eventually walked behind the building and disappeared.

Mr. Tony took a drag and continued, "I saw you come down and stop; I figured he cornered you. So, what did he say that got you blowing chunks?" His face was serious, and his demeanor was unlike anything I had ever seen from him. However, it was exactly how Donte would and did react. Damn, this is where he gets that from, huh? The damn Wright men! I reconsidered the "nothing" reply again, but I knew that wouldn't suffice. So, I told him everything, including what happened the night with Roy. He just nodded without ever looking in my direction.

When I finished, Mr. Tony hugged me tight and said in my ear, "You ain't got nothing to worry about, baby girl; we got you." He kissed my cheek, and we walked back to the party. Once we were with everyone, Mr. Tony was all smiles and jokes with people who passed us by. Then he went off to play spades but not before whispering something to Miss Chyna. She stared in my direction and nodded, then continued mingling with people.

Unlike Mr. Tony and Miss Chyna, I couldn't just snap back just yet. Trav had left the party, but I was still reeling from our interaction. I sat on a vacant picnic table and watched as everyone mingled. I tried to hide my anger, but it showed. Donte was talking to some guy he knew when he glanced in my direction. He was about to approach me, but Rayna intercepted him, causing him to go towards Miss Chyna.

"C'mon, Shar, let's get a drink," Rayna whined.

She now smelled like she had one too many, but I decided I would indulge her. If I kept an eye on her, I could release my thoughts for a bit. She grabbed two cups, and we sat back down at the table and people watched.

"Girl, I'm so glad to be home. I missed y'all so much." Rayna said with a very serious tone.

"We missed you too, Ray; life is different without you." I wanted to say more, but she wouldn't remember anyway. She smiled and gave me a side hug, then leaned her head on my shoulder.

"Man, I'm going to miss this place," Rayna said, then stopped as if she caught herself.

"Ray, what are you talking about?" Was she thinking about leaving? If so, why? As she was about to answer, I raised my cup to sip it. However, before it reached my lips, Donte took the cup out of my hand. He sniffed it and poured mine out along with Rayna's, not before she took a quick sip.

"Dang, Dee, what the hell you doing? Why you pour our cups out?" Rayna yelled with a drunk slur.

"My daddy's right there, ma dude!" Donte looked at me square in the eye and hissed, "We don't drink."

Then he walked away, ignoring Rayna's comment. It wasn't funny, but inside I was laughing. The "we" made my heart flutter, despite still feeling pissed.

As he was walking, Mr. Tony interrupted him and whispered something to him. He looked in my direction, even more pissed, and nodded, holding on to every word. Oh fuck, here it comes! I took a breath and anticipated Donte's reaction coming my way. P was now pissed as well, but with Rayna and her antics. He came over and scooped her up, saying, "I got her, y'all. She obviously needs to get some rest." Rayna sucked her teeth but didn't say anything as he ushered her off to the building to take her upstairs again.

A few minutes later, I was still stuck on what Rayna almost revealed, along with the bullshit from earlier. I didn't hear or even acknowledge Donte, who was now in front of me talking.

"Yo, you listening to me or nah?"

I snapped out of my daze. "Huh? What? I didn't hear you. What'd you say?"

Obviously frustrated that he had to repeat himself, Donte cleared his throat and said, "We done for the night!"

There was the "we" again. I didn't smile because this wasn't a smiling moment; he was really pissed.

"Yooo, you can't stay at your place tonight. Let's go get your clothes!" Now I was pissed. He helped me off the table, and we headed toward the building. I knew Mr. Tony had told him what happened. I was not in the mood for his attitude tonight. As we walked, he was on my heels, whispering to me, "Why you ain't tell me Trav approached you, Sharnel?"

I sucked my teeth as I walked but didn't bother to turn around to face him. His face was angry—no need to see that so soon yet again.

"Oh, you don't hear me talking to you again?"

I took a breath and finally replied as we walked, "Donte, you told me to chill, so I did. Ain't that what you wanted?"

He grunted, "You being funny now…I also told you to let me protect you, and yet again, you didn't listen!"

Was he serious? "I can't fucking win! Yet again, Trav does some bullshit, and I'm getting the brunt of it." Donte opened the building door, I got a front-row seat to his glare, and he got one to my eye roll.

When we got to my apartment door, he turned to face me. "From now on, you don't go in that place without me, you hear me?" he said, purposely pointing his finger at the door.

He was very direct in his tone, but I snapped back anyway, "Donte, you trippin…where am I supposed to go?" I just looked at him, and he didn't budge.

I knew the conversation was over, "You heard what I said, Sharnel!"

I sucked my teeth and unlocked the door to let us in. As we walked into the apartment, he was still on my heels. When we walked into my bedroom, I turned on the light and began packing my stuff.

"Why is Trav causing the drama, and I gotta pay for it?" The more I processed it, the more annoyed I became. I turned around to Donte, who was waiting in the doorway, and shouted, "Ain't nobody scared of Trav's punk ass, you know that, right?" I folded my arms and stood in front of him, waiting for a response. "Fuck this! Not only am I going to the beach by myself, but when I get back, I will stay here by myself."

Donte just looked at me and shook his head. He was getting more annoyed by the minute. He took a breath, calmly gritted through his teeth while using his finger to emphasize his point. "Wrap this shit up; we don't have time for this now."

I rolled my eyes and threw the stuff in a bag. He just continued to stare, unfazed by my actions.

When I was done, he grabbed the bags and carried them to the living room while I turned off my light. As we were headed toward the front door, I stopped. "I want to check Regina's room for a second."

Donte grunted and motioned for me to go ahead. I wanted to see if she was still packing or if she had even been home. She had already made the arrangements for the beach, but I hadn't laid eyes on her since our last interaction. When I walked into her bedroom, I stood in shock—the room was completely empty. Everything was gone: her clothes, shoes, furniture—nothing was left. Everything was still intact in the living room and dining room, but her stuff was gone. Donte could see me from the living room, so when I didn't make a move, he made his way to me.

When he came into the room, he was shocked as well. "Damn."

All I could muster up was, "She's…gone! She…didn't even tell me she was leaving so soon!"

Donte, unsure what else to say, just calmly muttered, "Let's go, Shar." When I didn't move, he gently ushered me out of the room.

The walk back to the living room was longer than normal. He picked up the bags, and I turned off the light by the door. As soon as I opened the door, Mr. Tony was right there, scaring the shit out of us.

"Y'all good?" We nodded. I locked the door, and we all headed upstairs. As we made our way upstairs, I was dazed that Regina left. I knew she was going, but now she was really gone. I really was fucked! As we walked, no one said a word, but Donte kept his hand on my back as we walked upstairs together.

When we made it upstairs, Mr. Tony let us in, and we walked in. Miss Chyna was in the living room but didn't say a word. Donte guided me to his room and closed the door. The last couple of hours had been too much for one day. I just wanted to shower and go to bed. "I'm exhausted. I just want to shower and go to bed."

Donte just nodded. I went to the hall, grabbed a towel and washcloth, then made my way to the bathroom. Donte went to the living room to talk to his parents. I let the water just run all over me and washed until my skin hurt. When I finished, I went to Donte's room to get dressed; the bathroom was too hot, and I needed to breathe.

When I opened the bathroom door, the house was dark, so I knew everyone had gone to bed. Donte was still up, sitting at his desk and working on something when I came in. Without looking up, he said, "I can leave while you get dressed."

I immediately replied, "No, you good." He nodded and kept doing what he was doing. I put on my body oil, got dressed, and tied my hair up, then slid into bed. Like clockwork, Donte got a shower himself and came back into the room to get dressed. By the time he returned, I was facing the wall; he knew I wasn't asleep, just staring at nothing. When he got dressed for bed, he turned off the light and slid into bed.

"Hey…" I rolled over to face him.

"You good either way. Everything happens for a reason."

I just nodded and moved closer to him. He embraced me with a hug and kissed my forehead.

When Donte fell asleep, I was still wide awake. I couldn't process what my life was in that moment. I was going to take the time I needed on this getaway to enjoy this break. Regina had abandoned me, but there was no way I was going to fail! I would show her. When I came back from the beach, I would have plans for going forward. As my thoughts turned to Trav's foolishness, I got angry all over again. No one was going to run me away; I ain't afraid of nothing. I heard what Donte said, but Trav made this personal, and I didn't like that. I'd see him before he saw me; that was a promise.

A few hours later, when Donte woke up, I was still awake. However, I was now facing the ceiling, still having a mental dialogue with myself. He gently turned my head to look at his face.

"You ain't been to sleep yet?" he said while he turned his head so he could yawn.

I turned my face back toward the ceiling and then responded, "I can't sleep; too much on my mind."

He nodded, took a breath, and gently turned my face again. "Look, I know you can handle yourself, but this time…" He made sure I saw his eyes. "Don't do nothing, Sharnel. Remember what we talked about."

I looked back at the ceiling. I heard him, but I couldn't guarantee anything given how I felt. He turned my face to him one more time.

"I got this…I got you! I'm asking you, please do this for me…" When I didn't respond, he followed with, "Do it for us, please," then he kissed my lips. Urgh, how the hell could I go against that? I waited so long for us, and now that I had it, I couldn't risk it. He waited for a response; I just nodded and looked back at the ceiling. He kissed my cheek, then went to use the bathroom while I kicked myself for agreeing.

"I hope I can keep my word," I said aloud. I rolled over and finally fell asleep before Donte came back.

CHAPTER 19

When I got up the next morning, I decided I needed to head to the beach sooner rather than later. While Donte slept, I got out of bed and texted Regina, telling her to move the reservation up to today. Once she confirmed, she told me where to find her car keys. I needed a break from everyone and everything; despite being exhausted, I was ready to go. So, I went to the bathroom and got myself together. When I came back to the room, Donte was awake, sitting on the edge of the bed. We didn't even say good morning to each other. He looked just as tired as I was. So, I sat next to him on the bed, and he lifted his arm so I could lay on his chest. My leaving early wouldn't make him happy, but I hoped he would understand.

"I'm leaving for the beach today. I just need a break…I gotta get out of here, Donte."

He didn't say anything, never made a sound, which surprised me. We sat quietly as he still held on to me. As I was about to look up at him, he finally mumbled, "Okay, Sharnel."

A sense of relief came over me. We both got back in bed, and I laid on his chest as he held me. Not saying a word, we fell asleep for another hour or so. When I woke up, I felt energized and ready to tackle the next step before heading out.

I went back to the apartment to pack for my trip, of course with Donte. He sat on my bed while I sat on the floor with my suitcase open. He didn't say much; he just flipped through his phone while I pulled clothes from my drawers and closet into the suitcase. Although I had a playlist playing, I wasn't really listening to the music. I wished he would say anything, but he didn't. We hadn't spoken since I told him I was leaving today. I was over the silence between us; it was bad enough I wasn't going to see him daily. I wanted our last moments together to be different from this.

So, I finally spoke up, "Why so quiet today?"

He closed his phone and looked at me. "Nothing, man…look, I know you're tired of hearing this, but I don't like this," he said, pointing at the suitcase.

"You're right…I am tired of hearing it!" I snapped back. He was annoyed, but I needed to say it. "But I hear you, and I get it! But even more now…I need this break!" I calmly said.

He was still displeased but nodded. "Look, man, I need you to do some things while you're away!" I stopped and looked at him. I'd do anything he needed if it meant he would relax.

"When you get on the road, I need you to check in every time you stop. When you get there, let me know you have arrived."

This was simple; I could do this, so I thought. However, Donte wasn't finished. "When you go out of the room, let me know where you're going. When you get back, let me know you're safe. Then text me when you get up and go to bed."

I frowned; this wasn't just some things—it was a whole fucking agenda! "You can't be serious! With all that checking in, I might as well stay here!" I said, trying not to laugh.

"Fine, stay your ass here then!" he said, frustrated. I folded my arms and waved him off. "Do I look like I'm playing, Sharnel? If I don't hear from you, I'm coming for you! If you think I'm playing, try me!"

I knew he was serious, but part of me was intrigued at the thought. I rolled my eyes. "All that is a bit much, but I'll try!" I said, slightly laughing.

"You heard what I said, Sharnel!"

He went back to his phone, and I finished packing. I held up several of my bathing suits to decide if I should bring them.

"Why the fuck are all those suits see-through or look too fucking small?" he said, annoyed.

"Yet another thing to complain about," I said, letting him know I was over him. "Plus, I like them!" I eyed one that included mesh and had cutouts on the sides.

"Yeah, leave that one here!" he said, pointing to it. I grunted then put it off to the side. Donte then proceeded to veto several swimsuits and other stuff, which resulted in more shit outside of the suitcase than in it. I added a few cover-ups, shorts, and dresses to my bag. I grabbed my sandals and put them in bags.

"Why do you need heels at the beach, Sharnel?"

I grunted again. "Damn, why don't I just throw all this shit out!" I snapped.

Donte nodded and closed his phone. "Cool!"

I was officially over Donte, but he didn't care. I added a few more things and zipped up the bag.

"Glad that's over!" I said as I stood up. Donte was still sitting on my bed, so I sat down next to him and leaned my head on his shoulder.

"Can you do what I asked…please?" he said. I rolled my eyes.

"Yes, Donte! I will do everything you asked!" He lifted his arm and put it around me, and I laid my head on his chest.

"You gonna miss me?" I said, smiling.

He replied quickly, "Nope!" I lifted my head to glare at him.

"I bet you won't, since I'll be telling you my every damn move!"

He looked at me and kissed me. "Whatever, Sharnel! Don't make me come looking for you!"

I waved him off and stood up. "I'll be fine! Besides, ain't no one thinking about me!" I said as I walked toward the bedroom door. I was joking, but as the words hit the air, they pained me like I had smacked myself in the face.

Donte got up, reached for my hand, and hugged me. He held me tight, then whispered, "You know that's not true!" I nodded, and he held me for a while longer.

After our hug, he rolled my suitcase to the front door. When I grabbed the keys to Regina's car, we headed toward the parking lot. When we got to the car, I started it, and he put my bag into the trunk. I approached the trunk, which was still open.

I smiled, but his face was serious. "Don't give me the straight face before I leave!" I said, putting my arms around him.

"Be careful, Shar! For real, man!" Aww, he was worried. I smiled and tried to make a joke to soothe him.

"I will… I promise I'll talk to strangers, drive too fast, and post a vacancy sign on my door!" I laughed, but Donte did not; if anything, his annoyance was apparent again.

"That shit ain't funny, Sharnel!" I laughed again, but his face remained serious.

"Lighten up, Donte! I was joking!"

He shook his head. "Now kiss me one last time before everyone else comes out, please!" He obliged my request, kissing me slowly, just like the night of the necklace debacle, which included some rubs and squeezes.

Just as we finished, I heard Keith yelling my name as he ran toward the car. We let each other go, and he closed the trunk. I could see the family coming in our direction.

"Shar Shar!" Keith said as he stood on the sidewalk; he knew he wasn't allowed on the street. We walked to him, and he jumped into my arms.

"Keithy face! I'm gonna miss you!" I said, kissing his cheek as he put his head on my shoulder.

"I miss you too, Shar Shar!" he said, about to cry.

The moment was too real. I was leaving not just Donte but the family. It was almost becoming too much.

"Aww! Don't cry; I'll be back in 7 days… you know how many 7 is?"

He lifted his head and showed me on his fingers. "That's right! I'll be back in that many days! Plus, you can call me anytime, okay?"

He nodded, then reached for Donte. A sad Keith never sat well with me, so I had to sweeten the deal.

"I'll bring you back something, deal?" He nodded instantly and smiled. Donte and everyone else shook their heads. I hugged the rest of the family, and we said our goodbyes.

Mr. Tony and Miss Chyna headed inside after I hugged them, while Rayna, Donte, and Keith stayed with me a bit longer.

"I can't believe you're leaving me!" Rayna said, annoyed.

"Girl, how do you think I felt? You just left me for a few weeks!"

Rayna nodded. "Whatever! I'm gonna be calling you all the time, so you better pick up!"

I nodded and hugged her again. "Alright, y'all, I'm out!"

Rayna took Keith from Donte, and he opened my door. I smiled at him, and he partially smiled back. I got in, closed the door, and let down the window. I whispered to him, "I'll call you later! I love you!"

He nodded. I knew he wasn't big on PDA; if that was a thing, we'd do it in private whenever we decided what we were. So, I didn't expect a hug or anything. I was just happy he was seeing me off.

However, Donte leaned in and kissed me on the lips. He didn't rush or even try to hide it… it was perfect! He put "our thing" on blast, and I wasn't mad about it.

However, Keith felt a way. "Donte, don't kiss my Shar Shar!" he whined.

"I love you too! Be safe… remember what I said!" He stood up and returned to the sidewalk with Rayna and Keith.

I beamed at the sight of him, while Rayna looked shocked.

She mouthed *WTF*! She motioned that she would call me, which would be momentary, knowing her.

I selected a playlist and pulled out of the space. That was the perfect goodbye; I was ready for my trip and my break from my reality.

Thanks for reading! Peace, love, and blessings from a lady on her way.

Part 2… COMING SOON!

BACK COVER

Welcome to my world; don't count my sins, and I won't count yours… Show me your hand, and I'll show you mine. Maybe love, Sharnel.

Sharnel is the story of Sharnel Grace, as she embarks on a new phase of life that will test her resilience and belief that there's more to her already beautiful, chaotic life story. She has all the freedom in the world, thanks to Regina, her mother, who is financially stable but emotionally bankrupt. So, Sharnel fills her emotional cup with those in her building, which includes her best friends Rayna and Tonya. While keeping her on her toes, they are consistently stepping on them or causing more drama in her life to unfold.

Navigating life after graduation is proving to be more of a challenge when it seems everyone has a plan for their future but her. Beyond her writing, love for music, and flair for drama—which is a constant in her life—Sharnel can't get out of her own head and see what's next.

However, when she finds herself infatuated with an unexpected confidant, a new battle stirs within. After putting all her cards on the table, she finds that love doesn't come easy and questions if it's even worth it.

- Will Sharnel keep her cool and see beyond her circumstances to create a plan for her life?
- Will her "supportive" inner circle become gatekeepers, adding more drama to her life?
- Is Sharnel self-sabotaging to stay complacent in the life and mindset she's always known?
- Will showing her cards cause her to fold, leaving her sitting at the table alone?